Praise for *The Sta*

"In *The Starlet Spy*, Rachel Scott McDaniel [...] torical novel full of romance, mystery, and in [...] come to love through her previous books. Set in Sweden in the 1940s, McDaniel brilliantly ties fiction to real-life events in the midst of WWII. With the plot embedded in the deadly world of spies and counterspies, this novel was a page-turner and had me guessing right along with the heroine on who to trust. Historical romance perfection!"

–Rebekah Millet, award-winning author
of *Julia Monroe Begins Again*

Praise for *In Spotlight and Shadow*

"This book satisfied every need in my variety-hungry soul, and I couldn't love it more! It's deep without being somber, witty without being overdone. It's a perfect balance of romance, intrigue, and suspense, with some historical elements thrown in, all wrapped up in glorious Christian principles that feel natural and uplifting. Once I started, I could not put this book down! I never guessed at the threads that tied the two stories together; it was even better than I imagined! This book has easily catapulted into my category of top favorites, and I know I will enjoy reading over and over through the years."

–Jessica Harwood, @lovelybookishdelights

"I was captivated by the first page and couldn't stop reading until the very last. With the suspenseful romance set in a dual timeline, reading this book was medicine for my soul. Love, forgiveness, and acceptance poured off the pages, and I made sure to drink every last drop."

–Shannon Hargreaves, @the_reel_bookery

Praise for *Undercurrent of Secrets*

"Rachel skillfully binds dual-timeline love stories together against a fascinating backdrop—the *Belle of Louisville* steamboat. I thoroughly enjoyed uncovering the twists and turns of the mystery surrounding a woman who went missing a century before. Surprising. Heartwarming. A beautiful overlapping of past and present."

–Becky Wade, Christy Award-winning author
of the Misty River Romance series

"Anchored by a historic riverboat, *Undercurrent of Secrets* links past and present in a tale featuring two sweet love stories. Readers will enjoy the lively banter and the relatable themes of finding yourself and following your dreams. Romance, adventure, and mystery abound in this charming split-time story!"

–Denise Hunter, bestselling author
of the Bluebell Inn series

HEROINES OF WWII

THE STARLET SPY

RACHEL SCOTT McDANIEL

BARBOUR
PUBLISHING

The Starlet Spy ©2023 by Rachel Scott McDaniel

Print ISBN 978-1-63609-613-1
Adobe Digital Edition (.epub) 978-1-63609-614-8

All scripture quotations, unless otherwise noted, are taken from the King James Version of the Bible.

This book is a work of fiction. Names, characters, places, and incidents are either products of the author's imagination or used fictitiously. Any similarity to actual people, organizations, and/or events is purely coincidental.

Cover Image © Ilina Simeonova / Trevillion Images

Published by Barbour Publishing, Inc., 1810 Barbour Drive, Uhrichsville, Ohio 44683, www.barbourbooks.com

Our mission is to inspire the world with the life-changing message of the Bible.

Printed in the United States of America.

DEDICATION

To the resilient souls of the 1940s. You stared into the face of undiluted evil and refused to back down. Among your great lot was my Poppy—a fighter pilot ace and the best grandpa a girl could ask for.

A WORD FROM THE AUTHOR

Dear Reader,

This is my first foray not only into WWII fiction but also into placing a story in an international setting. If you've read my previous stories, you know I adore slipping as many historical elements into my books as possible. This one has by far the most truth woven into each chapter. So I encourage you to read the Author's Notes at the end. You might be surprised at what's actually true.

⮚ CHAPTER I ⮘

October 1943

Everything around me whispered lies.

Artificial moonlight spilled into a manufactured alley, slowly filling with fake fog. Real haze didn't have a stench. Yet the vapors reeked of burnt toast—most likely a reaction from chemicals exposed to the heating element. But I, Amelie Blake, didn't get paid to analyze components of a Hollywood fog machine. I got paid to deceive. To trick the multitudes into believing I was someone else—otherwise known as an actress.

A menacing figure stepped from the shadows. "There's nowhere to run." The man's voice carried as much steel as the gun in his gloved hand.

My face obediently twisted, feigning a panic I didn't feel. I was entirely safe. On this imitation backstreet inside Stage 23, my only possibility for harm would be a foolish trip over camouflaged wire.

"No!" I reeled, my shoulder blades scraping the artificial wall. "I beg you!"

The assailant raised his weapon higher, my cue to release an ear-splitting scream. Passable, but not my best effort. How could I feel anything but an imposter, staring down the barrel of a pistol, while millions of soldiers across the Atlantic faced weapons that shot more than full-load blanks?

The world was being ravaged, but in this corner of the planet, I stood in a shimmering evening gown designed by Orry-Kelly, playing make-believe in front of a boxy camera.

The villain's thumb clicked the gun's hammer. "No one to save you now, lady."

"That's where you're wrong." Phillip Gregory, the other top-billing actor, lunged in front of the enemy, and the choreographed fight scene commenced. A dodged punch here. A jab to the gut there.

Once—just once—I'd love a role where the leading lady joined the fray, helping the hero in the climactic attack rather than standing aside as a horrified spectator. Better yet, what if the heroine defended herself from the get-go? Such a move would defy the age-old damsel-in-distress formula, but wouldn't it be more inspiring to have the bad guy subdued and bound *before* the hero arrived?

But that wasn't how the script went.

Keeping angled toward the camera, I shrieked and gasped at the appropriate times until the gun fell from the villain's limp hand. Hopefully, this actor could play dead better than the gentleman from my last picture. I swear one could see the rise and fall of his chest from a kilometer away.

The camera swung to me, and I threw my arms around Phil, thankful my tear ducts produced the right amount of drips down my cheeks. If not, the director would force a retake and dump glycerin on my face. "I was so scared. It was horrible," I said on a sob, inwardly wincing because, once again, the writers made my character a raving idiot. Which would only confirm what the average moviegoer already suspected. All of America, perhaps the world, thought me the brainless blond. "I knew you'd come."

He crushed me to his chest and kissed me. "I'll always come for you."

"Cut!" Our director's booming voice could split the concrete beneath my heels. "That's a wrap, folks. Send it to the team for edits."

The crew dispersed in a chaotic din. Microphones lowered. Lenses capped. The villain, who was actually a gentle father of four, revived and dusted off his trousers.

I disentangled from Phil's arms, and he shot me a wink. "What do ya say, Amelie? Want to grab a celebration lunch? I sniff an Oscar with this film."

I sniffed something spicy. Phil was notorious for drenching all his clothes, costumes included, in his expensive cologne. Though now the scent clung to me, thanks to the embrace we just shared. "Sorry, Phil. I can't."

He waved at the prop director, then focused those dark eyes on me with a dimple-dented grin. "Dinner, then? I can make us a reservation at the Ferris Wheel."

The Ferris Wheel? Phil wasn't after a meal but publicity. The swanky restaurant stocked more tabloid reporters than filets. There were already bogus rumors about a hot romance between Phil and me. Showing up together at a place like that would only douse that spark of gossip with kerosene. No thank you. My heart still bore third-degree burns from the last actor who'd placed fame over human decency. "I can't because—"

"She already has plans." A well-dressed gentleman, no more than a few years older than my twenty-six, stepped between Phil and me. "Miss Blake, I'm Henrik Zoltan's driver. I'm here to pick you up for your lunch meeting."

It was a struggle to keep my brows from lifting. I hadn't spoken to Henrik since my return from the capital, but I was certain we hadn't anything scheduled. Henrik Zoltan was an illustrious movie producer and director. A soft-spoken, middle-aged Hungarian, he was responsible for several propaganda films, boosting the morale of a battle-wearied country.

He was also a spy.

My mouth slanted into a smile. "I must've forgotten. How silly of me."

"*The* Henrik Zoltan." Phil's eyes widened. "You're not going to sign a contract with him, are you?" His voice lowered. "What about the plans for our sequel?" An admirable job of keeping the desperation from his tone, but he failed to keep it from his eyes.

I shrugged. "It's only lunch."

Phil led me aside, shooting skeptical glances at Henrik's driver. His voice dipped even more. "Henrick Zoltan's a Hungarian. You can't trust foreigners."

"So I can't trust you?" I asked in a chipper tone, which only made the confusion on his face all the more satisfying.

"But. . .I'm American."

"And I'm Swedish." I gave his tie a playful tug. "Which makes *you* a foreigner to *me*."

He breathed a laugh. "I forget you're not from here. You fit in so naturally."

That wasn't always the case. The move to America had been more difficult than I imagined. All the hours with a voice coach to strip the accent from my tongue. Lonely evenings and holidays because my sole family member stubbornly remained in Stockholm. And now a global war separated me from reaching her. "I shouldn't keep Henrik waiting."

After a swift change from my gown to a smart dress suit, I followed the hired driver outside to where a Plymouth sedan sat idling.

The rear passenger door opened, and cigar smoke billowed out in lazy plumes.

I leaned down, peering into the haze. "Have you come to challenge me to another game of billiards?"

"No." His eyes narrowed behind his glasses. "Hop in, Amelie. We've much to discuss."

I lingered an extra second, inflating my lungs with a fortifying breath, then lowered onto the plush seat. "Much to discuss?" I asked when the driver shut the door. "I don't remember planning this little tête-à-tête."

Henrik tapped his stogie on a bronze ashtray on the seat beside him with two decided raps. "We'll talk in a few moments." Then he shifted his gaze out the window, puffing on his cigar as if it were his only source of company.

The car left the studio lot. I itched to question him, but that wasn't how Henrik operated. He would only speak when ready. So as the car's cabin plugged with smoke because Henrik wouldn't crack a window, my mind filled with questions. Block by block we moved almost in a crawl, Henrik taking drags on his cigar, me waving a hand about my airways, hoping he'd catch a hint. He didn't.

Unlike most wealthy producers, Henrik wasn't flashy. Thin-wired spectacles perched upon a knobby nose. A suit, the shade of a mud puddle, stretched over a paunchy frame. One would peg him as a languid fellow who spent the day on a park bench tossing breadcrumbs to pigeons. Dull. Unassuming.

But Henrik Zoltan was shrewd, multilingual, and no doubt neck-deep in covert activities. Something I'd discovered when he'd approached me last month.

The driver pulled onto a lot beside a café I'd never visited and promptly got out of the car. But instead of opening my door, he strolled to a cluster of outdoor tables on the far side of the building and sat.

With the chauffeur gone, Henrik slowly faced me. "Let us talk here.

When we're finished, we'll have lunch."

Henrik wasn't long-winded but more like long-paused. He took his time between remarks, as if his mind sorted and sifted each word before allowing it to leave his lips. I expected this conversation to stretch well past lunchtime, threatening to impose on my afternoon *fika*. The British may be devoted to their teatime, but the Swedes are downright adamant about their coffee break. Though not as strong these days due to rationing.

I settled against the seat. Might as well get comfortable. "This isn't about a role in your pictures, is it?" Henrik wouldn't act this secretive only to offer me a part. No, he would've summoned me to his office for that sort of business. Which only meant he needed my assistance for something else. I almost didn't want to ask.

He finally stubbed out his cigar. "Maybe I'll consider it after your service is over."

Perhaps I was wrong. "You mean, contract? I'm an independent performer now." Once my contract was up with MGM, I hadn't resigned. Just like Carole Lombard, I wished to have the freedom to select my own roles with any studio. It would be a shock to the world to watch me in any other part than the dumb blond. An opportunity I savored. "I can work wherever I like now."

His half-lidded eyes met mine. "The service I speak of is for the Allied benefit."

Ah, there it was. "Let me guess—you'd like me to sell war bonds?"

"No."

"Hmm." I made a show of tapping my chin as if in deep thought. "Am I to join Bob Hope on his next tour entertaining troops?" Though teasing, this was a sore topic for me. I'd never been asked to publicly contribute to the war effort. Fellow actors held rallies or drives. They'd use their off time to visit troops in France. All the while, I was excluded to the point society had taken notice. I'd even spotted articles speculating my loyalty.

"The call you put in to King Gustav was effective." Henrik's mild praise returned me to the moment.

"I can't take the credit. All I did was plead with him, but he was going to open the borders to the Danes anyway." I nibbled the edge of my lip, recalling the brief conversation. The king's decision to allow refugee Jews and Christians into Sweden made me proud of my homeland. When war had broken out, my country firmly embraced the same stance it had during the first great war—neutrality.

But neutral didn't always mean safe. Denmark, Norway, Belgium, and the Netherlands didn't take sides yet were invaded by Germans nonetheless. Sweden held its breath, tiptoeing that fine line of nonbelligerence, not wanting to give the Nazis any cause to attack. By welcoming the Danes, and even the Norwegians before that, Sweden took a great risk.

Henrik made a noise. It wasn't one of assent or disapproval but one that told me absolutely nothing.

"I'm serious. King Gustav would've received the evacuees with or without my begging." Henrik had introduced me to the head of the Office of Strategic Services, Bill Donovan. I'd felt foolish when Bill had asked me to accompany him to the capital only for a transatlantic voice radio call. While international calls were extremely rare, I'd believed myself too insignificant to sway the heart of a king. King Gustav had listened to my argument, but I didn't believe I'd influenced him one way or another.

"Donovan disagrees. So does Stephenson."

As Bill Donovan was the head of clandestine operations in the United States, William Stephenson held the same role for the British. I'd spent time with both men during my visit to Washington.

Henrik pushed his glasses up the bridge of his nose. "They believe the king softened at your influence."

"But it wasn't only me. Some scientist also pleaded with the king to give the Danes asylum."

Henrik's head whipped left. Gone was his lazy approach. An uncomfortable severity sharpened his gaze, darkening the shadows under his eyes. "What do you know about it?"

My heart jumped under his intense perusal. "Only what I said. The king mentioned a scientist who spoke on behalf of the Danish Jews."

"Is that all you know?"

"Yes."

He nodded, the line of his shoulders relaxing. "The scientist is Dr. Niels Bohr. He barely escaped the Nazis' clutches in Copenhagen." He slouched in the seat, reclaiming his comfortable position. "The point I'm making is, that call proved you're an asset."

We were talking in circles. Was this some sort of spy mind trick? Or perhaps he was stalling, trying to gauge my reaction. "The rescue was a success, right? Isn't that all that matters here?" More than seven thousand Danish Jews had been smuggled into Sweden over the past month.

"Yes. But there's more work to be done."

Of course there was. There was a powerful Nazi empire to subdue, an entire race of Jews to protect, and a world to rebuild after so much devastation. *More work* was a pitiful understatement. But since Henrik had brought up my call to the king, I suspected he wanted to make use of my connections to the Swedish officials. "Okay. Out with it, Henrik. What is it that you need me to do? Write letters? Make more transatlantic calls? Tell me my role."

His gaze latched onto mine and held. "What if I asked you to return to Sweden as a spy?"

≡ CHAPTER 2 ≡

Outside the car window, the breeze pulled through the palm trees. People luncheoned on the café terrace, their smiling faces and laughter a stark contrast to the heaviness sifting through me.

I hadn't been on Swedish land for four years. Forty-eight months without swimming in the Baltic. Running my fingers over the wildflowers or glimpsing the sunsets over the skyline of Stockholm. And more than that, since embracing Mamma. But as much as I longed to breathe Scandinavian air, I knew more than anyone of the risks. "You realize I'm more intelligent than the idiot roles I'm in."

Henrik nodded. "I do realize. In truth, I'm banking on that very fact."

"Are you?" I twisted on the upholstered bench, angling toward him. "Because last time I checked, Sweden's trapped by Nazis." The bordering nations of Norway plus Denmark were occupied by Germans as well as an entire ocean filled with U-boats. "I can't just waltz into Sweden."

"You're right. It's dangerous."

"More like deadly." I arched my brow. "Or have you forgotten what happened to Leslie?" Earlier this year, fellow actor Leslie Howard, who'd charmed the masses in *Gone with the Wind,* was shot down by Luftwaffe over the Bay of Biscay. He was visiting Portugal giving lectures on the film industry, but there were rumors it was all a cover. Could he have been working with Allied intelligence? Why else would the Germans invade neutral skies and shoot down an unarmed civilian plane? "Was he one of your recruits too?"

Henrik's expression turned somber; even his jowls sagged lower. "That was unfortunate." He tugged his glasses off his face and wiped them with a handkerchief from his pocket. The move seemed more to buy time than to clean the already spot-free lenses. "We can get you in." He slid the frames back on and regarded me. "I've been informed there's a window."

Even that window could be shot full of holes. And I wasn't about to inquire who the word *we* included. Though I had my suspicions it was the OSS. "What is all this about?"

"You'll be on a treasure hunt."

I frowned. The more he spoke, the more all this sounded like a terrible B-movie plot—the actress with questionable roots sent to her homeland in search of…what? A priceless painting? A valuable heirloom? A pouch of diamonds? Wait. Diamonds. I caged a groan even as I shot Henrik a look. "Is this some sort of joke?" At my last film's premiere, a prominent gossip columnist called me the Queen of Diamonds, some foolishness about my eyes. Now I couldn't quite shake the nickname. It clung to me like an ill-fitting gown, always uncomfortable. I couldn't fully believe Henrik would resort to childish games, but I'd learned from years in Hollywood that people weren't always as they claimed.

He stiffened as if my question finger-poked his self-importance. "No. Most certainly not. My time is too costly to waste on pranks."

His offense would've made me snicker if the moment wasn't so serious. Perhaps this wasn't a ploy, but Henrik wasn't giving me much to work with. "What kind of treasure?"

"One that many are after."

"Are you purposefully being cryptic?"

At this, he smiled. "If you choose to go, we'll tell you all you need to know."

I was to blindly decide? Risk my life for a treasure I knew nothing about? How or where to find it? "What makes me right for the job?"

He took a moment, as if considering how much he could detail. "We need a Swedish citizen. Someone who can mingle with all classes. With your fame and status, you can gain access into places most couldn't."

I mulled over his choice of words. *All classes.* He knew of my connections to high officials, but was he aware of my past? He couldn't be. No one knew except for Mamma.

"And you possess the key skill required for every operative."

My brows lifted. Had Bill Donovan told him of my oddity? I hadn't meant to reveal to the OSS head my rare talent.

Henrik sniffed as if I was to know the answer. "Acting. An excellent operative must fool the world around them."

Ah, my profession. Not my gift. "How important is this so-called treasure?"

"If it falls into the wrong hands, it could change the dynamic of the entire war."

Now this was getting a bit showy. Alter the entire war? I found that difficult to believe. "I should've brought popcorn." I folded my arms. "I didn't realize the conversation would turn theatrical."

"No exaggeration." He was silent for a few heartbeats, then heaved a sigh. Which sounded very much like resignation. "Niels Bohr, the scientist King Gustav mentioned, is an atomic physicist. The Germans were after him, but he escaped Copenhagen. With Bohr's extensive knowledge of nuclear weapons, it would've been a disaster for our side if the Germans succeeded in their capture."

Look who finally decided to get talkative. "It seems we dodged a bullet there." More like an atomic bomb.

"Dr. Bohr arrived safely, but his research did not." His gaze remained steady upon me. "We're sending you to recover Dr. Bohr's manuscript."

My hand flew to my collarbone, my heart pounding wildly beneath my fingertips. So that was the *treasure*. Not precious stones or metal but paper and ink. Yet the knowledge within those pages held power to destroy. "Do the Nazis have it?"

"We're not entirely sure but suspect not yet." He dotted his brow with his handkerchief. "If you accept this assignment, Bill Donovan will tell you more about it."

My guess was correct—the OSS was behind all of this.

"I don't have to explain how this could affect the outcome of the war. Dr. Bohr said this would be tragic if his work fell into Nazi hands."

"No pressure or anything," I mumbled. But there were more problems than just finding a missing manuscript. "I haven't been able to get into Sweden for four years. It'll look suspicious if I just show up."

"Donovan just sent a man over to promote the business interests of the States. You have a better reason than that." He met my gaze. "You'll be visiting your dying mother."

"What?" The word barely scraped out of my throat. What was he talking about? I'd just received a letter from her. Henrik must be wrong. "It can't be."

"She's fine." He flashed his palm and shirked away as if unprepared to handle an emotional female. "She's fine, Amelie. It's a cover we created."

"You could've led with that." Then my heart rate wouldn't have spiked. I took a calming breath. Mamma was fine.

"You more than anyone understand the power of the press. Thanks to some well-placed tips to the prominent papers, all of Sweden thinks the famous starlet's mother is at death's door."

My head spun, trying to place all this new information. The OSS had invented a reason for my being in Sweden, but Mamma was okay. If I agreed to this crazy mission, I'd get to see her. My heart ached at the thought. But another question surfaced. "You said many are after this treasure, Bohr's work. Do you mean—"

"The Gestapo? Yes." He nodded solemnly. "There are many in Sweden. Along with Swedes who are Nazi sympathizers. Swedish soil may not be stained with blood, but there's war there, nonetheless. Stockholm's currently a hotbed of spies and counterspies. Propaganda warfare." He fixed his gaze on mine. "In your language, it's the *Casablanca* of the north."

A frustrated breath parted my lips. What did I know about being a spy? Nothing. This would be dangerous work. If I messed up, there were no retakes. Failure meant the Nazis possessing notes from a man who could construct a powerful bomb. That weapon could secure Germany's world domination. It sounded dramatic, even for one whose entire life was drama.

Yet it was possible.

"You really can get me there?" I couldn't believe I was considering this. But. . .when was the last time anyone asked me to do something worthwhile? I'd placed a call to King Gustav on the Danish Jews' behalf, but it seemed effortless compared to the thousands who forfeited their lives to protect mine. Was I worth dying for?

Henrik nodded. "Like I said, there's a window. We'll fly you to Scotland, where you'll meet our Swedish pilot who'll take you into Bromma."

Bromma was less than ten kilometers from Stockholm. Could I do this? There was a chance of leaving here and never coming back. "You're asking the unthinkable."

He considered me for a long second. "I remember a story of another young lady who was asked to do the unthinkable to save others from destruction."

I stilled. "A true story?"

He nodded. "I'll paraphrase what someone told her." A spark entered his dull eyes, lightening the gray irises with sudden brightness. "If you choose to remain silent at a time like this, deliverance for the Jews will come from someplace else. But who knows? Maybe you were brought to this place for such a time as this."

Conviction pricked. My breath seeped out slow. He referenced the story of Esther from the Old Testament. Henrik was Jewish. I was Christian. We both knew of the young woman who challenged the odds to rescue God's chosen people.

My lungs pinched the meager breath I pulled in. I folded my hands in my lap to keep them from shaking and met Henrik's eyes. "I'll go."

His chin dipped in a grave nod. "We'll do everything we can to help you. The next course of action is to pack your bags. You leave tonight."

My stomach clenched. That was sooner than I expected. "For Sweden?"

"No, first you must spend some time at the Farm."

The morning skies sprawled over vast grounds. Apparently the Farm was less cows and roosters and more barbed fences and cement block buildings.

My military escort—a man named Glen—drove us down a gravel drive, the wind through the open window tousling my hair. Henrik had arranged my boarding a small plane that left California late last night, more like very early this morning. Glen had been waiting for me at the modest runway outside of Toronto, Canada. The lanky gentleman had used the overt signal Henrik told me to watch for—two taps on the edge of his cigarette, then flicked it on the ground, extinguishing it with his left heel for five seconds. It seemed a bit over the top, but who was I to question clandestine procedures?

For the past hour, I had noticed Glen sneaking several glances my direction. He no doubt knew who I was but was too professional to bring it up. And I'd been too exhausted for conversation. Though the scene ahead—a secret training ground for spies—snapped my nerves to attention.

Another jeep sped down the narrow lane toward us, clouds of dust billowing behind it. Glen pulled over, the tires bouncing on the uneven ground. The other car parked as well, and out jumped a man I'd met four weeks prior.

Bill Donovan. The head of the Office of Strategic Services for the United States. His white hair was dutifully combed back, his cleft chin freshly shaven. Like most military men, his gait had the bearing of order and confidence, but his bright blue eyes held an untamed look.

"Amelie." He rounded the front of the vehicle to my open window. His tone was warm and friendly, as if greeting me in his family's living room rather than on the side of the road in the middle of nowhere just across the American border. "Welcome to the Farm." He exaggeratedly swept his arm. "Or as the upper officers call it, Camp X."

I offered a tired smile. "You mean this isn't the Ritz-Carlton?"

His chuckle carried on the light breeze. "I was certain you wouldn't agree to all this, but I'm glad to be wrong." He nodded to Glen. "I'll take it from here, Sergeant. You can put Amelie's things into the guest suite."

Bill opened my door, helping me out. Glen saluted and drove away.

We climbed into Bill's jeep, which made me thankful I wore trousers and sturdy oxfords. He gave me a vague tour as we drove the remaining stretch of gravel. "The camp spans 275 acres and is situated right on the shores of Lake Ontario. To my right." He pointed to a long stucco structure. "That's the communications building. And speaking of communications." His expression turned serious for the first time. "The cadets go by first names here. No last."

I opened my mouth to speak, but he beat me to it.

"Yes, most will know who you are. You'll attract attention but hopefully not as much as you would were you in any OSS school in the States. We can hide you better here."

An office building stood on my left, which he'd said was designated for high-ranking officials. There was a shed with high windows in the distance, but Bill didn't divulge its use. I assumed it was better not to ask.

I swung my gaze to the opposite side of the lane and noticed tall wooden platforms in the open field. "What are those for? That is, if you're allowed to say."

"Those are the jump towers for parachute training."

My eyes widened. Surely they weren't expecting me to jump from an aircraft. In all my films, I had a stunt double. A stand-in to perform any scene that posed the risk of injury. I often wondered how well I'd fare if I performed the stunts myself. In Sweden, I'd be all on my own. The thought was alarming but also thrilling.

"That right there"—Bill leaned, his arm outstretched—"is the lecture hall. That's where you'll spend most of your time."

"And how long am I to be here? Henrik sounded as if the mission was important."

His lips tightened. "It's crucial."

"Then why the delay?"

He parked before a large building. "Henrik Zoltan taught you the *why* of the assignment but not the *how*. You'll be here for the next forty-eight hours learning the ways of clandestine operations."

Two days. "Is that enough?" I felt there was so much I needed to know.

"Our recruits are here for at least a month, but we don't have that much time to spare." His left brow climbed his lined forehead. "Remember what you told me in Washington?"

My nose scrunched as I thought. "That I'd vote for you if you ran for president?"

He quirked a smile. "No, about your special talent."

"Oh, that." My oddity.

"Yes, that." He gave a decisive nod. "Do you know how valuable it is? What comes naturally to you takes most people years to develop, and, even then, it's not certain. This is why you're perfect for this mission. Your Swedish citizenship, your fame, and your acting ability all are key components, but your memory is what will prove the most useful." He moved to get out of the jeep, but I laid my hand on his arm, pausing him.

"It's not my whole memory."

"Pardon?"

"It's only if I *see* something. If my eyes take it in, then I'll remember." Which had been why I'd excelled at acting. I only had to read through a script once. "But not my other senses. If I hear or touch something, there's no guarantee I'll recall it." The winter I'd turned eight, I'd suffered a series of earaches causing temporary hearing loss. I relied on my sight more during that time, and, ever since, my brain processed in a bizarre fashion—a photographic memory.

The older man seemed to take that in. "I still believe you're the best candidate for this operation."

Doubt crawled under my skin as I exited the jeep.

He opened the door to the lecture hall and let me pass through first. The walls were painted a drab gray, fading into the concrete floor. But there was nothing drab about the activity within this building. Men moved with purpose, darting in and out of different rooms.

"There's our Axis powers room." Bill motioned to a door on the left. "It has uniforms, samples of money, and weapons the enemy uses. Our spies need to memorize as much as they can. It prepares them for warfare." He looked at me. "But the warfare in Sweden is different. It's a battle of information and misinformation. And today, we'll inform you of all you need to know."

I nodded, trying not to reveal how overwhelmed I was. We walked through a series of corridors. Most of the doors were closed, and Bill didn't offer any explanations.

He slowed to a stop. "I know you're tired, but I'm hoping to brief you on the particulars of your assignment. Then Commandant Skilbeck will help with the rest." He led me into a space set up like a conference room. There was a long table with chairs situated around it. Seated at the head was a man dressed in military uniform. He stood as we walked in.

"Commandant Skilbeck," Bill acknowledged him. "This is Amelie."

The commandant's light eyes fixed on me like a target on his radar, but I didn't squirm. When he opened his mouth, he let out a string of German.

My lips pulled into a smile. "I'm very well, Commandant. Thank you for asking, and my favorite color is blue." I extended my hand in greeting.

The man, whom I guessed was mid-to-late thirties, shook my hand with a nod of approval. "When Donovan told me you speak German along with your native language of Swedish, plus English"—he released my fingers with a growing smile—"I wanted to test you and see if there was an exaggeration on Donovan's part."

"If anything, you underestimate her." Bill tugged the door shut behind him. "Now you can see why her disguise is perfect."

My gaze toggled between them. "But. . .I wasn't given a disguise."

Bill shrugged. "Hollywood already gave you the perfect cover."

My mouth parted. "You mean. . ." Oh, anything but that. "You want me to be the blond bimbo?"

Both men nodded.

I ran a hand down my face. "Why did I agree to this?"

"Because you're doing a service for the Allies. And because, like the rest of us, you can't stand to see evil win." Bill stood a little taller and adopted a determined tone as if encouraging a legion of soldiers rather than one reluctant actress. "As for your disguise, people already expect you to be dull-witted. You're just playing the part."

"Most will feel comfortable around you." The commandant pressed a tin mug of steaming coffee into my hands. Bless him. "If they don't think you're bright, they won't be as guarded with their talk."

Bill nodded and motioned for me to take a seat. "If they still aren't divulging, then you charm the answers from them."

"I'm not a femme fatale." If these men believed I'd use my body in a compromising way, I might as well leave.

The officer caught my meaning. "We're not asking you to seduce and kill. Only to use your acting ability to siphon information. Your main target is already enamored with you. All you probably need to do is smile at the poor chap, and he'll likely tell you anything."

"He?" This was the first time a specific person had been mentioned.

"Your main target." Commandant Skilbeck dropped a file in front of me. "His name is Finn Ristaffason."

I inhaled sharply. Finn Ristaffason was a wealthy Swede. A shipping magnate. And a man I'd promised I'd never speak to again.

⨯ CHAPTER 3 ⨯

Inside the folder, a photo of Finn Ristaffason topped the stack of papers. He was formally dressed in a tailored tux. The picture was black and white, but my imagination filled in the color. The gleam of his wavy golden hair. Perfectly sloped nose and full molded lips set in the face of the broodiest man in all of Sweden. My profession always placed me near attractive men, but with Finn, it had been different. He didn't wield charm to slay the female hearts. No, his influence was more subtle but no less felt. A trip of my pulse. A catch of my breath. All with a single gaze from his Baltic-blue eyes.

Judging from the scores of girls who'd attempted to throw themselves at him, I wasn't the only one he had that effect on. But I'd been the only one far beneath his notice.

I swept aside the picture to the paper-clipped document beneath.

"Those are details about Ristaffason's life. His business." Bill tapped the paper. "Read through it all. May help you get an understanding of how to approach your mission."

I took a slow sip of coffee, savoring the warmth. "How is he involved in all this?"

Bill lowered onto the seat beside mine. "Niels Bohr gave his atomic research to his associate, Stefan Rozental. Rozental put the manuscript in his briefcase to carry over to Sweden. In all the confusion that goes along with an evacuation in the middle of a dark and stormy night, the briefcase got left behind on Danish shores."

My gut dropped. "So the briefcase is still in Denmark?" If traveling to Sweden was thought dangerous, entering and traipsing around a

Nazi-occupied country was a death sentence.

"No." Bill leaned back in his seat. "The Danish resistance found the briefcase the following morning while erasing any trace of the rescue. They sent it over the Sound to Sweden during the next evacuation." The Sound was English for *Öresund*, the strait between Denmark and Sweden. "The majority of the boats used in the rescue were Danish, but some Swedes pitched in. The boat the briefcase was in was from the Ristaffason boatyard."

"So Finn Ristaffason worked with the Danish resistance?" That didn't sound like the self-serving man I'd encountered. But then again, I hadn't seen him in years. Perhaps he'd changed. "Then why's he a suspect?"

"More like a person of interest. Ristaffason helped with the rescue, yes. He also aided the Allies in another operation, but there's been questionable activity at his docks. Plus, Ristaffason has ties to known Nazi sympathizers like Erik Bruun."

My fingers slipped on the mug's handle, coffee spilling over the brim. "I'm sorry. That was clumsy of me."

Commandant Skilbeck grabbed a cloth from a nearby cabinet. "We've run across our fair share of counterspies. Those working both sides of the fence, ready to hand over their loyalty to whoever benefits them most."

He wiped up the slight mess, and I smiled my thanks. "Was Ristaffason helping rescue Danes or helping the Axis powers retrieve Bohr's work?"

Bill leafed through the pile of papers, stopping at a page in the middle and pulling it from the stack. "Here's a rough sketch of the boatyard." He placed the drawing in front of me. "We haven't been able to get any of our men near that place. Or its owner. We need you to find a way to get there and search the boats. It could be that the briefcase was misplaced."

"Which would make my job a lot easier." The boatyard was in Malmö, a half-day train ride from Stockholm. Purchasing a rail ticket was simple, but somehow I felt dropping in on the bachelor's doorstep would appear suspicious.

Bill nodded. "But if Ristaffason has the manuscript, he could be waiting for the right price or time to turn it over to the enemy."

"Just to be clear, you want me to get close to him and see if he has Dr. Bohr's document?"

"Yes." Bill refilled my coffee. "Ristaffason's boatyard is the best place to start. Question his employees and dockworkers. We also need you to attend social events. Rumors circulate among the elite. You never know what you might hear."

It could be fatigue setting in, but my thoughts knotted, and I wasn't sure where to begin untangling. I skimmed through the file. There was a thorough list of the man's relatives, employees, and contacts. My gaze stilled on the record of his past lovers. Heat crept up my neck. It was uncomfortable reading a detailed account of someone's entire life. "You know, it's quite possible Finn Ristaffason may not want me following him around."

Amusement lit Bill's face. "Oh, I'm pretty certain he'll welcome any attention from you. Read the section about his hobbies, the last one especially."

I quickly found the part he mentioned and read aloud, "Film collector. Amelie Blake."

Bill's lips twitched. "He has his own projector and private theater in his home. He's purchased all your films. I believe the man has a crush."

I sat, unmoving, unblinking. The great Finn Ristaffason was a fan of my films? I couldn't picture the stoic-faced gentleman being entertained by any Hollywood production, let alone my movies. But the OSS had somehow dug up this secret, proving yet another reason why I was recruited for this mission. Finn may know *of* me, but I would wager he didn't know he'd actually met me.

I browsed the second file, filled with lists of restaurants and hotels considered pro-Nazi. The OSS also compiled several pages of Swedes suspected of working with the Germans. I read everything placed in front of me until my eyelids felt as if they'd been stuffed with lead.

"Come on," Bill said. "Looks like you need some rest."

I said my goodbyes to Commandant Skilbeck and followed Bill into the hall. He brought out a set of keys from his pocket and opened a large wooden door to what looked like. . .a janitor's closet?

"Is that. . ." I peeked inside the small storage space, spotting a three-drawer dresser and a cot pushed against the side wall.

"Your quarters for your stay." He pushed the door wider, and I saw my bags were already there. "There are only barracks for men, since we don't train women here. You're the exception."

I nodded.

He tugged the key from the door and handed it to me. "Sorry your accommodations aren't what you're used to." His lips pressed together in an apologetic expression. "You shouldn't be bothered at this end of the hall. Recruits don't wander this way in fear of the commandant. His office is close by."

"Thank you, Bill." I knew once my head hit the pillow, I'd be out.

He turned to leave, then paused. "Amelie, you need to be careful on this mission. War is never a fair fight." He scratched a gray tuft of hair. "You may find yourself in dangerous and compromising situations. Which is why after you've rested, Skilbeck is going to teach you how to defend yourself."

"This fountain pen squirts cyanide." Commandment Skilbeck pointed to an innocent-looking writing utensil that was alarmingly lethal.

Any exhaustion from only four hours of rest on a wobbly cot vanished. I gaped at the pen. Working in Hollywood for the past eight years, I was familiar with props that looked the part but didn't function as intended. This room took that mindset to a whole new level. There was an explosive appearing as a loaf of bread. Cameras tucked inside cigarette lighters. Ordinary sewing needles laced with poison so that a light jab on the throat brought instant death. The hair on the back of my own neck pricked at the thought.

"It was short notice, but our team came up with a few items tailored to your mission."

I blinked. "But I only agreed to go to Sweden yesterday."

He stroked his mustache, barely hiding his smile. "Henrik Zoltan has yet to fail in recruiting his actors."

My lips parted. Who else had Henrik persuaded to spy for the cause?

The commandant reached for a brass-plated hairbrush. "This unscrews." He twisted the top to the right and separated the brush pad from the handle, exposing a hollow opening. His fingers dipped inside, retrieving something. "These are lockpicks. May come in handy to get into cabinets and drawers."

He demonstrated how to use them, then had me pick an office drawer open. It was surprisingly easy. "This is all very impressive, if not overwhelming."

He nodded. "Seems like something from a movie."

I forced a slight smile of agreement. "Only, we have blanks in our pistols."

"You familiar with weapons then?"

"Just the fake kind."

His eyes narrowed in determination. "We'll fix that."

For the next several hours, I stood in the open field, in the shadows of the jump towers, shooting a dummy target. Then we switched tactics, and he instructed how to effectively strike a person. It was somewhat bothersome. But if I trembled at attacking a cotton man, how would I be with one of flesh and bone?

The commandant taught me how to use parts of my body to inflict harm in delicate places. I would never look at my wrist the same again.

Once Skilbeck was satisfied I could defend myself, he wrapped up the lesson—but not before pressing into my hand a revolver sheathed in a leather holster. "Wear this on your thigh and carry it everywhere you go."

I shook my head. "I'll be searched as soon as we land in Sweden. Customs prides themselves on their thoroughness."

He tugged the dummy off the wooden stand, his gaze squinting in the late afternoon sun. "The Swedish police are diligent in keeping weapons out. As soon as a US plane hits Swedish soil, they disarm our men. But this is where your disguise comes in handy. If you're searched, just smile sweetly and tell the guards you always carry the gun to deter raving fans with pushy advances."

Tension built behind my eyes. How was this going to work? There were so many ways this mission could go wrong. "Once I'm in Sweden, am I basically on my own?"

"It's all in the file Donovan gave you." He maneuvered the dummy under his arm.

Exhausted, sweaty, and sore, I trailed him through the tall grass.

"Our agent will meet you at the airfield, and you'll check in with him during your stay. His real name is Axel Eizenburg, but when you meet, you'll use his code name: Wolf. And he'll address you by yours."

I slowed my steps, a light breeze pulling the hair across my cheek. "I have a code name? What's the point if most already know my identity?"

"It's to protect you. Your code name will only be given to a select few. It's like a password of sorts. If the agent calls you *Gyllene*, you know they're on your side."

Gyllene. I smiled. That's the Swedish word for golden. I understood, more than most, the importance of adopting a new alias for safety purposes. My stage name, Blake, was a shortened form of what I'd gone by in Sweden—Blakstrom. Though even that wasn't the name I was born with. "Anything else I should know?"

He adjusted his grip on the dummy. "A fair warning about Axel Eizenburg. He's a bit of a ladies' man, but we trust him."

An ego-inflated man? No problem. "I'm guessing he's Scandinavian?" The surname was a giveaway.

"Axel's a Swede." He paused, his face growing somber. "Be wary when interacting with him in front of others."

I swallowed.

"You also need to be careful in hotels and restaurants. There are many Swedes who are pro-Nazi that have been recruited to spy on patrons. They'll snoop in the rooms, eavesdrop on conversations. Someone is always watching and listening."

If that didn't give a girl insomnia, what would? I shoved a wayward lock behind my ear. "What you're saying is. . .trust no one."

"Precisely."

———— 〜 ————

Morfar, my mother's father, had been a fisherman and absorbed all the folklore and superstitions that accompanied the trade. He'd rattled off tales to anyone who'd listen. Often it had been me. One myth, in particular, was the legend of the *Näck*.

"The Näck is a shapeshifter," he'd said in that hushed way of a storyteller, hinting at mystery and intrigue. *"No man has ever seen its true form."*

The sea creature could morph into a handsome man to entice women to the ocean's edge. Become a drifting rowboat to lure sailors. The cruel beast transformed into any image with the sole intent of destroying.

This morning I'd faced my own version of the Näck. German U-boats. Because just like the sea monster, those boats were filled with every sort of evil, waiting in the seas to kill anything entering their domain. As the legend went, to destroy the Näck, a cross must be hurled into the deep. This morning, as I'd crouched on a wooden bench in an unmarked military plane, I hurled the depths of my heart into prayer, clinging to the power of the true cross. The one where my Savior delivered me from all death.

By God's mercy, the plane landed in Leuchars, Scotland, and I was hustled onto another aircraft before I could catch my breath. The pilot, a sturdy man named Brent, insisted we fly to Bromma immediately since the fog was thick.

"If we don't go now," Brent said, "we'll have to wait until the skies are dark enough to travel through undetected. Last crew I took waited two weeks."

The unarmed B-24 had been painted dark green, the benches situated lengthwise, leaving the middle open for supplies and whatever got hauled back and forth. I'd noticed recognition in Brent's eyes, but he'd treated me like I was just another Swede making the passage into my homeland. Which was the truth. Mostly.

My stomach rolled as the plane cut through choppy skies. How could Brent navigate us so confidently with no visibility? What if he misjudged and we landed in occupied Norway? He'd assured me he'd flown this route over a hundred times, which helped chisel down the spikes of dread. Whether it was true or not, I had no idea.

Three hours later, we landed on a narrow airstrip, and I was reunited with the land I love.

Brent retrieved my bags and helped me onto the cement runway. My legs shook and my bones hummed, a residue from the engine's angry buzzing. I gripped my stomach, unsure if the nausea stemmed from nerves or intense hunger.

Two men rushed toward me, waving their arms, demanding to see my traveling visa. The navy uniforms, with two lines of brass buttons descending into a wide *V* above their armed belts, betrayed their position. Police.

It was time to step into my role.

The shorter of the two reached me first, a scowl marring his round face. But then his hasty pace slowed, and his firm frown wiggled into a grin.

"Amelie Blake! You've come home!" he exclaimed in Swedish, then summoned his comrade with an enthused wave.

I extended my hand to the fellow but was tugged into an awkward embrace. Weren't these officials the least bit suspicious that I'd just dropped from the sky, leaving the safety of America and challenging Nazi territories to get here? By their enamored expressions, I'd guess not.

Brent chuckled behind me.

"Axel Eizenburg is here." The taller officer stepped toward me. "I wondered why such an important man had time to dawdle at our humble airfield. Now I have my answer." He waggled his brows.

Eizenburg. My contact.

I greeted the officers with a friendly expression. After being away for years, I expected I'd need a second to adjust to conversing in my native language, but I fell right into the exchange as if I hadn't left.

I smiled brightly, but my insides quivered. According to procedure, my bags and my person were to be searched. The commandant had been convinced I wouldn't be detained, but my spiked pulse wasn't as persuaded. I remembered my disguise and adopted a somewhat blank look. "Thank you, officers. I'm happy to be home. It's much nicer than being not at home." I caught a flicker of their confusion at my oh-so-intelligent remark, before turning on my heel toward the small terminal. Inhaling, I concentrated on keeping the tension out of my movements. Easy strides. Poised shoulders. I'd walked red carpets with quivering knees, affecting confidence I didn't possess. But this stretch of concrete proved my most challenging jaunt.

"Wait!" The first policeman strode toward me with determined steps. "Wait a minute!"

My joints locked. The gun on my thigh seemed to triple in weight. I knew my exit wouldn't be so easy. I swiveled, facing the officer, tilting my head in question.

He reached into his pocket and tugged out a crumpled slip of paper. "Could you sign this for my younger brother? He's a bigger fan than I am."

Oxygen re-entered my lungs. "Of course."

He handed me a pen, and I signed a rumpled ticket stub. After autographing something for the other officer, I glided away.

Once out of earshot, Brent leaned closer. "That was brilliant." He readjusted his grip on my bags. "Nobody ever breaks protocol."

I offered a tight nod, knowing I wouldn't be at ease until I was safely off the airstrip.

A well-dressed man appeared at the exit gate leading to the lot. He tipped his hat but fixed his gaze on me. "Axel Eizenburg at your service." His mouth tipped into a warm smile. His face was the kind of attractive arrangement most women would give a second—or third—glance at.

I returned his smile and held out my hand. "How do you do?"

He wrapped my fingers with a gentle yet masculine grip. "It's likely you're going to be sought out everywhere. Normally, I'd say I'll be your guard dog, but you need something more aggressive. Just call me Wolf."

⧉ CHAPTER 4 ⧉

I'd never been more appreciative of leather car cushions than at this moment. After being jostled on an uneven wooden bench inside the airplane, my every muscle seemed to sigh as I sank onto the upholstered seat. But I'd withstood more than hours of unending jolts to my body; my mind had also been tested, keeping vigilant and alert throughout the flights. In those few instances I'd begun to relax, my imagination so graciously supplied all the various scenarios of how I could die.

Yet I'd made it home.

I tipped my head back, ignoring the hidden revolver chafing my thigh, and slid my eyes shut for several calming breaths.

Axel settled behind the wheel and started the Volvo's engine, a soft purr compared to the vicious roar of the plane's motor. After he'd introduced himself on the airfield, he'd also whispered my code name, giving me even more incentive to trust him. "I let my driver have the day off. Thought we should be alone for this conversation." There was nothing suggestive in his tone, but a curious note of something else.

"Certainly. Commandant Skilbeck warned me about eavesdroppers." I locked my jaw to trap the pressing yawn. I wanted nothing more than to hug my dear mamma's neck, then curl beneath the covers in my bed. Surely the U.S. government wouldn't begrudge me this small thing. I'd feel much more primed to save the world after a long nap.

"The commandant is right." Axel pulled onto the main road, leaving the airfield. "Eavesdroppers. Snoops. They're everywhere. I'm staying at the Grand Hôtel, and just this morning caught a maid riffling through my desk papers. I bet she's on the Gestapo's payroll." He shook his head.

"Point is, don't give your trust too easily."

I'd only been a spy for two and a half days, but my suspicious nature had developed long before that. Hollywood had prepared me. I'd grown accustomed to others invading my privacy. I learned that even after the cameras stopped rolling, people continued pretending, stuffing ugly motives beneath pretty words. Speaking of hidden things. . . "Are you German, Herr Eizenburg?"

A half smile crept over his lips. "Please call me Axel. And no. Austrian. My parents moved to Stockholm when I was quite young." He cut a curious glance. "How'd you guess?"

"The way you say your Rs." While the Swedish dialect was considered North Germanic, the trill of our Rs was more relaxed. The Germans put a heavier accent on the consonant along with a rough trill. Axel's Swedish was a slight mixture of both.

"I'm impressed." He propped his left elbow on the open window, casually draping his arm over. "Most don't catch it."

I shrugged, gazing out the windshield, taking in all the afternoon country views before we entered the heart of the capital. Parks and lakes dotted Bromma's borders, the touch of fall evident in the golden foliage. "I've been away from Swedish conversation for so long." There wasn't exactly a host of Swedes filling up California. "I suppose my ears are sensitive."

"They're lovely ears. As well as the rest of you." His flirty remark was surely meant to steer attention away from himself. But I didn't get a chance to call him out because he moved on. "Did you pack anything formal?"

I looked at him warily. "Yes." Henrik had made it clear I was to mingle among the swells so I had brought some of my favorite gowns.

"Good. Because you're attending a charity benefit at the Grand Hôtel tonight."

Pussa adjö. Kiss goodbye to my beloved nap. I slouched lower in the seat, crimping the rising groan. My eyes burned from lack of sleep. My bones felt brittle with fatigue. Tonight, I needed my nightgown, not an evening gown.

Axel grimaced. "Finn Ristaffason's attending the benefit."

Ah, this evening I was to meet the man with questionable loyalty. Years ago, I would've practically swooned over a forced rendezvous with Finn, but now I couldn't even summon a heart palpitation. "Are we even sure he has the document?"

He shrugged. "He may. He may not. But it was last seen at his boatyard. It's important for you to at least check, as unpleasant as it is." Axel's tone had all the enthusiasm of a funeral. By his set jaw and narrowed eyes, it was evident Finn Ristaffason wasn't Axel's favorite topic of conversation.

"Are you going to introduce me to him?"

"I'd rather not talk to the guy if I can help it." He scratched his neck. "I'll think of a better option."

So I was correct. It seemed I wasn't the only one who claimed a not-so-favorable history with Finn.

The gentle rattle of the car's springs tried to lull me to sleep, but I kept awake as we drove into the capital. With the Riddarfjärden (the easternmost bay of Lake Mälaren) to my right and Stockholm to my left, I took in all the familiar sights. The hum of the city pulsed life into my sluggish veins. Bicycles outnumbered cars. People strolled cobblestone paths. The bright shops boasted roofs with jaunty angles.

Axel turned toward Östermalm, and I blinked at him in surprise. "You know where I live?" It had taken a near miracle to secure an apartment in the eastern part of inner-city Stockholm. Mamma preferred a location where she could be within walking distance of everything she needed and, more importantly, live in a safe area of the city.

Axel pulled in front of the large stucco building dating to the late 1800s but updated for luxury. Mamma had fussed when I purchased the five-bedroom penthouse overlooking a beautiful park, but if anyone deserved a good bit of spoiling, it was Elsa Blakstrom.

A large hand settled on mine. I glanced over and found Axel's gaze on me. "Are you certain you're ready for this? I feel like I'm throwing you to the hounds."

I smiled, though I wasn't certain if he was referring to Finn or the Gestapo. Either way, I had a job to do. "I knew it was dangerous from the start. I'm going to follow through with it."

Something hinting of admiration stirred in his gray eyes, and he gave my hand a friendly squeeze. After parking the car, he hauled my luggage into the posh apartment building.

No attendant at the front counter. We took the lift to the top floor. Anticipation mounted within me. I was only minutes from seeing the only person who ever loved me for who I really was. The true me. Not the Hollywood-manufactured glamour girl. But Amelie Blakstrom. A nobody from the Stockholm slums.

We approached the bright blue door. One thing I adored about Sweden was its cheerful palette. In a world of dark skies and sinister winds, the colors were a balm to my soul. I turned and thanked Axel for all his help. "I can bring my things inside." It was better to say our goodbyes here. I wanted privacy for this impending reunion.

His chin dipped in understanding. "I'll be back around seven to escort you to the Grand." He gave a parting smile. "See you tonight then."

If only I could manage to stuff my tired body into a snug gown. "Looking forward to it."

I waited until he was out of sight, then flattened my palm on the door, my head bowing as emotion gathered in my chest.

Finally, after so long, I was here.

With one more calming breath, I found the spare key Mamma kept hidden in the potted fake plant by the door, and I let myself inside. The high-angled ceilings, exquisite parquet floors, and turn-of-the-century details gave the space an air of grandeur, but the scent of peppermint oil and coffee said nothing but home.

Home. Such a peculiar word. Especially since at present, I felt like I didn't belong anywhere. I was a citizen of Sweden, but I'd lived in America these past years, often visiting before the Nazis ruined everything.

I scanned the rooms. Everything appeared as if time hadn't marched forward. As if the rest of the world wasn't dueling with evil. I should call out, make my presence known, but my lips seemed to press tighter together, my heart savoring the quiet. Sunlight streamed through the floor-to-ceiling windows, adding extra warmth. I moved down the hall, knowing exactly where I'd find her, stopping at the arched entrance of the library.

There she was. Sitting on a wingback chair by the unlit fireplace, a blanket tucked over her legs. She turned the page of a thick book. No doubt a medical volume. We'd both been forced to quit our schooling at a young age, but she'd devoted any extra time to learning, tutoring me, and passing on her love of knowledge. So absorbed in the words before her, she hadn't realized my presence.

She'd slimmed a bit, but I'd seen her thinner. During our early years, when food was scarce and money was scarcer, she'd only eat after I had my fill. She'd claim she had no appetite, but I knew her stomach cramped with hunger. Then without any nourishment, she'd leave for work and toil endless hours.

Yet as I observed her now, she still had a glow of health. A miracle really, considering the years she'd worked as a charwoman and then as a maid. Despite breathing soot and bowing over a bucket, her lungs and back had remained strong.

God knew I needed her.

"I'm afraid if I look up, you'll disappear." Her gentle voice surprised me.

I laughed even as tears filled my eyes. How long had she known I was in the room? "I'm really here, Mamma." My feet couldn't carry me fast enough. I caught her in a hug just as she was rising. We both almost fell back into the chair.

How long I clung to her, I had no idea. She finally pulled back, studying my face with her maternal look. "Did you bring Cary Grant with you?"

I smiled. "He's remarried now, Mamma. You missed your window." I played along, knowing full well that if the famous actor were truly here, Mamma would no doubt give him the side-eye. She had long held a prejudice against overly handsome men. Even though Cary was pretty close to Mamma in years. Having had me at the young age of seventeen, she was often mistaken for my sister. I squeezed her again. "I missed you."

She cracked a smile. "How do I look for being so near to death's door?" She released me and tugged a piece of paper from the desk. "I got the strangest letter a couple weeks back. Hand-delivered too." Her eyes, the same blue shade as mine, glanced down at the page. "Saying rumors would be spread about my health and to *lie low* for a while." She regarded me with a skeptical expression. "That it all has to do with you."

I blew out a breath. "I'm not sure how much I can explain."

She looked me over. "Just answer me this: are you in any trouble?"

"No, nothing like that." At least not yet. There was potential for lots of trouble, but I held that tidbit back. "My work brought me here."

"Shooting a film?"

I shook my head, unsure what else I could detail. I should've asked more directly about what I was allowed to confess.

Mamma's gaze was long and searching until, finally, she expelled a tiny sigh. "You're here and you're safe. That's all I ever care about."

No truer words had been said. She'd always put me first, caring about my well-being above her own. Which was why I'd been so driven to be a success in the States. I wanted to take care of her, give her everything she wanted, and provide for her so she wouldn't have to lift a finger the rest of her days. Though that hadn't stopped her from volunteering her time at the city health clinics.

"Will your *work* allow me to rejoin the land of the living? The hospital is currently understaffed."

"The hospital is always understaffed." I gave her an affectionate smile. "And yes, but I think a slow re-emergence into society would be best." It would make my actions more believable. If the country thought her truly ill, it would make my moving about all the more suspicious. "But how is it here?" In her letters, she'd either been vague about war conditions in Sweden or wouldn't mention the war at all. "I know you never wanted me to worry, but have you need of anything?"

She sighed. "We can't complain. Everything is rationed, but everything is available. If that makes any sense. I've never once used up all my coupons. Well, except for coffee. Sometimes I had to reuse my grounds." She made a face. "And Stockholm only gets two days of hot water a month. If we want hot water any other time, we have to boil it."

I'd heard of the limits on coal consumption. "Anything else?"

"Not much to make an ordeal about, Mel." She shook her head. "We aren't suffering like most countries. You'll see for yourself. Things aren't in abundance, but you can find pretty much anything you want. Especially if you have the kronor to pay for it. As for now, let me mother you. Are you hungry? Can I make you anything?"

"No, but I suppose we should boil some water. Because I need to steam an evening gown."

The bell rang precisely at seven. I kissed Mamma's cheek with a goodbye and then answered the door. Axel stood in the hall, resplendent in his black tux and confident expression.

His gaze drifted over me, slowly down and then up. "You're not playing fair, *Fröken* Blake." He shook his head with a grin. "Maybe your code name should be Helen. For Helen of Troy. Because now, I can see how war can break out over one's beauty."

"That's a bit much." I returned his smile. "But I'm nervous. So I'll take the compliment without refuting." I ran a hand over the studded bodice of my gown. The dress was one of my favorites, a royal blue with silver motifs. It hugged my curves and flared at the bottom. With my yellow locks and blue gown, I was a breathing Swedish flag. That was, if I could even draw a breath in this dress.

I grabbed my hooded cape—a lightweight velvet with pockets—and Axel helped me into it.

I slid my hand into Axel's waiting arm, and such began my first evening working for the OSS. With my hood drawn, I walked the crowded streets with anonymity. The moon perched in the inky sky, half-obscured by wispy dark clouds. But we didn't need the moon to light our way because between the streetlamps, glowing storefront signs, and sconces lining the restaurant terraces, Stockholm shone bright.

Right now, all of England huddled under a blackout. Boarded windows, doused streetlights, every note of light extinguished in fear of the enemy. Remembering this dimmed my mood, weighing my mission even heavier on my heart.

Having already discussed the specifics of the evening, Axel and I kept to dull conversation until reaching the Grand Hôtel. The eight-story building overlooked Norrström River, opposite the Royal Palace and Old Town. Lights splayed on the pale-gray stucco walls, even as a gentle breeze rippled the many flags crowning the roof. We paused before the steps leading to the stately entrance flanked by door attendants.

Axel lowered his chin, peering underneath my hood. His face close, he repeated his question from earlier, "Are you ready for this evening?"

Was I? Tonight was my first step into the murky waters of espionage. If I found myself too deep, there was no easy drift to the shores of safety. With a prayer on my heart and a gun strapped to my thigh, I nodded. "I'm ready."

☰ CHAPTER 5 ☰

Since 1874, the Grand Hôtel had hosted kings and queens, dignitaries, Nobel laureates, and some of the most influential personages in the world. My hand rested in the crook of Axel's arm as we walked through the sizable lobby, which boasted ornate pillars, detailed crown molding, and crystal chandeliers.

Axel led me to the coat check-in, situated to the left of the counter. I peered from beneath my hood. People meandered about, but I caught several pairs of eyes locking on Axel.

"Good evening, Herr Eizenburg." The cloakroom attendant approached, his bright red hair glistening from too much pomade.

I moved to lower my hood, but Axel's fingers caught mine.

"Allow me." He leaned in and whispered, "It'll add to the effect."

I stood still as his hands drew back the velvet covering, his thumbs trailing along my collarbone, his gaze on mine.

Gasps, clearings of throats, and murmurs of my name rippled across the lobby.

Axel's eyes glinted. "How's that for an entrance?"

The unmistakable sound of camera shutters yanked my attention to a cluster of men with press badges stuffed in their hatbands. Journalists.

Axel followed my stare. "The Grand is the hub for all war talk. News correspondents gather here day and night. I'm surprised they don't set up cots in the lobby."

"If they're so keen on catching the latest scoop about the war, I wonder why they'd bother to snap my picture?"

His lips tilted in an amused smile. "It's not difficult to guess." He handed the young man my cape in exchange for a claim ticket. He looked down at me. "Shall we make our way to the great hall?"

I nodded, and he took my hand. Aware of the open stares, I pasted on a flighty smile and forced an airy bounce in my step. We approached the large room filled with grandeur and possible enemies.

"Amelie, I should warn you." He kept his voice low. "I arranged for you to meet Ristaffason in an. . .unconventional way."

I stilled beneath the entrance's archway. "How so?"

He opened his mouth to speak, but a woman bounded toward us. Her neck, wrists, and fingers were so heavily decorated with jewelry, I was amazed she could move at such a swift pace.

"Axel!" she called out, causing even more heads to turn. "Thank you for bringing our greatest showpiece." Her lipstick bled into the cracks of her lips, like red webs framing a giddy smile. "Fröken Blake, how good of you to contribute. I know tonight will be a success because of your kindness."

Axel tensed. "Uh. . .yes." He patted my hand on his arm. "Amelie, may I introduce you to *Fru* Ingrid Gelvig. She's planned this entire event on behalf of the Ristaffason family."

Wait. This charity ball was held by Finn's family? Why hadn't Axel mentioned this? And what had Fru Gelvig meant about a showpiece or my contribution to the evening? My guarded heart pounded harder as if in warning, yet the woman continued smiling, awaiting my response. "How do you do, Fru Gelvig?"

"Very well." She bobbed with excitement. "I told the master of ceremonies to call your name first."

The confused blond was no longer an act. I disliked being left in the dark, especially when it concerned me. My gaze toggled between Axel and Fru Gelvig, hoping one of them would expound.

No such luck.

Axel only adopted a polite smile. "Are any members of the Ristaffason family here?"

The older woman shook her head, her earrings jiggling against her fleshy jaw. "No. I assumed Anna Ristaffason would send her grandson to attend, but we all know Finn does as he pleases."

What? Finn wasn't coming? I sent a discreet glare at Axel. He at least had the grace to look abashed.

"It's almost time to start." Fru Gelvig's grin widened. "I'll see you in there." Then she skittered off with not-so-quiet whispers about my presence.

I gave Axel my sweetest smile even as he ushered me further inside the ballroom.

His head tilted. "Why do I get the feeling you're envisioning my demise?"

"So Finn Ristaffason isn't here. I sacrificed rest for nothing." I was all for charity. Since the war began, I'd donated far above my usual giving. But this evening's attendance wasn't as crucial to the mission as Axel had insisted. "And somehow I'm a part of this event, to which I assume *you* arranged but have not yet explained."

His gaze flitted about, and I noticed several young ladies trying to catch his eye. "There's an auction every year."

I spied lots of sparkling gowns, waiters holding trays of schnapps, and men in white or black dinner jackets. What did I not see? Any auction tables or displays. Where were the items up for bid? A sickening sensation crept over my gut, climbing to my squeezing lungs. "What showpiece did you bring, Axel?"

His expression turned sheepish. "Right here." His hands bracketed my shoulders. "The men will bid on the first dance with you."

"No. Absolutely not." I tensed. "I'm not a taxi dancer."

His brow wrinkled. "A what?"

In America, men would pay a dime a dance for a girl to partner with them. Those girls were called taxi dancers. "Forget it. I'm beginning to understand. In the car earlier, you said you'd thought of a better option to introduce me to Finn. Then a moment ago, you said it was unconventional. The auction was what you meant, wasn't it?"

His lips broke apart with a sigh. "I knew he wouldn't be able to resist you. What man could?"

"You know the old adage—flattery will get you nowhere? It's wrong. Because flattery will get you a nice dip in the Norrström." I jerked a thumb over my shoulder in the general direction of the river.

"I'm sorry, Amelie." He did look somewhat chagrined. But he might be a better actor than I was. "Finn isn't amused by anything unless he can win at the venture. The auction would play to his driven nature to conquest."

"Oh now, that's absurd."

"And I confess, I took pleasure at the thought of running up the bid. Might as well make him pay for it, right?"

Men. "So because of your grudge against Herr Ristaffason, you volunteered me without my permission?" My nerves tingled with equal parts tiredness and frustration. "I don't like you very much right now."

Something sparked in his eyes. I knew that look. It was one of a guy rising to a challenge. "I wager I can change your mind." Now his lips joined in the menacing, arcing in a crooked smile. "I'll make it up to you. I'll be sure I win the bid for your dance."

Not the consolation prize I hoped for. "What specifically is the charity?" For all I knew, it could be a fundraiser for the Third Reich.

"To improve literacy for children. The foundation purchases books, stocks libraries, and offers free tutoring to those in need."

My chest tightened. What I wouldn't have given for that sort of aid when I'd been young. "All right." I exhaled a noisy breath. "I'll go through with it." What was one dance if it helped get books into children's hands?

He reclaimed my hand. "Thank you, Amelie."

And, perhaps, I would do some spy work after all. Just because Finn wasn't here didn't mean I couldn't poke my nose around. There were lists of names in the OSS file. Surely there were other persons of interest present. My mood turned hopeful as we stepped into the ballroom, which seemed to stretch long. The second floor was open, allowing an impressive overlook of the orchestra, refreshment tables, dance floor, and stage.

A short, plump man, with a strong resemblance to W.C. Fields, waddled to the platform even as the strums of music quieted. "Ladies and gentlemen, we're about to begin the dancing portion of the evening. It's tradition to auction the first dance of one of our esteemed guests." He leaned forward as if about to reveal a great secret to a hundred attendees. "But tonight, we've the privilege of offering two dances for bidding." He then detailed the auction process with great animation, emphasizing this event was for charity and in good fun.

While the auctioneer prattled on, I openly scanned the crowd, offering a breezy smile if I made eye contact with anyone. But my search was limited. Axel and I stood on the fringe. Therefore, the majority of my view was backs of glossy heads.

"Amelie Blake, the renowned movie star, is here tonight," the emcee announced with an exaggerated sweep of his hand.

Applause followed. Many craned their necks, gazes drifting until landing on me.

I tipped my head in a friendly nod, acknowledging them.

"She's auctioning her first dance. Fröken Blake, please come to the stage, and we'll begin the bidding."

I gave a final look to Axel and walked unhurriedly across the room, the crowd parting as I made my way to the platform. Too many eyes trained on me, making the tendons behind my knees quiver. I didn't fear the crowd but my own legs, my left one specifically. How was I going to dance with a pistol strapped to my thigh? The odds of a gentleman pressing me close—and with that, our legs brushing—were uncomfortably high. I should've stored the gun in my satin clutch.

Too late now.

"Shall we start the bidding for a dance with Amelie Blake?" The auctioneer's voice was slightly nasal. "Let's start with fifty kronor. Is there a bid for fifty?"

"One hundred kronor." Axel lifted his hand and looked at me with a pleased smile.

In American money, that was roughly ten dollars. But it still made the older ladies twitter and the younger ones cup their gloved hands over their giggling mouths.

"One hundred fifty." Another man in the back waved his top hat to be seen over the crowd.

The bidding between Axel and several other gentlemen climbed to a thousand kronor, or one hundred U.S. dollars.

"Two thousand kronor." Axel took a commanding step forward, his hand raised as if ready to claim his prize.

Irritation spiked within. There was nothing worse than a smug man. But I had a part to play, and now seemed the perfect time to step into my role.

"Two thousand kronor going once." The emcee's face brightened. "Going twice."

I clasped my hands together. "Three thousand kronor."

The room fell silent.

The auctioneer's eyes rounded, and his mouth hung open, making him look like a stunned fish. "F-Fröken Blake, you can't bid on yourself."

"Why not?" I blinked innocently. "Isn't my money good enough?"

He gave a nervous chuckle. "Of course. Of course. But it's just not how it's done."

"I've never won a whole dance before." I pitched my voice higher, giving it a touch of airiness. "Just think, I could do whatever I choose with it." Like sit it out and not run the risk of shooting myself in the foot.

The announcer tugged at his already too-tight collar. "I—I don't see why you couldn't participate."

"Oh, that's ever so good of you." I patted his cheek with a giggle.

He reddened. "Continuing the bid. Three thousand kronor going once."

Just for fun, I almost raised my own bid, sealing the deal on my stupidity. But there was such a thing as overplaying a role.

"Going twice."

I lifted my chin in a triumphant smile. See, I didn't need Axel's rescue. "Sol—"

"Nine thousand kronor." A man stepped from a cluster of guests.

Finn Ristaffason.

He'd filled out since the last time I saw him. His strong shoulders and expansive chest tapered into a lean middle over long legs. Of course, the man would be even more appealing. But what remained the same over the years? His arrogant expression. It was no wonder the OSS cast me in the role of the ninny. My simple-minded facade would only play to Finn's self-imposed superiority.

"Nine thousand, ladies and gentlemen." The auctioneer grew flustered, flapping his hands against his sides. "That's triple the going bid!"

Everyone wore the same shocked expression as the master of ceremonies. One could buy a luxury motorcar for the amount of money Finn had bid. Yet his tall frame leaned against the marble pillar, indifference lining his handsome brow, as if he'd just tossed a few coins into a well.

"Any challengers?" The auctioneer leaned toward the crowd, his gaze swooping like a vulture.

No one dared twitch an eyelash.

The paunchy man faced me. "Fröken Blake, care to counter?"

"Oh, I wish. But stash anything more than three thousand kronor, and it starts to show." I glanced pointedly down my person as if I'd stored wads of bills beneath my dress, despite the perfectly serviceable clutch in my right hand. A few snickers and well-placed clearing of throats followed my remark.

"Then sold." The emcee's voice seemed to reach the high-vaulted ceiling. "Fröken Blake's first dance goes to Herr Finn Ristaffason for nine thousand kronor."

The man himself approached the stage, outstretching his hand, beckoning. "Fröken Blake."

I almost startled at the deep rumble of my name but kept my composure, slipping my fingers into his grasp.

His piercing blue eyes solely focused on me. His masculine form, impeccable in evening wear, was broad enough to give a woman a sense of safety and warm enough to coax her to cozy up to him. I could see how legions of ladies would swoon at his nearness.

Years ago, I'd have relished this moment, but now I wasn't certain if the fingers wrapping mine had also shaken hands with Nazis.

He led me down the stairs and off to the side. "It seems there's no need for introductions."

My brow scrunched. He wouldn't possibly remember me from Count Vernalette's estate, would he?

He motioned toward the stage. "The emcee introduced us in a roundabout way."

Ah, so he didn't recall that humiliating day. I wasn't sure if I was relieved or annoyed. Still, I mustered a sweet smile. "That's a lot of money to pay for a dance."

"It's my family's charity. I was going to spend that amount anyway." Finn's Swedish was refined, no trace of any dialect. But I already knew he'd been privileged with an upper-class upbringing.

"Do I hear fifty kronor?" The auctioneer's voice crashed in my ears, interrupting my set down. Perhaps it was for the best.

I shifted to get a clearer view of the next unfortunate young lady whose dance was up for bidding.

My pulse jolted.

Rosita Serrano.

Fröken Serrano batted her lashes prettily. She was dressed in a flowing gown, her dark locks piled upon her head, highlighting her graceful neck. The woman was stunning. She was also on the OSS watch list.

I could picture the page from the file—three paragraphs from the bottom. Second line down.

Female. Age: 31. Nationality: Chilean. Occupation: Singer.

Followed by the woman's photo.

Fröken Serrano played to the crowd, laughing and blowing kisses, stirring up bids left and right. But what was she up to? Moreover, why was her name on the list?

"You seem very interested in Fröken Serrano." Finn broke into my thoughts.

"Oh, she's just lovely." I made a show of studying her. "I can't decide if her dress is Parisian or French?"

He gave me a strange look, and I repressed the urge to laugh, choosing to beam at him instead. Maybe acting brainless could be more diverting than I imagined.

I tilted my head. "Perhaps we can ask her? But I haven't been introduced to her. Do you know her?"

"She sang at a nightclub I visited." Only Finn could wear a bored expression and look appealing doing so. "She's touring the country. Came here straight from Berlin."

From the heart of the Nazi empire. Was she running from the evil or spreading it? "Now that I think of it. . ." I paused as if straining to piece my *feeble* wits together. "I've heard some rumors about her."

He lowered his voice. "You mean about her dining with Hitler and gaining the distinct favor of Hermann Göring?"

Hermann Göring was the leader of the Third Reich. Interesting. This woman had possibly been in the inner circles of the highest-ranked officers in the war. My suspicions soared. "Oh," I said flippantly. "I meant the rumor about her mouth. I heard she stuffed tissues beneath her upper lip to make it fuller. How silly. Even I know one can't sing with a mouthful of cotton." Slight fabrication. But there were many women in my profession who went to such lengths to alter their appearance.

His lips pressed together, making a dimple dent the right side of his mouth. "As to that, I don't know."

"Sold for seven hundred kronor," the auctioneer announced and gently led Fröken Serrano to. . .Axel. During my conversation with Finn, I hadn't realized Axel had been bidding. If I knew Fröken Serrano was on the OSS watch list, so did Axel. I guessed his win was deliberate.

"Jealous?"

I turned to find Finn watching me observe Axel. "Not at all." I smoothed my hair over my shoulder. "Why would I want to dance with Fröken Serrano?"

"No, I meant. . ." He wasn't charmed by anything I said but rather seemed annoyed. Wasn't he supposed to be a devoted fan of mine? Because eye rolls and bored grimaces weren't signs of an admirer. "Never mind."

The orchestra played a swift overture. The dancing was about to start. My thoughts traveled to the gun on my leg. I'd secured it tightly but not overly where circulation would cinch. But what if I began to sweat? Would it slip?

Finn escorted me onto the dance floor, and then. . .off it? He paused before the ornate double doors. "Would you mind if we stepped out onto the terrace?"

"I thought you were going to dance with me."

He leaned close. "I intend to."

CHAPTER 6

Of course, the moon would choose this moment to appear, bathing the balcony's dark stone with an ethereal glow. Between the muted strums of the orchestra, the glistening current of the river beside us, and the golden good looks of a Scandinavian Prince Charming—well, could-be charming if he put forth any effort—it was very much a semblance of a fairy tale. We even had the Royal Palace as a backdrop.

But just like Swedish folklore, I was immune to fairy tales. I knew too much of the deception squeezed between "Once upon a time" and "Happily ever after."

So it was best to ignore the attractive blue eyes fastened upon me and the shiver chasing down my gloved fingers.

"Are you cold?" Finn's brow dipped. "I thought it would be better to dance out here, away from prying eyes, but I forgot about the chill."

The gentle fall breeze was refreshing compared to the stifling ballroom. Yet there was another advantage. The music was quieter, making conversation effortless. Not only would I not have to strain to hear, but we had the balcony to ourselves. The only eavesdroppers present were the few gnats circling my face. I swatted them away, then smiled. "I like it here." After setting my clutch on a patio chair, I faced him. "Shall we, Herr Ristaffason?"

"Please call me Finn." He gave a slight bow and reached for me. My hand slid into his, even as his other arm curled around my waist. We fell into an easy rhythm.

There were certain signals a man gave while holding a woman: The pressure of his palm, the clasp of his fingers. If a gentleman's grip was

limp, it betrayed his uncertainty. A tight grasp? The man was overconfi-
dent, dominating. I was confident Finn would embody the latter, but his
technique was smooth and sure, telling me he was comfortable having a
lady in his arms.

"How long is your stay in Sweden?" He peered down at me as we
swayed to the gentle music.

"I'm not sure." I wasn't given a departure day. Once I recovered the
document, I was to take it to Strandvagen 7. The OSS had claimed a
floor in the American Legation. Though, I'd been warned to keep clear
of the fancy waterfront building until I completed my mission. Bill
Donovan didn't want anyone discovering my connection to the OSS.

"I hope I see more of you during your stay." Most would take that as
a flirtatious remark, but his bland tone and neutral expression revealed a
forced politeness.

"Sorry, but no one *sees* more of me than this." I dipped my chin,
gesturing to my gown. "But I wouldn't mind spending time with you."

He gave a tight nod and spun me under his arm.

I twirled, my skirt tangling between us, my grin slipping free.
But that wasn't all that slipped—my holster! I gasped, sucking in one
of those wretched gnats, then proceeded to choke. My legs squeezed
together, trapping the gun with my knees, even as I bowed over with a
wracking cough.

Finn's hand was on my back. "Are you okay?"

"I. . .swallowed. . .bug."

He straightened. "I'll fetch you a drink. I won't be long." He strode
through the doors.

With tears welling in my eyes and my breath wheezing, I shuffled
toward a darkened corner. Hiking my dress, I fumbled with the leather
strap, my glove making the effort more difficult. I used my teeth to tug
the glove off my clammy hand. Once free, my fingers deftly unbuckled
the holster. By this time, my cough had subsided. I lowered my gown
and shoved the gun, holster and all, into my clutch.

I was composed and breathing evenly when Finn returned to
the balcony.

"Sorry it took so long." He pressed a glass into my hand. "I had to
hunt down a pitcher of water."

I didn't doubt it. At events like these, alcohol flowed like an endless fountain. I took a tentative sip, relieved to find Finn's words true—only water. "Thank you."

"Glad I could help." He searched my face. "Feeling better?"

I took another sip. "Yes, though I can't stop thinking that I'm currently digesting an insect." I shuddered, even as a laugh sputtered from my lips. Thanks to my disguise, there was no chance of dazzling Finn with my intellect. Which had only left my poise and charisma to snag his interest. But nothing killed that impression more than gulping gnats, then coughing hard enough to dislodge organs. So much for that. I wasn't one to dissolve into giggles, but I found my shoulders shaking as I tried to suppress the rising laughter.

Finn watched me as if I was some strange creature whom he didn't know how to approach. Likewise, pal.

I moved to the iron railing overlooking the water, pulling in deep breaths, reclaiming composure.

Finn joined me, his arm brushing mine. "Are you looking at the palace?"

It was almost impossible not to. The enormous U-shaped building was lit with spotlights that reflected off the river. No turrets or high towers, but the roman baroque structure still drew the eyes. While commanding, the palace wasn't what held my attention. "No, the water." There was something mysterious and unsafe about the deep, yet also beautiful and graceful. "My morfar was a fisherman."

"I know."

My brows rose. "You do?"

His eyes met mine. "My *farmor* speaks of him often."

I shook my head, barely comprehending. Finn's grandmother knew my grandfather? That was a new revelation. Our families moved in vastly different circles.

"She's told me stories about his youth."

How I would love to hear those. Morfar. His gruff and rigid exterior housed the softest heart. My chest tightened. Perhaps Finn just handed me a key to unlock the next step in this charade. "Can I meet her?" I bit the edge of my lip, even as an idea formed. "Oh, how marvelous it would be. I've heard you own boatyards. Does your farmor live near there? Because then I can see the boats and talk to her." I sighed dreamily. "I know Malmö's a good distance from here, but it would be like hugging my dear departed morfar."

His gaze tracked my face for a heart-pounding second. "How could I refuse you?"

"Easily with the word 'no,' but I'd rather you say 'yes.' "

"Then yes."

I beamed at him. "Thank you, Finn."

"Farmor is at the Malmö estate, which links to the docks. You're welcome to stay as long as you want." He nodded, but he didn't seem as enthused at the prospect of spending time with me as Donovan had implied. If I hadn't seen it myself in the OSS files about Finn purchasing all my films, I'd assume the man had no regard for me whatsoever.

Axel stepped through the double doors. "There you are, Amelie." His gaze shifted to Finn. "I didn't realize the dance floor extended to the terrace." He didn't bother to disguise his unfriendly tone. "Ristaffason."

Finn seemed unfazed at Axel's cold greeting. "Eizenberg."

How long had Finn and I been out here? The orchestra had moved on to another song. Or had more than one passed?

Ignoring Axel completely, Finn channeled those blue eyes on me. "I plan on returning to Malmö in the morning, though you can visit when convenient for you."

This was my chance. "I'd like to go with you."

≡ CHAPTER 7 ≡

I swept up the side of Mamma's hair in a red crystal comb and ran my fingers through the curls in the back. "There." I patted her shoulders, pleased at the becoming style. "You look just like Lana Turner."

With a light scoff, she twisted on the vanity seat. "Aren't you acting suspicious this morning. First you cook my favorite breakfast. Now you're fixing my hair. I thought you had a trip to get ready for."

Suspicious? More like guilty. I hated leaving her for Malmö. Though I wasn't exactly certain if Finn was serious about taking me. Or even if I should go. It was hard to judge a man's sincerity by only a handful of minutes in his company.

Because the more I'd thought on it, the more absurd it sounded. What woman would travel several hours by train, only to stay at an estate belonging to a man she'd only just met? I'd practically thrown myself at Finn. What if he expected an indecent favor in return?

My stomach soured, but I summoned a smile for Mamma. "I packed last night." After those moments on the balcony, Finn had disappeared from the charity event as mysteriously as he'd arrived. As for Axel, I'd been correct about him keeping an eye on the singer Rosita Serrano. He'd admitted to winning the auction for an opportunity to speak with her. After her departure from the Grand Hôtel, Axel and I danced a couple of songs and then left. I'd returned to the apartment by nine, and though exhausted, I'd enjoyed catching up with Mamma. "Besides, aren't I allowed to pamper you?"

She rose, her blush-toned dress enhancing her ivory complexion. "It seems all you do is take care of me."

"Nothing wrong with that." I swiped my hat from the vanity and pinned it on my head at a jaunty angle. The red felt matched the piping on my navy-blue traveling suit. "I was hoping—"

"Ah, there it is." Mamma folded her arms with a knowing look. "I told you last night not to feel guilty about leaving."

Yes, I was hesitant about going to Malmö, but there was another reason. I was painfully aware of how she felt about that area of the country. She'd fled Lomma, Malmö's neighboring fishing village, when she was seventeen and never returned. Though she'd sent me there almost every summer to stay with Morfar. "What if..." I took a steady breath. "What if you came with me?" It would take some juggling on my end, between seeing to her comfort, uncovering Finn's political loyalties, and searching for the document, but I was nothing if not efficient. "We can face what has haunted you, together."

Her shoulders lowered with a sigh. "I swore to never go back. I've stayed away, first out of pride. But now..." She shook her head, her forehead creasing. "There's nothing for me there anymore."

I wasn't certain if it was regret in her tone for not attending her pappa's funeral. Or if something else evoked the somber notes in her voice. Regardless, she was resolved not to join me.

I gave a resigned nod. "Okay, Mamma."

Her gentle hand slipped over my shoulder. "But if you would, can you please tell Anna Ristaffason thank you on my behalf? She'll know what you mean."

My brows drew up in confusion. Thank Finn's farmor? I opened my mouth to ask, but a knock at the door interrupted. "That must be Herr Ristaffason."

She pulled me into a hug. "I've long heard about this man. It's rumored he's a trifle good-looking." She said the last word as if her lemonade was too sour.

I might as well inform her now. Of all the prejudices a person could have, nothing provoked her displeasure more than a handsome man. "It's not a rumor. I'm sorry to report he's incredibly attractive, Mamma."

Sighing, she lightly patted my back as if I were a child needing consoling, then she eased away. "But what kind of mother would I be if I didn't warn you?" Her eyes implored mine, and I knew not to take this topic lightly. "The forbidden road is often heavily worn." She conveyed a message deeper than just reciting the Swedish proverb.

I gripped both her hands in mine. "Then I'll be certain to keep my feet on the straight and narrow."

Another rap.

"I shouldn't keep him waiting." I glanced at my reflection, then at Mamma. "Maybe you should remain here."

She shook her head. "I think I should meet him."

"You're supposed to be recovering from a life-threatening illness," I reminded her, but she was already moving out of the bedroom.

I followed with a roll of my eyes. It didn't take much to see where I'd inherited my stubbornness from.

Mamma repositioned the parlor chair to face the entryway. "I'll just sit right here." She plopped onto the tufted cushion and snagged the blanket draping the armrest, tucking it over her lap. "I can act tired and frail, if that helps." Her chin sagged even as her shoulders drooped. "How's this?"

A laugh danced across my lips. "I'm sure resting in the chair will be enough." I kissed her head and moved to answer the door.

Finn stood behind the threshold. He wore a suit of dark brown, heightening the blues of his eyes. I heard a tiny gasp behind me. I should've prepared Mamma for the Finn Effect—a term I'd coined years ago but had forgotten until this moment.

He removed his hat, revealing his wavy blond hair. "Good morning, Amelie. Are you still up for retreating to the estate?"

Nodding, I motioned to the bags I'd placed by the door earlier. "Yes." Seeing that Mamma had no idea about my *disguise*, I kept my words to a minimum.

I introduced Finn to Mamma, who now eyed him warily. According to her, the handsomer the man, the more dubious the character. Poor Finn had just landed top billing on her mistrust list simply because of his unfortunate good looks.

Feeling the emotion of our upcoming separation, I hugged Mamma tight with a goodbye. I grabbed my clutch from the side table, which had been emptied of any lethal weapon. While Mamma had slept in and then bathed, I'd spent the morning familiarizing myself with the spy trade. I'd practiced holding, unloading, and reloading the pistol. Had gone about picking every lock in the penthouse. And had tested various spots on my leg, finding the best position for the leather holster. I could now proudly dance, run, and jump without it budging.

Finn reached for my bags, even as a large man approached the doorway.

"A message for Amelie Blake," he announced, holding out a small envelope. Though he donned a uniform and cap, I'd never seen a messenger *boy* in his midthirties with a military bearing. He was obviously an OSS courier.

Feeling both Mamma's and Finn's eyes on me, I accepted the missive. "Thank you." I reached into my clutch, fishing some coins out for a tip.

He mumbled his appreciation and left.

"Whoever it was may have called," Mamma remarked, looking pointedly at the note in my hands. "Seems a lot simpler."

"Yes," I verbally agreed, but knew the phone line was not a trusted means of communication. It could easily be tampered with. "When does the train leave?" Because I hoped to escape for a few minutes to read the message in private.

Finn glanced at his pocket watch and grimaced. "Actually, really soon. We should head to the station."

Trapping the rising disappointment, I stuffed the envelope in my clutch as Finn gathered my belongings. Hopefully, the contents weren't urgent.

I said another farewell to Mamma and followed Finn out. He led me to the hired car where the chauffeur held open the back door. Finn placed my bags in the trunk, and I lowered onto the car's bench.

My breath seeped out in a slow contrast to my racing heart. Could I do this? My gaze drifted over Mamma's apartment building. Sunlight dappled the stucco exterior. I was leaving her behind, my only family, for a job that was potentially dangerous. But then again, how many husbands, fathers, and sons had left their families to fight in a war with no guarantee of a safe return?

I would do my part.

———— ≈ ————

The Stockholm Central Station had linked all of Scandinavia by rail since 1871. Yet what was considered ideal and convenient could also be judged as detrimental. Because up until two months ago, those same tracks had carried Nazi soldiers and supplies into Norway. Germany had attacked our neighboring country and used Swedish railways to carry out their dark plans. Allied forces had pressured Sweden to forbid passage to the Germans, and thankfully, they'd listened.

Central Station was a hub of activity. Beneath the skylighted dome, Swedes from every background milled about, some in more haste than others. I'd enjoyed blending into the sea of people, until the gentleman manning the newspaper stand yelled my name across the concourse.

I was certain Finn was used to a good share of public attention, but even he seemed surprised, if not alarmed, by the swarming crowd. But I loved it. These were my people. If we hadn't been pressed for time, I would've gladly remained and chatted. Such as it was, I could only dole out smiles and well-wishes along with a few autographs.

The conductor called "*Ombord!*" and we gravitated toward the designated platform.

Movement to my left snagged my attention. A man frantically jumped and waved in our direction.

Finn's mouth pressed into a scowl. "Excuse me a moment." His long strides ate the distance between him and the panicky fellow.

I couldn't catch their words, but the shorter man did the speaking, Finn listening with the scowl cemented on his face. Finn's eyes narrowed, making my chest constrict. What were they discussing in heated tones? My skeptical nature feared they were talking about me and my bogus cover.

Breathe in. Breathe out.

Finn ended the exchange with a terse nod, then rejoined me in line. The crush of people boarding the train prevented any discussion. With our bags already checked, the porter showed us to. . .our private cabin? Of course Finn would travel this way. The coach car seemed beneath a person like him.

Yet I was hesitant. A few hours in a secluded cabin with a man I hardly knew?

Finn seemed to catch my reluctance. "Do these accommodations suit?"

With a tight nod, I stepped inside. There were two plush benches opposite each other. The walls above slightly bulged, indicating sleeper units. Because this was a day journey, the beds had been stowed and locked.

The porter wished us a good journey, then left, closing the door behind him. Usually, I selected the seat beside the window, but I found myself remaining near the exit. Something that didn't escape Finn's notice.

He sat on the other bench, a comfortable distance away. The tense set of his shoulders and fixed frown told me he was still bothered by the conversation with the man on the platform. Or maybe it was I who bothered him. Perhaps he was now aware of my motives for traveling with him to Malmö.

I swallowed. "Don't you like him?"

"Hmm?" He snapped his gaze from a blank spot on the floor and settled on me.

"You've been scowling like this"—I imitated him with a bit more exaggeration—"since talking to the guy out there. You must not like him."

He shook his head, but at least the glower was gone. "No, he's only the messenger. I was disturbed at the message. But I won't bore you with the details of my boatyard business."

"Really?" I perked. "I heard there's been a lot happening in your boatyard over these past weeks."

"What. . ."—he leaned forward, his gaze smoldering with interest—". . .exactly did you hear?"

My throat burned dry. From his dodgy dismissal about his interaction with the guy on the platform to his sudden curiosity about what I knew about his boatyard, it was clear something was amiss. Perhaps the OSS were wise to suspect Finn Ristaffason.

I reclined against the seat and studied the red polish on my nails. "Only that you helped with the Danish rescue." I looked up to find him staring.

"A lot of Danes arrived at my shores." He nodded, relaxing slightly. "And some of my boats were involved."

I pressed my lips together, inwardly tired of feigning confusion. "But I thought the Danes used their own boats."

He stretched out his long legs, the soles of his shoes almost tapping against my bench. "A lot of them were Danish, but we lent some of ours on some rescues."

Donovan had said the briefcase was aboard Finn's boat. So far, Finn's answers seemed to line up with what I'd been told. But deception was often couched in truth. The train rolled out of the station, slowly gaining momentum. For better or worse, I was headed to Malmö. "How many boats do you have?"

"A lot." Finn rested his bent elbows on his knees and leaned forward. "You're quite inquisitive. Does that mean you'll answer my questions too?"

As if he considered his cryptic responses *answers*. It irked me that he'd been purposefully vague, then in the same breath demanded honesty from me. I rounded my eyes, taking the naive approach. "It all depends."

"On what?"

I shrugged. "On if I know the answer."

"I noticed you spoke to everyone who approached you at the station." His gaze melted into mine. "Why did you talk to them?"

My heart sank. Exploring this topic would stir up long-buried memories, awakening my insecurities. Today, I needed my wits sharp and my emotions dull, and this was one subject that would bring the reverse. I took a deep breath. "Why did I *talk*?" I tapped my chin, then dropped it as if the answer just hit me. "Because that's the easiest way to communicate."

His jaw tightened. My foolishness was irritating him, but I couldn't blame the man. I found it annoying as well. "I'm asking why you took the time?"

I twirled a lock of hair around my index finger. "Why shouldn't I?" Of all the moments I'd loathed my disguise, this topped them all. For years, I'd longed for an opportunity to knock Finn Ristaffason from his high pedestal. I'd imagined scenarios in which I'd be the one who delivered the perfect knockdown, finally vindicating myself. Seemed ironic that when the rare chance finally arrived, I was required to be the idiot. Again.

He peered at me as if I were a puzzle he couldn't quite put together. "It was. . .unexpected."

Something sparked in my gut. Of course anything that resembled human decency would surprise him. I was keenly aware of how he'd treated those he'd deemed below him. Maybe it was fitting this subject arose, if only to remind me to squash any hints of attraction to him. Because while the world thought me brainless, I'd rather be missing the vital organ in my skull than the beating one in my chest. "I talked to them because it's the kind thing to do."

His gaze briefly swept my face, but he said nothing. If the man was so disinterested in me, why spend a small fortune to win my dance? Why bring me to his home?

Stifling a sigh, I turned to peer out the window. I found comfort in the beauty of my homeland. Outside the capital, the country was mostly forest. The scene glided past in colors of vivid greens and golds.

As a child, it always reminded me of the turning of a kaleidoscope. I remembered pressing my face against the glass, gazing everywhere, afraid of blinking in fear of missing something extraordinary. How Mamma had sacrificed to put me on those train trips. We hardly had enough kronor for food, yet she'd insisted I visit Morfar each summer, claiming I needed a fatherly influence in my life. Those precious months were filled with laughter, swimming in the Öresund, and reading letters Mamma had sent.

Wait. Letters.

The missive!

I'd completely forgotten about the message I'd received at the penthouse. Though I knew better than to open the envelope in front of Finn. I gathered my clutch and rose, drawing Finn's attention. "I think I'll powder my nose."

"Of course." He nodded.

I slipped out of the cabin and drew a full breath. One unfortunate difference between Sweden and America was the bathroom fee. But I'd gladly forfeit a krona if that meant privacy. I pushed the coin through the metal slot and turned the lock, opening the door. Once inside the compact lavatory, I tugged the envelope from my bag and gently tore it open.

Hoping to catch you before you leave. Ristaffason can't be trusted. Postpone your trip to Malmö until we speak.

Wolf

⅀ CHAPTER 8 ⅀

After reading Axel's warning, I'd been restless to reach Malmö. On the five-and-a-half-hour trip, I'd finagled ways to keep from being alone with Finn in the cabin. We'd visited the dining car for lunch, to which I'd become the world's slowest eater. Then, of course, I had to have fika—though a cup of coffee only lasted so long. Thankfully, by the time we had returned to our secluded compartment, we were approaching the station.

Several moments later, Finn helped me down the train's narrow steps onto the platform. He released my hand, and I breathed in relief. I didn't know what prompted Axel's message, but I was determined to remain guarded.

A gentle breeze rolled off the Öresund. Malmö was as bustling as Stockholm, yet it claimed a small-town feel with its cobblestone square, half-timbered buildings, and charming cafés. I'd only visited Malmö a handful of times, since Morfar's fishing business was about thirteen kilometers north in Lomma.

Finn's driver met us near the station's entrance and proceeded to load our things in the trunk, while Finn opened my door. I nodded my thanks, and then we were on our way to his estate.

"Are you sure your farmor won't mind me staying?" I asked, feeling guilty for having not thought this before. "I don't want to upset her."

"You won't." He sounded so certain. "I'm more concerned she won't let you leave."

Finn's remark caused me to hope Anna Ristaffason had a hospitable nature, one her grandson seemed to lack. Throughout our journey, he'd been well-mannered but continued his display of indifference, stirring my curiosity. Bill Donovan had painted Finn as my admirer, but I wasn't sensing anything but polite tolerance from the man sitting beside me.

Finn's driver slowed the car, allowing a tram to cross the intersection on a ribbon of rails. I noticed there weren't many automobiles on the streets, the effects of gasoline rationing.

But there were locals displaying their wares on street corners. We passed stalls of balloon bundles, bouquets of flowers, and late-season vegetables. Boats bobbed in the harbor. Several pedestrians huddled around a fishmonger, stuffing paper bags with crustaceans. The tiny, sweet-fleshed Baltic shrimp were only found in southern Scandinavia and had been Morfar's main source of income for decades. He'd sold them straight from his boat just as these men were.

Finally, the car pulled onto a drive leading to a palatial home—the Ristaffason residence. I almost laughed. Because, though grand, the house before me, with its cheery yellow plaster and ivory trim, had an inviting aura of warmth, vastly contrasting the personality of its owner.

For some reason, I expected the house to be secluded from the rest of Malmö, but it was as if the city wrapped itself around this three-story estate, just as much a prominent part of its history as St. Peter's Church or Malmöhus Castle.

I twisted on the seat to ask Finn a question, only to find him watching me. Was he observing my reaction to his beautiful home? I sloughed off the thought. He'd already proven he didn't put much value in my opinions. "It's lovely." I smiled. "When was it built?"

"In 1750." Traces of pride were in his tone.

I let out a low whistle as the chauffeur slowed the car to a stop. "I hope I age as well as your house."

"It's a constant flow of repairs." Finn glanced at me. "A lot of money's required to touch up the exterior."

"Same could be said for a lot of actresses I know."

"That so?" was all Finn's response, but I could've sworn I heard his driver snort.

The chauffeur opened my door, then rounded the car to Finn's side. But to my surprise, Finn retrieved my things from the trunk.

I followed him down the manicured walkway and up the limestone steps, but Finn paused before the front door, leaning toward me.

The late afternoon sun touched his face, highlighting faint stubble along his sharp jaw, bringing my attention to the silver starbursts ringing his pupils. Yes, I'd danced with him last night, but I'd never been this close in natural light. His eyes were truly remarkable.

His gaze pierced mine. "You're bound to hear gossip about some unfortunate events." His voice was a deep rasp. "I ask you to do me the justice of not trusting the sordid rumors as truth."

My gut pinched. Rumors? What kind of unfortunate events? Also, the man had the entire day to spring this important piece of news upon me, and he waited until we were seconds from entering his house? Why? Ah, but I knew. He hadn't wanted me peppering him with my foolish questions. Well, too bad. "How will I know what to believe or not?" I innocently batted my lashes. "Should I come to you first? Ask you if what I hear is right?"

He considered my words with the sort of painful expression one would have if they stubbed their toe or suffered a toothache. Was my company that tiresome to him? I recalled all our conversations today and had to conclude—yes. Yes, my ninny facade proved to be a colossal failure in getting on Finn's good side. The OSS was comprised of the smartest people in America, but somewhere along the spy chain, someone had goofed. Perhaps Finn was a Rita Hayworth fan.

Finally, he looked down at me. "Of course, Amelie. You may approach me whenever you like." He opened the front door, allowing me to enter before him.

The inside was just as bright. Satin damask wallpaper of powder blue flowed into the elegant crown molding. A grand staircase centered the room with white polished banisters and a light gray runner.

"There you are!" A feminine voice jolted me from my appraisal.

A tall, older woman rushed into the foyer, followed by a younger lady shuffling at a more hesitant pace.

Anna Ristaffason, I presumed, moved swiftly toward her grandson. "I'm so glad you're home, Finn. Johan is still—Oh." She caught sight of me and froze, her aged face slacking in surprise. "Amelie Blake?" Her gaze briefly drifted to Finn, then returned to me. "Amelie Blake!" The next few seconds blurred as an eighty-plus woman careened toward me, catching me in an embrace.

"*Hej*," I said hello, somewhat baffled. I'd never met the matriarch of the Ristaffason family, but she clung to me as if I were some beloved relative. She hadn't even hugged her own grandson yet. Speaking of which, Finn rounded us, giving me a full view of his reaction. Instead of appearing bothered by his farmor's slight, his eyes lit with. . .amusement?

The older woman released me with a growing grin. "I'm so thrilled to meet you at last."

Finn stepped forward. "Enjoy her company, Farmor. I spent nine thousand kronor to claim a private moment with her to get an autograph for you."

My brows dipped. "But you didn't ask me to sign anything."

He shrugged. "I brought you here instead."

A soft gasp escaped my lips. What? So that hefty sum he'd doled out for a dance had nothing to do with any infatuation. He wasn't enamored by my charm. He was only thinking of his farmor. Well, if that didn't humble a lady.

"Finn spoils me." She sent him an affectionate look. "He purchased all your films for me. I can't begin to tell you how many times I watched them. He even had the old music room refurnished into a charming theater. So I overlook him never joining me." She gently squeezed his arm. "Though I tell him over and over he'd enjoy your movies if he gave them a chance."

Finn's disinterest finally made sense. He wasn't my biggest fan. His farmor was. The man hadn't even seen any of my films. The boys at Camp X had been so sure Finn would be eating out of my palm, when in reality, he was more likely to brush my hand away.

And now I was trapped hiding behind a silly facade that irked the man I was supposed to get close to. One would think Finn would savor having a silly female hanging on his arm. The lower the intellect of those around him, the higher he was to look down upon them. Though I didn't have the time or energy to pick apart Finn's complicated personality. Despite the somberness of my newfound situation, I forced a chipper expression. "Thank you for the kind greeting, Fru Ristaffason."

She returned my smile. "The granddaughter of my childhood friend is always welcome here. And you must call me Anna." Age had matured her face and whitened her hair, but she was hearty and had a glow of health.

Anna waved to the woman who'd seemed to fade into the tapestries. "Let me introduce you to my secretary. This is Margit Lastrand." Anna leaned in and lowered her voice. "The child's a bit shy. I blame her home, a small village in Gotland. But she's a steady girl."

I exchanged hellos with the young lady who appeared a few years younger than me. Her pale blond hair had been parted in a severe line down the middle of her scalp, making her sharp nose the prominent feature of her face. She wore a button-down gingham dress that had been patched in a few areas.

Anna placed a gentle hand on my elbow. "I was just about to go to the parlor for afternoon fika. You're most welcome to join me, or I can show you to your room."

I was exhausted, mentally and physically. But I had a job to do. If I couldn't get close to Finn, I'd have to get to him through the only woman he seemed to love—his farmor. I smiled sweetly at the man of the house, which prompted his brow to raise, then beamed at Anna. "I never turn down coffee."

She gave a pleased nod. "Wonderful. I'll have your things sent to your room." She turned to her secretary. "Margit, please fetch my calendar. I need to clear my schedule for our guest." I began to protest, but Anna stilled me with a smile. "I insist."

Margit retreated silently as I followed Anna into a charming sitting room with two plum sofas positioned around a marble fireplace. Finn didn't join us, not that I'd expected him to. The man was probably elated to be free of me.

The coffee was on the bland side but not the company. Anna was charming. As if sensing my fatigue, she had kept the conversation light. Margit had come and gone, her movements timid and quiet. After the last pastry was consumed, Anna showed me to my room on the third floor.

She paused at a door at the end of the hall. "I hope this one will suit you." Her brow lowered. "Most of our guest rooms overlook the back garden, but I'm afraid they're being repapered." The buttons on her sleeve clicked against the brass doorplate as she turned the handle. "The prospect out the window isn't as pretty with the boatyard in the distance."

Perfect. "This is a fine room." And it was. The furnishings were soft blue with gold drapes. "Thank you."

With a graceful smile lining her face, she nodded. "Dinner's served at eight. I hope you can rest until then." She patted my elbow and left.

My things had been set by the door. It would be wise to select a dress for dinner and let it air out. I moved to open the suitcase but stilled. One of the latches had been tampered with. And the cuff of my houndstooth suit poked out from the left corner. Last evening, I had everything neatly organized and folded. Heart pounding, I laid the suitcase on the floor and opened it.

I gasped. My clothes were crumpled. My cosmetic bag had been emptied, my ivory powder spilled about. My head spun, taking in the disarray.

Someone had rummaged through my things.

≣ CHAPTER 9 ≣

I straightened my suitcases and separated the makeup-soiled clothes to be laundered. I didn't know who'd carried my things to my room. Had it been Finn? A maid? Some other house staff? Unease pricked. No one would possibly know I was in Malmö to locate Dr. Bohr's document. . .would they? Was that the reason my luggage had been opened and searched?

Of course, there could be a simpler explanation. Perhaps whoever moved my luggage had been careless and somehow knocked it open, accounting for why all my things had been stuffed back into the suitcase as if in haste. If the culprit had been from the house staff, I could see why they'd be hesitant to confess. Having an employer as difficult to please as Finn Ristaffason could be nerve-racking. I puffed out my cheeks and exhaled slowly. Whatever the reason, it only strengthened my resolve to be more watchful.

I slipped on my dark green velvet dress and readied early for dinner, giving me time to explore and acquaint myself with the layout of the house.

High-heeled pumps weren't conducive for covert activities. At least when one was walking on hardwood floors. I slipped off my shoes and made my way to the first floor without being detected.

What I'd gathered from the short jaunt to the sitting room this afternoon was that the west portion of the house held the dining hall, parlors, and a formal ballroom. All the social spaces. Which made me guess the east side would be the family wing. Finn's office, perhaps?

Oil paintings lined the halls. But there were also portraits. I stopped in front of a young couple. The clothing style was early 1900s, not quite the turn of the century but definitely not the from the twenties. Which made me suspect I was looking at a portrait of Finn's parents. His parents had tragically passed in the sinking of the *Titanic*, leaving Anna to raise an infant Finn and his older brother Rolf. As for Rolf—

Muted voices pulled my gaze to a room a few yards away. I eased along the wall, keeping my footfalls quiet, until I reached an ornate wooden door, half-cracked open.

I stole a swift glance inside. A young woman stood in the center of the room, her face buried in her handkerchief. Finn hovered near, that frown I'd viewed all day still marring his mouth. His hand rested on her back, comforting her the way he'd consoled me during my coughing fit last evening. I'd forgotten the warm pressure of his touch until this moment.

"I've looked everywhere." His voice pitched low. "All without success."

She sniffled. "I should give up the search."

I perked. Her Swedish wasn't as polished as Finn's and hinted at a local dialect. Whoever this woman was, she was not high society.

"No, we won't give up." Determination hardened his tone. "I'll keep looking. I give you my word."

Finn was vowing to find something. My suspicions soared. Did he mean Dr. Bohr's research? The OSS had emphasized the possibility of Finn already having the document. So why would he be searching for something allegedly in his possession? Of course, the OSS could be mistaken about assuming Finn had the document, just like they'd been wrong about his regard for me. Or maybe...Finn wasn't referring to the document at all. Perhaps he was looking for something else entirely to assist this mystery woman.

My temples throbbed as my thoughts knocked about in my head. This spy business was complicated.

"But why did you invite Amelie Blake at a time like this?" Her tone didn't exactly say adoring fan. "I'm sure you mean to entertain her during her stay. Wouldn't she interfere?"

A slight pause. "She's here for Farmor. Not me."

"Are you sure about that?"

Of all the...

My blood fired through my veins at her insinuation. Yes, I was indeed here for Finn, but not for a romantic liaison as the lady concluded.

The shuffle of footsteps spurred me to duck into a shadowed alcove. I caught a flash of blue from the mystery woman's dress as she passed, Finn's determined strides not far behind her. I pressed my spine against the wood paneling and waited until they were gone.

After a few steadying breaths, I cautiously stepped into the hall. Instead of returning to the main foyer, I decided to check Finn's office. If I wanted to get a firm grasp on his character, looking through his business affairs and personal effects would help. The door was shut, so I tried the knob.

Locked.

Ugh. Why hadn't I brought my lockpicks?

Frustrated, I trudged farther down the hall, hoping for an alternative route to the foyer, but another door caught my eye. I pushed it open, and my mouth dropped.

The enchanting scent of paper and dust clung to me as I stepped inside an expansive library. My spirits lifted at the sight of towering shelves. This was a room I could spend days in. My fingertips itched to run along the embossed spines. I had a library at my home in Beverly Hills, which I was slowly building. But this—this!—collection appeared as if it had taken a lifetime to complete.

There were a lot of volumes on business and ships. Some titles on Swedish history. An entire section devoted to architecture, my favorite area of study. So much intricacy was involved in the art of buildings. To design a structure to be both beautiful and useful. Sturdy. Symmetrical. It all fascinated me.

I almost tugged free a book, if only to sniff the pages and breathe in the scent of learning, the fragrance of words. But I couldn't get distracted. Because what better place to hide a manuscript than in a library? I skimmed rows of titles, pulling out books and opening them, making certain there wasn't anything hidden in the pages. But in a library this size, it would take excruciatingly long to examine every book.

I reshelved a volume and browsed an edition of older Swedish homes and villages. There were a lot of German titles, but that was hardly surprising with the country being so close and Sweden having Germanic ties for generations.

I narrowed my eyes on a book that stood out from the others—*Atomic*

Theory and the Description of Nature.

By Niels Bohr.

I stared at the unsuspecting book lodged among other scientific tomes. How clever would it be to slip the missing manuscript into *this* book? Anyone who'd stumble upon it wouldn't flick an eyelash at the content. For they'd expect to see expositions and studies on atomic theory.

But I was now at a disadvantage. The book stood on the sixth shelf up, out of my reach. I frowned. Shouldn't there be a ladder? I turned a full circle, scanning the room.

Nothing.

I glanced at the door. Exactly how much time had I wasted here? There wasn't a clock anywhere. What if dinner had already started? No way my absence wouldn't be noticed. But then, I could easily rattle off the excuse I'd gotten lost.

I set my heels on the floor and braced my hands on the shelves. I hung on the bookcase, testing its strength. It didn't even shake. Good sign.

I stepped high onto the second shelf and hoisted myself up. If only my directors could see me now, they'd throw a tantrum. But Bill Donovan hadn't sent along a stunt double, so I was all on my own. And it was fabulous.

I pulled my weight onto the third shelf. It was somewhat scandalous, with my skirt hiking up my leg, but I was alone. Besides, I was nearly there. I stretched my right arm high. The tip of my middle finger could...almost...touch the—

"Need some help?"

I yelped, and my foot slid off the shelf. Books cascaded over my head. My hands grappled for something, anything. Arms flailing, I flopped backward, landing hard on my hindquarters. In the movies, the heroine always fell into the handsome hero's arms. Sadly, this was real life.

Finn hovered over me, his arms outstretched, joints locked, as if trying to show me his botched rescue attempt. "Are you okay?"

I winced at a sharp jab in my hip. The edge of a book poked me. I shifted and cleared it away.

He stooped. "I'm sorry for startling you." His tone was sincere, and there was a touch of regret in his eyes.

"I'm fine." My backside throbbed in protest to my lie. I resisted the urge to rub it. "I was just in here looking for. . ." I picked up the closest book. "This edition on. . ." I skimmed the cover and inwardly groaned. *The Mating Principles of Dragonflies.*"

His brows rose. "A topic that intrigues you?"

A blush crawled up my neck, and I averted my eyes from his piercing gaze. It must be my unfortunate lot in life to make an utter fool of myself in front of this man. It had begun at the age of thirteen, and the streak continued.

He pressed his fist to his mouth but not before I glimpsed a rare sighting—his smile. It was small, the charming display ending before I could fully appreciate it. Yet it was there, and something akin to attraction swelled within me.

I shook it away. As if one half smile could erase the scene I'd witnessed of him and the mystery woman, plotting to keep me from interfering with whatever they were searching for. Once composed, I glanced up at him. By the expectancy in his eyes, he awaited my response about his wretched dragonfly question. "No, I don't care much for insects."

"I noticed they're not appetizing to you."

I blinked. His remark was a direct reference to my bug feast last evening, but I couldn't determine if he was teasing or taunting. "I need this book for its width." I held it up. "My en suite door keeps closing, so I thought this would be a good doorstop." I scrunched my nose, realizing just how mammoth the volume was. "Though who would guess there'd be so much information about this. . .umm. . . subject?"

His lips twitched. "I have no idea. That particular book was purchased before my time."

My gaze swept the books beside me. There it was. Dr. Bohr's book, the one I'd intended to retrieve, had been in the literary avalanche. "I'll just clean this up and head to dinner."

He stretched out a hand to help me to my feet. "The staff can do it."

I batted his hand away, trying not to look as annoyed as I felt. "I'll do it." I understood it was their job. Yet having worked as a housemaid alongside Mamma, I also knew how frustrating it was to be yanked from routine duties to attend to the smallest mess so easily tidied by the hand that had created it.

His head tilted, as if unsure what to make of me, then he crouched, helping me pick up the surrounding books. I nodded my thanks and grabbed the ones around me, Dr. Bohr's first. The pages had been glued to the binding and were yellowed at the edges. This was the original book, not the missing research. But maybe I could use this to my advantage. "This is by Dr. Bohr." I glanced at Finn, who paused to read the cover I held up. "I wonder what it's like to meet an atomic scientist. I heard Dr. Bohr came here from Copenhagen." I drenched my words with enthusiasm. "Did you see him?"

"He was brought over before the mass rescue." Which confirmed the story Henrik and Donovan had told me. The Gestapo had planned on capturing the atomic scientist, but the Danish resistance was able to smuggle him out. "I didn't meet him."

I let my shoulders curl forward. "Oh." I sighed. "I guess a part of me would love to know what it's like to be a genius." I slightly pouted, making sure I didn't overdo. "Not that I've ever been called one." Which was the truth. The tabloids had never once praised my intellect.

With everything scooped up, Finn reached out his hand to me again. This time I took it. He tugged me to my feet with a surprising strength I wasn't prepared for. I almost knocked into him, bracing my hand on his chest, nearly dropping the books I held in the other. I was close. Too close. I breathed in notes of his aftershave. Caught sight of the shallow dip right beneath his full lips. My eyes traced his sharp jawline. The man really did have a nice face. A face that could very well belong to a Nazi sympathizer.

"Sorry," I mumbled and stepped back.

"No." He swallowed. "It was my fault."

I turned my attention to returning the books to their rightful spot.

He stepped beside me, sliding a biology digest beside a horticultural encyclopedia. "My operation manager met Bohr's assistant when he came through our marina." Finn unexpectedly resumed our conversation. "If you're truly interested in what it's like to meet a genius scientist, you can talk to him. His name's Danikan Skar."

I was making progress! And Finn was being kind to me. I shouldn't reveal how pleased I was, but I also didn't want to say something stupid, making him retreat into his surliness. I tempered my smile and met his eyes. "I'd like that."

He nodded, then gently extricated the dragonfly book from my hand and placed it on the shelf. "I'll find you a proper doorstop. Are you through in the library?"

Oh, my shoes. I quickly slipped them on. "Yes, all done."

"May I escort you to dinner?" He held out his arm.

I slid my hand through the crook of his elbow, and he led me back the way I'd come—past his office, his parents' portrait, and through the foyer. He hadn't said a word as we moved into the west wing, reaching the area connecting the dining hall. A young man I hadn't met yet stood beside a large vase, talking to Margit. Finn's farmor was chatting with—judging by the perfume—the mystery woman from Finn's office. I took in her measure just as she did mine. Her wide-set eyes were framed by a heart-shaped face, giving her a unique but lovely look. Despite her well-arranged hair and flawless complexion, her clothes were frumpy. The robin's-egg-blue dress was a pleasing color but too large for her willowy frame. Out of my peripheral, I watched Finn's reaction to the woman. But there was nothing. No tense muscle beneath my fingertips. No pause in his steps upon seeing her. In fact, I don't think he even spared her a glance.

Odd.

Finn stepped aside as Anna glided toward me. She clasped both my hands in hers and smiled. "Our distinguished guest is here," she said to no one in particular. "I'll make introductions, and then we'll dine." Anna released me and stepped beside the mystery woman. "Let me present to you, Fru Birgitta Lindgurst. Her husband helps oversee the shipyard, but. . .won't be joining us tonight."

Ah, so the woman was *married*. Interesting. "How do you do?" I dipped my head with a smile. "I'm Amelie Blake."

She acknowledged me with a slight smirk. "I know who you are." Something skimmed beneath the polite surface of her words. She seemed quite recovered from her emotional bout in Finn's office. If I hadn't known, I wouldn't have guessed she'd been crying. "I hope you have a nice stay in Malmö."

I gave her a friendly smile regardless of her fake one.

The young gentleman I'd spotted a moment ago approached, nodding at Finn and then settling his gaze on me.

Anna gave him a doting motherly look. "Fröken Blake, may I present Elias Rickertz. Finn's business associate."

So this man worked for Finn. And Fru Lindgurst's husband did as well. Was it customary for Finn's employees to join him for dinner? Or was this a special occasion? I offered the man a warm smile. "Pleased to meet you." I shook his proffered hand. The glittering chandelier brought out reddish tones in Herr Rickertz's blond hair and highlighted a spray of faint freckles on his nose, a rogue one dotting his left lobe.

"Charmed to make your acquaintance." His voice was on the soft side, but he didn't seem shy like Anna's secretary, Margit.

"Shall we all go in?" Finn spoke from behind me, motioning toward the dining hall.

"May I?" Herr Rickertz kindly offered his arm, and I could've sworn I saw Finn grimace out of the corner of my eye. But when I looked at him, he appeared as disinterested as always.

"Thank you, Herr Rickertz." I smiled.

"Just Elias," he said, placing his hand over mine on his arm as we moved toward the door.

Fru Lindgurst cut in front, entering the room before me as if in spite.

"Don't mind her." Elias pressed his lips together. "She's distraught about her husband."

"Is he ill?"

"I'm sure you'd find out soon enough." Elias cast a look at his boss, then dipped his face lower to mine. "He helped with one of the Danish rescues but never came back."

⚏ CHAPTER 10 ⚏

Crystal chandeliers reflected off silver-plated candelabras as we ate from gilded-edged porcelain dishes. The Ristafasson dinner was quite the event. But the entrées were a simpler fare of fish and herbs.

Dinner conversation, led mainly by Anna or my new friend Elias Rickertz, remained within the confines of mild topics such as the weather, the success of Anna's charities, and the nightlife in Malmö. I'd been asked several questions about Hollywood and living in America. But no mention of important events, like Italy surrendering to the Allied forces and the mounting rumors that the Italians intended to declare war on their previous partner—Germany. It struck me as odd that no one discussed the local news of the recent Danish evacuations involving Finn's boatyard. My table companions did their very best to tiptoe around all war talk.

But I had successfully gotten more information from Elias when walking into the dining hall. According to Elias, who was now seated across from me, Birgitta Lindgurst's husband, Johan, had helped with the Danish rescue effort. He'd been responsible for logging each boat that had docked at the Ristaffason marina. Three weeks ago, during one of the evacuation nights, he'd disappeared and hadn't returned.

It seemed too much of a coincidence.

Had Herr Lindgurst stolen Dr. Bohr's research and chosen to lay low for a while? Was he planning on selling it to the highest bidder? I picked at my salmon, the flaky flesh crumbling around my fork. Or. . .what if he hadn't taken the research but had seen who had. Maybe the thief had kidnapped him. Or worse. Johan Lindgurst could be villain or victim.

And what about Axel's warning about Finn? How did that tie into everything? If only—

"Are you feeling well, Amelie?" Anna's voice broke into my musings.

I nodded. "I'm a bit tired. It's a long journey from Los Angeles."

Birgitta Lindgurst eyed me skeptically. "Quite a risk, if you ask me."

I smiled but said nothing, hoping she'd let the matter rest.

Instead, she lowered her fork and hooked me in her narrowed gaze. "Why did you come here in the middle of a war? You had to have flown over enemy waters."

It didn't escape my notice that she didn't specify who she considered the enemy. It was challenging to define others' loyalties and how deep they ran. I took a dainty bite and regarded her with a friendly expression. "I was told my mother was ill and wanted to see her." I shrugged. "I knew the right people to make it happen, and so I'm here."

"Yes, you're *here*." She gave a triumphant look as if my remarks had won her the argument. "Not where your mother is. If you're so concerned, I wonder why you're not by her side. The fact that you're in Malmö and not with your mother dilutes your point." A smirk lined her mouth. "Unless you're here for more advantageous reasons." She glanced at the others as if to get them to join the discussion that was more like accusation, but Anna's mouth was pinched in disapproval and Margit kept her eyes on her plate and Elias casually sipped his lemonade.

That left Finn. He was the last person I'd count on as a conversational buffer. If anything—

"I was unaware, Fru Lindgurst"—Finn's voice was gruff—"that tonight's dinner featured an interrogation."

I almost dropped my drink. Had Finn just. . .defended me? I wasn't the only one who found his scold unexpected, because Fru Lindgurst blanched. Honestly, I wasn't shaken in the least at her barrage of questions. I'd faced tabloid reporters more aggressive than this woman, but Finn's small show of support was oddly touching.

Her surprise quickly faded. Sitting taller in her seat, she shot back, "No crime in wanting to know Fröken Blake better."

My senses heightened. Did she want to know me better, or was this some sort of ploy? By aiming a spotlight on my situation, she could keep hers tucked in the shadows.

After Elias told me about her missing husband, I understood her vague conversation with Finn in his office. She must've been crying over Herr Lindgurst's disappearance, to which Finn had vowed to locate him. But there was a slight pinch in my gut. A warning, maybe? Because from Birgitta Lindgurst's darting glances to her fidgety mannerisms, it was clear she was hiding something.

And I intended to find out what.

The morning sun's warmth offset the chill in the air. Anna and Finn were occupied until the afternoon, so I embraced the opportunity to explore the boatyard. Though I was late leaving the estate because I'd wasted precious moments searching for my cashmere cardigan. I was certain I'd packed my cranberry short-waisted sweater, but I couldn't find it among my things. I somewhat panicked because my last wardrobe director had gifted me the custom piece, and the puffy shoulders and attached belt made it one of my favorite tops. Yet in the end, I'd settled for my dark rose argyle pullover.

Since the boatyard wasn't directly beside the estate, I'd walked through the gardens and past the Ristaffason's private beach. The water called to me, especially today being Morfar's birthday. Memories of those carefree summers floated to the forefront of my mind. How I wished I could spend this day reflecting on his life, but I needed to keep my mind clear and alert as I searched for any clue leading to the document.

Usually walking helped me think, but with every step, I grew more conflicted. Would I discover the manuscript today and be on a train to Stockholm tomorrow? Or would I uncover something bitterly dis-appointing? Time was already against me, given that a few weeks had passed since the briefcase had touched these shores. The research could've been found and sold before I'd stepped foot in Sweden.

Though the OSS had strongly believed the document hadn't yet reached Nazi hands. And something inside me seemed to confirm that. Over the years, I'd learned to rely on my gut rather than my head, clinging to the Proverb: "Trust in the Lord with all thine heart; and lean not unto thine own understanding." So instead of debating the what-ifs, I softly prayed as I approached the boatyard.

The docks stretched into the water like wooden fingers. Boats of various sizes and colors were coming in and going out. Three large warehouses loomed before me. A boatyard of this caliber could be intimidating, as well as the dockworkers and sailors who worked here, but this setting felt more like home to me than anywhere else.

I looked out over the Öresund. So familiar, the sights. So soothing, the whispers of its course. I'd swum its waters, floated on its current, and splashed its amusing spray on unsuspecting Morfar. A smile curved my mouth. These same waves had also carried the innocent to safety, nestling God's chosen people within its flowing arms. Sunlight danced upon its surface. The sky stretched like blue satin, so perfect and flawless. I peered out over the water, though now a heaviness tugged at my soul. Because about forty kilometers from where I stood, Denmark was being ravaged by Nazis.

"May I help you?"

I startled at the approach of a fifty-something man, whose confident gait told me he bore authority. His eyes scanned my face, even as recognition hit, stopping him midstride. "You're her, aren't you? The movie star."

I nodded. "That's me. I'm a guest at the Ristaffason residence." My profession put me in the public's view, but it always made me pause, thinking how people from all over the world knew me just by my face.

He puffed out his chest. "Just wait until my wife hears I met Ginger Rogers."

I laughed. That was what I deserved for vanity. "Ginger's a nice woman, but I'm not her. I'm Amelie Blake."

He looked me over again as if I could be mistaken. Then I noticed it—the tease in his eyes.

"Hmm." He rocked on his weathered boots, seemingly unconvinced. "I heard Amelie Blake was taller."

I expelled a mock sigh, playing along. "I wish I was. Then I wouldn't trip over the hems of my gowns." My return jest finally cracked his smile. "But perhaps you may know me through my morfar, Herr Strom. He once owned a modest fishing company a stone's throw north of here."

He scratched his silvery whiskers, brows pulling together in thought. "Sven Strom? He hailed from Lomma."

Strom had once been Mamma's surname as well. But after she'd fled to Stockholm, she wanted a fresh start and had changed her name to

Blakstrom. "He did." I swept a hand toward the shore. "You see? The love of this water is in my blood."

He gave me a hearty nod of approval. "I never met him, but I've heard your morfar was a good man."

"The very best." I beamed. "Which is why I had to take a stroll along the shores my first morning here. And you are?"

"Danikan Skar." He held out a calloused hand. "I'm manager around here. Well, one of them."

I suspected the other was Herr Lindgurst. Wait. Skar. Wasn't he the man Finn had mentioned met Dr. Bohr's assistant?

Herr Skar glanced over my shoulder, his mouth crimping into a scowl. I turned to find several men huddled beside an upturned boat, lolling in their duty of scraping sediment off the hull.

"May I ask you a question?" I continued as if I weren't being watched like a flock of pelicans eyeing a herring.

"I was about to check the stern on one of our maidens." He jerked his head. "You can come if you like." Herr Skar glared at his men, intimidating enough to jolt them to work. With a satisfied nod, he motioned me to walk alongside him.

I smiled at my form of escort compared to last evening. Elias accompanied me into a glittering dining room, but I was more at ease here with a craggy boatman along the lapping waves of the Öresund. Pebbles shifted beneath my feet even as seagulls cawed overhead.

Herr Skar crouched low and examined something on the boat's frame. "I'll have to patch that," he muttered, then straightened. "Now what kind of question would a movie star ask a humble sailor like me?"

"I heard you met an atomic scientist. One who worked with Dr. Bohr." I gave a conspiratorial smile. Now to convince him why I was so curious. "There's a role in an upcoming movie about a scientist, and I'm thinking about auditioning." I pressed a hand atop my chest and adopted a dramatic inflection. "As an artist, it's important to get a feel for the character. To immerse myself until their perspective, their zest for life, becomes my own." I let my hand fall to my side and shrugged. "At least that's what my director tells me."

Herr Skar only blinked.

"So who's this scientist and what's he like?"

"His name's Stefan Rozental, and he's tiresome," he said without hesitation.

"Really?" I tried not to laugh. This man, with his soured tone and rough exterior, reminded me of Morfar. "How so?"

"That night of the rescue was stormy." Herr Skar puffed his leathery cheeks, then exhaled. "Families got separated during the run. They reached shore and were scrambling to find each other. It was pouring rain. Children were screaming. And this Rozental guy? He was complaining about a lost briefcase as if it was a matter of life and death."

He had no idea. "Did Rozental discover his briefcase?" Of course, I knew the answer, but I wanted to see if Herr Skar would provide any more information.

He pointed to the Öresund. "The Danes found it on shore and sent it over the next rescue. On this very boat, to be exact." He patted the exterior. "But it disappeared."

I let out a tiny gasp. "How mysterious." One thing about sailors. They enjoyed telling stories. So I let him.

"The fellow responsible for the briefcase said it vanished from thin air." He snapped his thick fingers. "One second it was beside him, and the next it was gone." He shook his head. "As if I hadn't enough duties that day. My hand cramping with all the paperwork and having to keep an eye on my boats. I didn't have time to report a missing briefcase. Too much work for one man."

I knew that Herr Lindgurst had disappeared, but where was Finn during all that chaos? Helping at his other harbor? "So very odd."

His gaze turned shrewd. "Not as odd as you and two other folks quizzing me about it."

People had been asking him about the briefcase? My heart jumped, and I couldn't help but relish the jolt of the chase coursing through me. I'd only been in Sweden three days, and I was already on the very shores of the scene of the theft. From Herr Skar's story, the briefcase had been removed from the boat. So it would be a waste of energy to search. "That *is* strange." I had to tread carefully here. I didn't want to appear overly aggressive in my questioning. "But then again, maybe not. I'm sure the others who asked knew Rozental. That's kind of them to want to retrieve his briefcase for him."

He shook his head. "I don't think so, fröken." He waved at a passing dockhand and then faced me. "He wouldn't give me his name." He snorted. "Though I wouldn't either if I was pretending to be someone I'm not."

A seagull swooped alarmingly low, but I didn't even flinch. "What do you mean?"

"He put on airs, dressing all flashy like he was from the well-to-do. But he was about as genteel as I am." Herr Skar held out his hands. "A man only gets swollen knuckles and coarse fingers from hard labor, and that's what the man had." He leaned in. "I suspect he once worked with machinery since the tip of his right pinky was gone."

Helpful. A bit gruesome, but helpful. "Who was the other person who asked about that day?"

"Birgitta Lindgurst."

⊰ CHAPTER II ⊱

Ristaffason Enterprises was a larger operation than I'd realized. Finn owned marinas catering to fishermen and their trade, but farther down his property was a harbor dedicated to his shipping business. The clanging of anchor chains, hollers of workers, and general hum of activity had left my ears ringing by the time I'd returned to Finn's house.

I walked into the foyer, surprised at how vacant the massive space felt. Of course, Finn and Anna were still out. And with the staff tending to dinner and other duties, it felt like I had the entire estate to myself. What better time to search Finn's office?

With my bedroom on the third floor, and in it my lockpicks, I decided first to check if Finn, or one of his staff, had left the study open.

I darted a glance to my left, then right. All clear. Moving swiftly through the halls, I reached my destination. I tested the door, and the knob turned easily. Success!

I slipped inside, only to discover I wasn't alone. Someone else had the same thought as me.

Birgitta Lindgurst was behind Finn's desk, trying to force open a drawer. So intent on her mission, she hadn't noticed my entrance. Should I alert her of my presence or simply slip behind the door and observe? The choice was decided as her gaze snapped up to mine.

She drew a sharp gasp, pressing a startled hand to her stomach. "Fröken Blake? I-I didn't see you come in."

I spun slowly in a full circle. "This isn't it, either." I shook my head with a dramatic sigh. "I've been searching an entire hour for the billiard room."

She released a nervous chuckle. "The Ristaffasons don't own any billiard tables."

"Ah, that explains it." Pity. A few rounds of pool always eased my nerves.

Her jumpy behavior matched her fidgety mannerisms from last evening. Though yesterday, she'd at least worked to conceal it. "I'm searching for some blotters. Herr Ristaffason said he left some on his desk, but I can't find any."

I clasped my hands together and approached her. "Oh, I do love a seeking game. I'm really good at it too, because look." I pointed at a stack of absorbent strips. "There they are. Right beside your left hand." It was apparent she hadn't been searching for something as obvious as the blotting paper.

She studied me beneath her long lashes, as if trying to gauge her next move. "Well done." She grabbed half the pile with a shaky hand. "I'll just return to my room and finish writing my letters."

Wait. "You live here?"

Her chin lifted. And just like that, she returned to the haughty creature who'd grilled me with questions at dinner like a crime detective. "I was invited to stay at the estate."

Yet she'd purposefully left out who invited her. Was it Anna? Finn? Would Finn risk a scandal by asking a married woman to remain at his house? Was it for her protection, considering her husband was gone? Or for romantic purposes? Only. . .last evening at dinner, I'd watched for hints of a relationship between them, for any shared looks or veiled remarks, but Finn seemed as indifferent to her as he was with the rest of the world's population. "Oh, how lovely! I hope your room has a lovely view like mine."

"If you'll excuse me." She hustled out of the study, leaving me staring at the open doorway.

I hurried to peek into the hall. Good, she was gone. I ducked back inside. Pushing past that awkward encounter, I returned to Finn's desk, skimming the surface. No personal papers or letters. Yet Birgitta had left me a giant clue. She'd fully concentrated on opening the lower left drawer, which made me curious about the contents within. Was that where he'd stowed important documents? Or maybe. . .atomic research? I was determined to return. Only next time, I'd bring my lockpicks.

I determined to keep an eye on Birgitta Lindgurst. I hadn't forgotten what Herr Skar had relayed. She'd been drilling him about the rescues. Most likely because of her missing husband. But then, why had she been in Finn's study? There were more questions than answers regarding the young woman.

Danikan Skar had also mentioned someone else who'd asked openly about the briefcase—the man who'd dressed as high society but had tell-tale signs of being a workman. The missing fingertip would be an easy identifier if I ever spotted the gentleman.

For now, I needed to get out of Finn's private study. I quickly exited into the hall and made it ten steps before the man himself turned the corner.

My heart squeezed against my ribs. He'd returned earlier than I'd expected. I'd been only seconds from being caught. But I wasn't in the clear yet. My mind scrambled for an excuse to be in this part of the house. He wouldn't buy my visiting the library again. Why would a flighty actress be interested in books?

His gaze collided with mine and his steps slowed. We met just shy of his parents' portrait.

"Hello, Finn." I offered a friendly grin he didn't return. A part of me wondered if I'd truly glimpsed his smile in the library yesterday. Or was I like one of those misled Swedes who scoured forests for sightings of mythical creatures? They'd so often deceived themselves into thinking they'd glimpsed something that wasn't there. That was how I felt about Finn's smile—that it had existed only in my imagination. "It's not that difficult, you know."

"What isn't?" His gaze flicked over my shoulder, then zeroed in on me. Was that suspicion narrowing his eyes? Was he questioning my presence in this hall? I needed to distract him.

"Smiling." I stepped closer, my ditzy mask firmly in place. "You move your mouth muscles like so. Let me teach you." Then I did the unthinkable. I reached up and cupped his face. Using my thumbs, I pushed on his cheeks, forcing his smile. I fought back a laugh. His mouth looked every bit like cranky duck lips. Yet despite the ridiculousness of the moment, my pulse leaped. Because beneath my fingertips was a strong, taut jaw, and less than an inch from my left thumb was that delicious dip in his chin. "See? That way," I murmured, disliking the breathlessness in my tone, "people won't think you hate them."

His hands wrapped mine, and he gently peeled them off his face. But instead of releasing me, he held my fingers captive in his. "I don't hate people."

I swallowed at his nearness, but I couldn't look away. "Your face says otherwise."

He leaned closer, his hot stare on me. "Maybe you just don't know how to read it."

An accurate remark if I'd ever heard one. I was accustomed to shallow men with flirty quips and roaming eyes. It was simple to guess what was on their minds. Not so with Finn. He had a complexity in his gaze that almost dared me to test its depth. But there was something else lurking in those blue and silver hues. Awareness. Hints that warned me he might see beyond my mask. Which meant, I'd better step away from his fiery touch.

So I did.

He cleared his throat and straightened to full height as if he, also, hadn't quite known what to do with all the sparks between us. "How was your morning?"

I thought of the boatyard and my conversation with Herr Skar. Then there was my encounter with Fru Lindgurst and my discovery of Finn's locked drawer. "I learned a lot."

"Pleased to hear it." He moved to brush past me, then paused. "There will be special guests for dinner this evening. A necessary evil in my business."

Finn appeared as giddy about a formal dinner party as a man who'd just slammed his fingers in a door. I brightened. "The more the merrier, right?"

"If you say so. Now if you'll excuse me. I have business that needs tending to." He gave a tight nod and stepped past me toward his study.

Would he notice anything amiss? Finn seemed the kind of man who had a certain spot for everything and would know if something was out of place. Which would rule him out as the person who'd rummaged through my luggage. I couldn't imagine Finn tossing my things about, let alone prowling in my room. An image of Birgitta Lindgurst bumbling about in Finn's study almost made me gasp. Had she been the culprit? It was evident she had no qualms about invading people's personal quarters.

She could've heard of my arrival and easily searched my room while I'd been having fika with Anna.

I hastened to my room, relieved to find things as I'd left them. Call me paranoid, but this morning I'd tugged a thread off my sweater and placed it on my luggage lid. It was still there.

After a short nap, I jotted a letter to Mamma and readied for dinner. I'd brought my favorite gown of taupe satin with a black netting overlay. Though the hooks in the back made it nearly impossible for me to fasten on my own. With a grimace, I rang the bellpull. A maid I hadn't seen before entered, her eyes downturned, her manners quiet.

She dipped a curtsy, and I noticed her knees quivered. "Yes, Fröken Blake?"

"Would you help me with my dress? I can't reach the back." I turned, and judging by the shuffling on the carpet, the maid skittered toward me. Her icy hands met my bare skin, and I struggled against a wince. She deftly took care of the hooks and adjusted the collar.

"Anything else?" Her voice was barely a squeak.

"No." I faced her with a smile. "Thank you."

She looked at me, a touch bewildered, as if she hadn't expected any kindness from me. Then with a tiny nod, she almost ran from the room. I reapplied my lipstick and gave myself a once-over in the mirror.

After grabbing my clutch, I moved into the hall and nearly knocked into a wall of a man. Finn. He caught my elbows, keeping me from stumbling forward.

His gaze swept over me, and his fingers almost reflexively tightened on my arms. "You look. . .satisfactory." Despite his underwhelming choice of words, I caught the definite marking of masculine appreciation in his eyes. So Finn wasn't as impenetrable as he'd like me to think. Good to know.

I smiled. "Thank you."

Once realizing I wasn't going face-first into the hardwood flooring, he kindly let me go. But didn't step away.

He glanced at my door, surprise hiking his brows. "Farmor put you in that room?"

I adjusted my glove, which had slipped during the altercation. "She said the others are being repapered."

"They are?" His bewildered expression could only mean two things.

Either he didn't know what went on under his own roof, or Anna had invented the excuse to put me in this wing of the house. Finn flicked a hesitant look to the left where he'd come from.

Just because one was a little old lady didn't mean she wasn't a conniver. A smile lifted my lips. "Is your room close by?"

"Two down from yours."

Anna must've known he and I were bound to run into each other, almost literally. I may have been playing the role of a ninny, but she took on the part of matchmaker.

I laughed. "We're neighbors!"

Finn didn't find it as amusing. With a somewhat resigned exhale, he offered me his arm, and we walked together downstairs.

There were only about twelve guests in the receiving room. I spotted Elias chatting with a few young ladies, including Margit. Fru Lindgurst stood off to herself as if lost in thought. She wore the same ill-fitting gown as last evening.

Anna waved me over, a pleased smile lining her mouth, and I broke away from Finn's arm. I was thankful for the chance to speak with her, for I'd completely forgotten about Mamma's request until this afternoon.

"You look stunning, Amelie." Anna practically glowed in her lavender gown, which complemented her complexion and silver hair.

"As do you," I replied. "My mamma wanted me to thank you on her behalf. She said you'd understand what she meant."

Anna smiled, but there was touch of sadness in her eyes. "You can tell her it was an honor."

I couldn't hide my curiosity. "I wouldn't guess you two to have ever met." How would Anna Ristaffason, the wife of a shipping tycoon, have any connection to Elsa Blakstrom, a housemaid in Stockholm?

"I suppose there's no need for secrecy anymore." Though she lowered her voice all the same. "I paid for your passage here all those summers. I knew how much it meant to Sven."

Shock parted my lips. Morfar must've been a closer childhood friend than I'd suspected. I had no idea Anna had been my benefactor. Only that Mamma was so relieved that I could visit. "Then I add my thanks too."

She took my hand and patted it, her gaze turning somber. "I don't deserve your gratitude. I had to right a wrong."

Her words made me pause. What kind of wrong? But I couldn't

press Anna any further because Finn approached, his gaze swiveling between Anna and me. Had he caught any of our conversation? Talking of Mamma reminded me of the letter I'd written earlier. I peered up at Finn. "I hope to go into town tomorrow to post a letter."

"Of course. I can accompany you." He didn't seem entirely thrilled at the idea. "Or you can give me your mail. I have a man who runs my posts for me."

More than letters traveled through post offices. From my experience, it was the best place to catch hints of gossip. But I couldn't let Finn know the real reason, so I chose an alternate one. "I don't want to trouble your staff."

"No trouble. He's taking mine, might as well take yours."

"Are you really going to make me give my ulterior motive?" I gave a small pout.

His gaze fell to my mouth, slowly sliding to my eyes. "I'll never ask you to give anything you don't want to."

"*Salmiak*. I haven't had any in years." This wasn't an actual lie. I had missed salted licorice. The Scandinavian candy wasn't available in America.

He stared at me for a long second, making me think he didn't intend to answer my nonsense. But then his mouth formed a ghost of a smile. "We'll get you some tomorrow. I know just the place."

I hid my surprise behind a soft grin. I didn't want to frighten the man away once he'd willingly agreed to spend time with me. "Sounds wonderful." If I'd known I could somewhat win him over by salmiak, I would've mentioned getting licorice yesterday at the train station.

"Is this the Queen of Diamonds?" An unfamiliar masculine voice sounded over my shoulder. "I was hoping to catch a glimpse of you."

I slowly pivoted on my heel, facing the stranger. Only to realize he wasn't a stranger at all.

I'd been trained to defend myself against surprise attacks. Yet I'd never imagined this scenario.

Because I stood a few feet from Herr Erik Bruun.

My father.

≡ CHAPTER 12 ≡

Moments like these tested my worth as an actress. Erik Bruun was the owner of a shipping empire, a native of Lomma, and the man who'd disgraced my mamma. I wanted nothing more than to call him out for his disgusting behavior. To expose him in front of his acquaintances. But instead, I remained poised, unaffected.

I glanced at Anna and found her gaze on me, brimming with compassion.

My gut twisted. She knew. But how? Was anyone else aware of my illegitimacy? Most of Sweden believed my father—or in Swedish, pappa—was dead. After the success of my first picture, the press hounded Mamma for the inside story about our lives. She'd struck a deal, giving them all the details of my background in exchange for them leaving her alone from then on. What she hadn't promised? The truth. She'd told the press my father had died before my birth. When I'd questioned her on it, she only shrugged and said he was dead to her the moment he'd refused to marry her.

But he was very much alive and staring at me.

My breath squeezed in my lungs even as Anna's hand cupped my elbow in a silent show of support.

"Amelie," she said kindly, "let me present to you, Herr Erik Bruun."

A woman about Mamma's age broke away from a group of guests and joined his side, all smiles.

"And this is Erik's wife, Hildi."

I couldn't help but scrutinize the woman. Her dark brown hair was the shade of her round eyes. She was lovely, and her smile seemed genuine. I wondered if she knew the caliber of man she'd married. Did they have children? That would mean I had half siblings. Over the years, I'd often wondered if I had any brothers or sisters but couldn't bring myself to discover the truth. Not that I'd be able to approach them without causing a scandal or bringing sorrow to Mamma. I pressed a fingertip to my temple in hopes of subduing a wave of dizziness.

Herr Buun grinned at me. "When I found out a movie star was staying at the Ristaffason estate, I thought I might as well invite myself to this gathering."

He didn't seem to recognize me. Not as his own child, anyway. Why would he? I'd never met him. Had never tried to contact him. There was nothing to connect us.

I studied his face, searching for any similarities. My eyes were the same color as my mother's, but their shape—oval with an upward lift at the outer edges—matched his. The off-centered widow's peak of my hairline matched his as well. Yet no one would know because my side part concealed mine. My heart grew heavy. I didn't want to share *any* traits with him, however small. But I was grateful our characteristics weren't blatant. No one should detect I was his daughter.

I'd yet to respond. But what could I say? I wasn't delighted to greet them. Nor was I glad they were here. For the first time, I was relieved to be considered the dumb blond. I wasn't expected to utter anything brilliant. "Are you in the shipping business like Herr Ristaffason?" I finally managed.

Both husband and wife gave eager nods.

"I hate to steal her away," Anna blessedly said. "But I've yet to introduce her to all the guests." And with that, she led me around the room, rattling off names I probably should've paid attention to.

An older woman, Fru Something-or-other, trapped Anna in conversation, leaving me to my thoughts. I needed to regain my composure or else I was bound to let my cover slip. I wasn't one given to tears, but the burning sensation behind my eyes wouldn't weaken.

"Are you okay, Fröken Blake?" Margit seemed to materialize out of nowhere.

Had she been beside me the entire time, or had she just approached? The young woman had quiet movements, able to blend into her surroundings. I'd once been like that. Easily overlooked. At the time, I'd hated it, but now? Well, invisibility seemed a luxury beyond my reach. "Thank you." I smiled warmly. "I'm just catching my breath."

She nodded, her awestruck gaze roaming the room. "It all seems overwhelming, but I'm sure you're used to it."

I didn't want to discuss what I was *used to* because nothing felt familiar, not even my own skin.

The butler announced dinner, cutting short our chat. Finn sought me out, escorting me into the dining hall and helping me into my chair. Sadly, I was seated at the place of honor beside him, meaning Erik Bruun was opposite me, his wife farther down beside Fru Lindgurst. At least Birgitta was far removed from me tonight, so I wouldn't have to endure her badgering.

I hazarded a glance at Herr Bruun. He looked at me with a gleam in his eye. If he even tried to flirt, I'd likely cast my accounts all over the fancy table setting.

"This is bound to be a tedious evening," Elias mumbled. Finn's assistant was seated to my left. Something I should've already realized, but I was still reeling from the appearance of my father. "At least I have a good-looker nearby to help me endure it." His wicked smile was something I hadn't been prepared for. During our previous conversations, I hadn't judged the man a flirt. It seemed surprises were popping up everywhere this evening.

"Oh, what a kind thing to say," I preened. "But I'm better than a good-looker. At my last checkup, the doctor said I have twenty-twenty vision. I'd say my looking is excellent."

Tally number one for outrageous remarks. I might as well make a game of how many silly things would flow out of my mouth before the night was complete. I ignored Elias' rapid blinking and swept my gaze down the table. There were fourteen of us. Several of which I couldn't recall names. It wasn't like me to be inattentive. The OSS had emphasized the importance of my ability to recall, but that talent only extended to what I saw, not what I heard. I needed to concentrate better. Listen better.

"What's that scowl for, Fröken Blake?" Herr Bruun's voice pulled me from my scolding thoughts.

"No reason at all." I falsely brightened.

With his steel-gray eyes focused on me, he proceeded smoothly,

"Wonderful. I'd hate for you to be in a foul mood at such a pleasant dinner." While deep lines etched his forehead and bracketed his mouth, he would still be considered handsome by most. During his younger years, I could see how he'd charmed scores of women and, consequently, broken their hearts. "In fact, when I heard you were residing at Finn's estate, I had to see you. I have something important to share with you."

My fingers imperceptibly tightened on my glass of water. Perhaps I was wrong. What if he *did* know I was his daughter and planned to announce it now? But how could he? During his time with Mamma, she'd gone by a different name. When she'd fled to Stockholm, she'd changed it to Blakstrom.

I took a long sip, purposefully making him wait. "I'm listening."

He scooted his chair forward. "I'm in the process of securing ice-breaker vessels to be used in the winter months in the Bothnian Sea. You see, Fröken Blake, the Gulf of Bothnia always freezes in November, preventing the passage of merchant ships. Every year we close our harbors in Luleå."

My toes curled inside my satin pumps. This wasn't a stunt to tell the room he was my pappa but a ploy to get at my money. I'd been subjected to hundreds of sales pitches throughout the years that I could identify a schmoozy spiel before the salesman ended his first sentence. Granted, Herr Bruun's delivery was polished but no less rehearsed.

"So instead of the iron ore being shipped out of Sweden, it must go by rail to Norway and out the Narvik ports." He shook his head. "It takes funds away from our ports, but we can do something about it."

Iron ore. Herr Bruun wanted his ships to carry the steel through the Bothnian Sea, which flowed into the Baltic. Nazis occupied the Baltic. That only meant one thing—he was transporting the iron ore to Germany. Germany would use the steel to forge more weapons to kill Allied soldiers, design more airplanes to shoot down RAF fighter jets, and create more propellers for their U-boats to sink American battleships.

My mind flashed to the OSS folder. I could see the very page in my mind. Erik Bruun's name was listed as a suspected Nazi sympathizer. And they'd been correct. The man whose blood ran in my veins sided with the enemy.

"When I heard you were in the country"—to my distress, he continued—"I knew you'd be the perfect one to help finance the icebreaker vessels. We can certainly use good backing from someone like you."

All conversation around the table had hushed, and I felt every pair of eyes pinned on me.

By sheer force of will, I kept my facial muscles relaxed. "Me? Why would I care?" But I did care, though not for the motives Erik Bruun presented. I cared about the millions of brave souls who'd sacrificed their lives in the name of freedom. I cared about seeing good triumph over evil.

Sweden's neutral stance came with the right to import and export from any country. There was nothing technically illegal about selling steel to Germany, but to me, it was morally wrong.

"You can triple your investment, Fröken Blake."

I wouldn't let my disguise slip. I refused to give Erik Bruun that power over me. Instead I feigned a yawn, which seemed to irk him. "I already have more money than I know what to do with." A maid set a bowl of soup in front of me.

"Nonsense." He chuckled as if good-naturedly, but it sounded forced. "I heard of your *high intelligence* and was certain you'd see the benefit in investing."

He was mocking me. I was certain of it. The man had a smooth resonance in his words, but he wasn't a good actor. I noticed the scornful glint in his eyes when he'd referenced my intelligence. And since he thought me stupid, he could speak confidently, believing I wouldn't grasp the insult.

But I caught it, and much more. Utilizing icebreakers in the Bothnian Sea would mean his harbors could remain open year-long. The Kiruna Mine in Lapland, Sweden, was the largest iron ore mine in the world. The world! It went without saying, the Third Reich was mostly dependent on Swedish steel, giving cause to believe that without it, the war would've concluded a while ago.

I hazarded a glance at Finn and found his searching gaze on me. Not Herr Bruun. There was something in his expression I couldn't read. Unlike Herr Bruun, Finn hid his emotions better. But if I had to guess, I would say he seemed conflicted. And I assumed it had to do with Herr Bruun's veiled insult.

If Finn defended me, it would draw more attention with the risk of embarrassing me, especially if he believed I hadn't caught the underlying meaning. But I had, and was most capable of defending myself even with my ninny facade.

"What's nonsense?" I gave a confused look. "I don't get it. Is it nonsense that I earn more money than everyone in this room?"

He bristled. "You don't make more than me."

"Hmm. I think I do," I said nonchalantly and took a dainty spoonful of soup. Honestly, I was unsure if I made more than he did. I only said so to get under his skin. Because if there was one thing I knew about arrogant men, they didn't like their pride bruised.

Something dark entered his eyes. "It's easy to say, but where's the proof?"

Finn set his napkin down and scowled at Herr Bruun. "Amelie doesn't need to prove anything to you."

But the horrible man didn't pull his glare from me. "Well, I refuse to believe it. Unless you can show me."

I shrugged. "Then I'm forced to believe you don't have a brain."

His face reddened. "Of course I do."

"Prove it. Can you show me?"

A few feminine snickers clashed with some clearings of masculine throats. Finn pinned me with a gaze I couldn't quite decipher, but I was in a battle of wits with a man I would never call Pappa.

I casually sipped my water as Erik Bruun sputtered, "Well, no. That's impossible."

"Then I believe you're brainless," I said as if I didn't care one way or the other. But the sad part was, this conversation troubled me. The world was in chaos, and it seemed the man was only concerned about expanding his fortune. But at what cost? The more iron ore shipped, the more supplies of weapons to the Nazis, and the more powerful they became.

It had to stop.

He finally seemed to realize the tense mood of the party, and that he was to blame for it. "It doesn't matter," he muttered, then sipped his schnapps. "I'll get the money from somewhere else."

⊱ CHAPTER 13 ⊰

I donned my nightgown and sat at the vanity, my hand curling around my hairbrush. With a sigh, I ran my thumb over the soft bristles. I didn't have the energy to put my hair in pin curls. Or anything else. I stared at my face in the mirror. How was it that now I could see even more of that man in my own reflection?

I am nothing like Erik Bruun.

But that wasn't the truth. I was like him. I'd almost dropped my fork when I'd caught Herr Bruun grabbing his. He was left-handed. Like me. The main course was cubed prime beef with potatoes and pickled beetroot. Herr Bruun ate everything except the beetroot—my least favorite vegetable as well. But tonight, I devoured those horrid things just to prove a point to myself. I could change my tastes. Maybe learn how to use my right hand more. But I couldn't change the blood coursing through my veins.

I rested my bent elbows on the glass vanity top and sank my chin into my cupped hands. It was clear Herr Bruun had come tonight to coax me into supporting his Nazi-leaning project. When he'd realized he wasn't getting any money, he had no use for me, and refused to look my direction for the remainder of the evening. It seemed the man held on to the habit of taking advantage of others for his own gain.

I forced my thoughts on another man who'd been as selfless as Herr Bruun was the opposite. Sliding my eyes closed, I pictured Morfar's face, trying to imagine the rasp of his voice, the coarse melody of his laugh. But it wasn't enough.

Before I could think better of it, I threw on my robe and darted out my door. The stairwell at the far end of the hall belonged to the house staff, but tonight it was my escape route.

I hustled down the steps until I reached the bottom floor. A doorway led outside, and soon I was taking in the night air. The smooth pebbled walkway was cool beneath my slippered feet. I moved swiftly through the garden, drawn by the sound of water just beyond.

This day was still Morfar's birthday, and I determined to spend the rest of it honoring his memory. I reached the Ristaffasons' private beach and shed my slippers, sinking my toes into the sand. The moon, a milky crescent, was framed by a host of stars.

My gaze fell upon the Öresund, and a sob caught in my throat.

"Both sand and stars surround us, Mel, but they aren't easily grasped," Morfar had said one night during my summer stay. *"It's the same with life. The sand's like lost opportunities. Things we try to hold on to, but sooner or later slip through our fingers."* He'd scooped up a handful of sand, the grains drifting through the cracks of his knuckles.

"The stars. . ." he'd continued, more like a philosopher than an aged fisherman. *"The stars are our dreams, always beyond reach. There's nothing we can do about the sand, the lost chances, but there's a secret about the stars. Did you know you can touch them?"*

I remember peering up into the sky and giggling. *"It's silly, Morfar. You can't touch the stars."*

He'd bracketed my narrow shoulders with his callused hands and leaned down, peering into my face as if he were about to reveal the grandest mystery. Then he'd scooped me up as I'd dissolved in laughter and had waded into the water. He'd pointed at the stars' reflections on the glass-like surface. *"See? Right here."* He'd set me down, the water hitting just above my knees.

I'd stretched my hand out, dipping my fingers into the glistening sheen.

He'd smiled down at me. *"You can always touch the stars, Mel. Just need to know where to find them."*

Nineteen years had passed since that night, but I found them once again. The starlight gently rippled on the current. The Öresund called to me, just as it had when I'd been seven. I bunched the hem of my robe and stepped into it, my heart quickening.

The water lapped against my shins with an icy chill, but somehow, I was warmed. Because I was here. Surrounded by glittering memories.

I took another step forward and reached down, skimming starlight, touching dreams as the rest of the world was rife with nightmares.

As I pulled my fingers through the water, the emotion that had been piling upon my chest. . .shattered. A tear rolled down my face. I dashed it away, but more followed. I could no sooner cease the flow than I'd be able to stop the Öresund's current pulling against me. Both were forces beyond my control.

So I gave myself to it, moving further into the water, crying freely, until numbness coursed every part of me.

"Amelie?"

No. Please, no. Finn was the last person I wanted to see in this state. What was he doing out here? He probably wondered the same of me. I had to have been so focused on my memories I'd tuned out the rest of the world. Which was completely unlike me. Tonight was not my night.

Still, I couldn't face him or even speak.

The swishing of water betrayed his movements. He was coming toward me. A senseless part of me wanted to take off toward deeper waters and swim far, far away. But I'd already lost feeling in my legs because of the frigid temperature.

Within seconds, Finn's large form shadowed mine.

He was silent for several seconds, but I could feel his gaze on me. "I heard you crying."

I nodded, still refusing to glance his way. Instead I focused on steadying my breathing. This kind of display of emotion was rare for me, but I'd learned over the years not to cage it. Doing so only drained my strength. I'd rather be tired from a night of sobbing than become weak by imprisoning the rising pressure. The former was easier to recover from than the latter.

Strong fingers wove into mine, and I froze. Finn Ristaffason, a man seemingly made of stone, held my hand, offering me comfort. Why that made my eyes sting all over again, I didn't know. Didn't *want* to know.

His bare arm brushed mine. Wait. Bare? I finally risked a look to my right. The austere millionaire was shirtless. And wet. The moonlight exposed rivulets of water cutting paths over the muscled angles and solid planes of his chest. I blamed my open stare on my complete and utter shock, rather than the obvious truth that the man was breathtaking. "H-Had you been. . .swimming?"

"I always do my training on the beach." He shrugged. "I got heated and dove in the water to cool off."

The Gulf Stream swept warm currents to Sweden's southern shores, making the fall season much milder than most expected for a Scandinavian country. Nevertheless, it was still October. And if I expected Finn to be embarrassed about his lack of attire, I'd be wrong. He wasn't the least affected. I wish I could say the same. A shiver rocked my body.

"You're chilled." He squeezed my hand. "Let's get you inside."

I dumbly followed as he led me. The water only met my calves, but we moved against the current, slowing my steps. Finn shortened his strides to match mine, remaining beside me, keeping hold of my fingers. I wasn't accustomed to this nurturing side of him. Which only made me wonder. "Finn?" My toes reached the sand, and I paused. "How long were you watching me?"

He released me and palmed the back of his neck, his bicep bulging with the movement, unfairly distracting me. "Since you first waded into the water."

I slid my eyes shut. So he'd seen all of it. My enamored show of touching the shimmering waters. My entire sobbing episode. I groaned. How many times could I embarrass myself in front of this man? "I'm sorry."

"No, please. Don't apologize." He reached for his shirt, which had been folded on a rock, and slipped it on. "I'm the one who's sorry. When I saw you, I should've returned to the house, but I wanted to be certain you were safe. Then when you. . .that is. . .when I saw your distress. . ." He let out a heavy breath. "I wanted to be sure you were okay. That you *are* okay."

It took me a long second to adjust to this version of him. Because the Finn I knew didn't care about others' feelings. *"Perhaps you read it wrong."* Finn's words from earlier, when we'd spoken of his facial expressions, resurfaced. Had I been mistaken about him? Though I was wary of tossing aside my entire perception of him based on a few moments of unexpected kindness.

I couldn't pinpoint the reason why I'd cried. Fatigue from the week? The burden of the OSS assignment? The world being in chaos? Nothing was normal anymore. All of that, coupled with the shock of seeing my father this evening. Of glimpsing his true nature. He would never be my pappa. I had someone who'd filled that role, and he was gone. "Today is my morfar's birthday."

"And you miss him."

I nodded.

The moonlight outlined his impressive form, but I could only focus on his face and the compassion written on it. "Tell me a memory."

My lips parted. "What?"

"I never knew my parents." His gaze lowered to the sand. "But Farmor would often speak of them. So I borrow her memories. Maybe if you share one, it might help."

Okay, now my caution flags were fully hoisted and flapping in the breeze of suspicion. This was *not* Finn. I blamed the atmosphere. There was something about the soft glow of the moon, the lull of the coursing water, and the stillness of everything else that must've drawn out his softness.

I slid my eyes closed, struggling with his request. I didn't want to act scatterbrained. Relaying a precious memory in a silly fashion went against everything in me. But I also couldn't betray my cover. Perhaps if I spoke in simple words, I could protect my image without betraying my conscience. "Morfar met my *mormor* at a *midsommar* festival." One thing I loved about the Swedish language was the distinction between grandparents. Anna was on Finn's paternal side, making her name farmor. Josefine Strom was on my maternal side, making her name mormor. I looked to Finn who watched me closely. "She passed when I was ten. Did you know she was American?"

"Farmor mentioned it. Is that why you know English so well?"

I nodded. "My grandparents danced the hambo at the festival. She didn't know what she was doing, and Morfar taught her as they went." The ¾ time variation of the waltz was considered Sweden's national dance. "They got married, and every year on their anniversary, they danced the hambo. When she was gone, he taught me." And we'd carried on the tradition, while creating a new one. Because we'd always dance on the last night of my stay in Lomma. He'd never owned a Victrola but would hum the melody with his croaky voice. Twirling me fast enough to make my girlish head dizzy, but I'd loved it. Loved him. "He's gone now too. I haven't danced the hambo since." Funny, I hadn't realized that until now. Those moments with Morfar had been the closure to my childhood. Because when I'd turned twelve, I'd started working alongside Mamma.

I hadn't attended any midsommar festivals, only cleaned up after them.

Finn was quiet. I'd spoken too much. Had I given myself away? I'd endeavored to use basic vocabulary, but perhaps I should've inserted some foolish remarks.

He moved closer, peering down at me. "Would you like to now?"

Huh? "To what?"

He swallowed. "Would you like to dance the hambo? With me?"

"Why?" I blurted. Probably not the best response, but Finn was acting so strange tonight.

"I don't like seeing you cry," he confessed in a deep rumble.

My brows jumped. He almost sounded human. Did Finn Ristaffason possess a compassionate heart beneath all those layers of surliness? I nudged his elbow. "And here I thought you didn't like me."

He didn't answer. I was well aware he wasn't fond of me and was only offering to dance out of kindness.

I gave him my fullest smile. "I'm happy to dance with you."

He nodded, stretching out his hand.

I placed my fingers in his and looked up at him. "Shall I hum the tune? Or should we count in our heads?"

"Let's just start." Which sounded much like *Let's get this over with*, but I wasn't about to complain.

With our hands linked but bodies apart, we stood side by side and stepped in unison with our left, lifting the opposite foot and extending the leg. Then we mirrored the same moves on our right, the standard opening of the hambo.

We joined together. The stance was different than a routine slow dance, for his hands spanned my back as I pressed mine to his, in more of an embrace.

Then we spun in a circle. Once. Twice. It was harder to turn and pivot on the sand like the hambo required, but I favored this setting over a crowded festival where these traditional dances took place. Not like Finn danced *traditionally*. He pressed me close. The warmth of his palm against my back, the press of his arms to my sides made something in me swell with. . .attraction?

I almost faltered.

Finn must've blamed my misstep on the uneven sand, because the next turn he smoothly lifted me from the ground.

Setting me on my feet again, he challenged, "Shall we go faster?"

"I'll keep up."

He quickened his steps, and I followed suit.

His arms anchored around me as we moved about the beach. The quicker we turned, the more I laughed. There was something freeing about slipping out of the confines of the rules, making the century-old hambo our own. Since our dance floor wasn't the smoothest, any time we came across a mound of sand, Finn lifted me from the ground without breaking step.

The folds of my robe swished around his legs. My hair loosened from its binding, falling around my face. Then we slowed as if we'd danced this way a thousand times together.

"Thank you," I said, breathless, my parted lips inhaling much-needed air. "I feel better. Happier."

His gaze skimmed my face, the night sky somehow making his blue eyes darker. "I'm glad for it."

"Yes, well. . ." Then I realized the view I presented him. My hair was disheveled, my complexion flushed, and the collar of my robe hinted slightly open, giving the impression of a woman after a romantic interlude. Not at all the image I wanted to convey.

I broke apart from him and moved to collect my slippers, seizing the opportunity to adjust my robe. I was thankful nothing more than a creamy expanse of skin around my neck and collarbone was revealed. But still. I had morals, and despite what magazines might print about me, I refused to give the idea of a temptress.

I combed my fingers through my hair, a poor attempt to subdue it. But what was more, I was flustered. My cheeks burned even while the hairs on my arms raised. We'd exerted ourselves in a high-movement dance, and with the temperature seeming to drop by the minute, it was no wonder my body responded with waves of heat and chills. Though, I knew the truth.

Finn Ristaffason was getting to me.

◗ CHAPTER 14 ◖

"Good morning, Amelie." Anna breezed into the breakfast room only a moment after me, appearing fully rested and arrayed in a day suit of pale blue.

I, on the other hand, was tired, and it most likely showed. After my late night with Finn on the beach, I'd had trouble falling asleep. "Hello." I gave my best effort at a smile and moved to the buffet table to retrieve some coffee. I also took a plate, adding a piece of toast with a slice of hard cheese and a boiled egg. I wasn't exactly hungry, but I was walking into town today with Finn and needed nourishment. With my coffee and plate in hand, I claimed a seat at the table.

This room was smaller than the others but lent a cozy feel, especially with the wall of windows providing a gorgeous view of the Öresund.

Anna fixed her breakfast and sat opposite me, her ivory complexion almost glowing in the streaming sunlight. Though her brow clouded as she looked at me. "I feel I must apologize for Finn's behavior last night."

I froze. Had she witnessed our dance? Had we been visible from some high window? Though innocent, I tried to imagine what sort of scene we'd created. Me in my flowing nightclothes and him spinning me in his arms, pressing me close. Finn would say he'd held me tight for safety's sake, considering the speed at which we danced. Most likely true, but was it wrong for me to have enjoyed it?

She shook her head. "Finn was raised with more propriety than to allow Herr Bruun's crass manners at the dinner table."

Oh, that.

She nibbled on her toast, her mouth scowling all the while. "It's unlike Finn. He should've defended you."

Yesterday I would've been confused by her words, but last night I'd glimpsed his protective nature. "I'm used to dealing with people." Hollywood was a jungle of predatory creatures with ulterior motives. Besides learning to adapt to a new country, I also had to sharpen my perception skills concerning those around me. I'd been successful until meeting William Graham. His deceiving words had rung true in my ears. I'd never been more blinded than that year I'd wasted believing I'd found someone who'd genuinely loved me.

"I suppose that's true." Anna's voice pulled me back to the moment. "But he still should've informed me Herr Bruun was coming." She set her coffee on the saucer with an emphasized clink. "I could've at least warned you your father would be in attendance."

I choked on my bread, coughing and sputtering without any grace.

Her face bled of color. "No. Oh no." She rose from her seat and smacked my back with surprising strength. "I'm sorry, Amelie. I thought you knew. And now I've gone and made things worse."

I clenched my eyes and swallowed once more, dislodging the rebel bite from its stubborn place in my throat. After a few deep breaths, I twisted toward Anna who lowered onto the chair beside me. "I know he's my father." And I'd suspected Anna, had been aware as well, but I wasn't prepared for her to confirm it so openly.

She pressed a comforting hand to my arm, much like my mormor had done when I was young. "It's awful to say, but I believe you were better off without that man and his influence. Some people never change no matter how much you wish them to." Her eyes turned sad, and I wondered if she was now thinking of her oldest grandson. Rolf Ristaffason had a wild streak that had gotten him killed. Rumor was, he'd provoked a barroom brawl and had died from his injuries. The Ristaffasons had paid the press to keep the incident quiet, but gossip always bled through.

With losing her son and daughter-in-law in the *Titanic* sinking, her husband to natural causes, and then Rolf to his own foolishness, Anna had endured significant loss. That grief must've also extended to Finn. My heart reluctantly softened even more toward the man. "Why did you say you felt guilty about my summers in Lomma?" I reached across the table and grabbed her abandoned coffee and plate, setting it in front of her.

She smiled her thanks. "I was the one who got your mother that domestic position at the Bruun estate. I'd heard rumors, of course, but it's difficult to determine which were true or not. I never imagined Erik Bruun would dally with the house staff."

Ah, so there was where her guilt had stemmed from. She'd found Mamma the job, which placed a pretty young woman in the home of a man with no morals.

I understood her heavy position. When I'd realized Mamma had fled her home because she was pregnant with me, I was weighted with shame. If not for me, Mamma could've remained in Lomma. Instead, she had been forced to Stockholm, separated from her family. "Mormor once told me never to take the blame for someone else's wrong actions." I gave a soft smile. "She'd probably say that to you too."

"Your mormor was a wise woman." She nodded solemnly. "Sven couldn't have picked a better partner."

I smoothed away a crumb from my finger. "How did you know him?"

"Sven's pappa worked for mine, so he was always around. He learned the trade of boatbuilding. Your morfar was one of the best in his field."

That confirmed the stories Morfar had always told me. He'd said he enjoyed being on the vessels more than building them. Though his knowledge of building and repair was invaluable in his fisherman business.

"Sven could charm any female no matter her station." Her smile was nostalgic, and I wondered if perhaps she may have been one of his admirers at some point. "He was very much like Finn in that regard." Her smile faltered a little. "Though Finn's money and position draw the wrong women. I believe it's made him bitter."

I understood that predicament too. I'd met several actresses on their third or fourth divorce simply because the men had married them for their status and wealth. At least I'd discovered the truth about William before we'd reached the altar.

She dabbed her mouth with a napkin. "He just needs to find the right woman."

I had to commend Anna. She was trying her best to pair Finn and me together. From placing our rooms close to each other, to this not-so-subtle conversation. I offered my vacant look with a small smile. Maybe if Anna believed I had no idea what she was talking about, then maybe she'd drop the topic.

"Finn doesn't give the best impression. He appears cold, unfeeling," she continued. "But we don't always show our true selves to strangers, now do we?" There was a knowingness in her tone that made me squirm.

Did she know I'd been acting silly on purpose? I wouldn't doubt it. She was sharp. Perhaps the OSS should've recruited Anna Ristaffason for their spy work.

Anna rose with a warm smile and pressed a hand on my shoulder. "Do you ever intend to tell Erik Bruun he's your father?"

I shook my head. "I don't think so."

She nodded her understanding. "I'm glad we had this talk." Her fingers gave a gentle squeeze. "I've been burdened with guilt for all your lifetime, and you removed its weight. Thank you."

"And thank you for your kindness." I'd always treasured those summers with my grandparents. And it was all made possible by her generosity. But my smile froze on my face at the sight of Finn in the doorway.

He gave me a curious look, and my heart sank.

How much had he heard?

———— ≈ ————

Finn and I walked into the heart of Malmö, which was hardly a kilometer from his estate. The morning sun swam in feathery clouds, shafts of light hiccuping through the line of birch trees, igniting the bronze and gold leaves.

But I couldn't enjoy the view because I'd noticed Finn sneaking looks in my direction.

Had he heard Anna reveal that Herr Bruun was my father? I glanced over and caught him watching me again.

I sighed and decided to call him on it. "Is there a reason why you keep looking at me?"

"Isn't it obvious?" His tone and his face were not at all flirty. If anything, he seemed annoyed, as if I should know the reason.

"No, that's why I'm asking."

"You seem troubled this morning." He exhaled. "And after last night..."

Was he baiting me? "Did you hear what Anna said earlier in the breakfast room?"

"Only parts." He rubbed his jaw. "It was unintentional. I was about to enter the room, but I heard Farmor talking."

I couldn't hold his eavesdropping against him. I'd done the exact same the other night outside his study. "What did you hear?"

"That she felt responsible for your mother's plight."

Anna had been so repentant, as if she'd carried the weight of it all. "It's not her fault," I said simply. "Is there a hat shop in town?" I hastened my pace, hoping Finn would let the matter drop.

But he wasn't deterred. "I also heard Herr Bruun's name."

I did not want Finn knowing my secret. Because it wasn't only mine. It was Mamma's. And she'd already borne enough shame to last several lifetimes. "We should visit a hat shop, and you can tell me which ones look best with the shape of my face."

"How is he involved? What does he have to do with you and your mother?"

The man was relentless. If he didn't find out from me, he'd no doubt badger Anna. Or worse, ask Herr Bruun. Fine. I gave him a pointed look. "And you think *I'm* clueless."

He stopped, his brows slightly rising as he put the pieces together. "Erik," he muttered. "Is he your. . ."

"Father? Yes, he is." I smiled grimly. "Now you can see why I'm so brainless."

He tucked my hand in his arm, either trying to slow my hasty strides or offering his support. "That's what upset you. Why you cried last night. It was about him."

I nodded. "Part of it."

"I won't allow him at the house during your stay." His adamant tone surprised me. "You're safe here."

I swallowed back the rising emotion. "Thank you."

"Does he know you're his daughter?"

"No." I shook my head. "Nobody does."

"Farmor won't tell anyone. Neither will I," he affirmed. "Not after everything we've gone through."

I glanced up at him, unsure of his meaning.

He trained his gaze on the narrow cobblestone walk. A muscle leaped in his taut jaw. "Every family has secrets."

Interesting, but I wasn't charged with uncovering his family's background, only his. What were *his* secrets? The obvious being he was a thirty-two-year-old businessman who clung to his bachelorhood. No woman had yet secured his commitment. Perhaps no powers had either. Bill Donovan had vaguely mentioned Finn had helped with an Allied project, though he still questioned his loyalties. I studied Finn's impressive profile. For some reason, I couldn't imagine him partnering with the Axis powers. Time would tell.

We approached the bustling part of town, and I was struck by its quaint beauty. Timber buildings were painted in bright colors of blues, reds, and yellows. Vendor carts perched on the corners, much like the day I'd arrived here. People milled about, some with purpose, others on a lazy stroll.

First stop was the post office. I had a scarf around my head and put on my sunglasses. I doubted any gossip would spark if people noticed me as I walked inside. I'd hoped to overhear something—anything—but everyone kept to themselves, with hardly any conversation. Trying not to be discouraged, I posted the letter to Mamma and rejoined Finn, waiting outside.

The walks were crowded, but from where we stood, I had a clear view of the row of doors on the main thoroughfare. I spotted Birgitta Lindgurst stepping out of a building to my right. She breezed right past…the Ristaffason maid? I almost hadn't recognized the young lady at first, but I most certainly identified what she wore.

Because it was mine.

The Ristaffason maid, who'd helped me with my evening gown last evening, loitered in front of the ice cream parlor, flirting with a young man. Which in itself wasn't a crime, but she was doing so wearing my cardigan. The one that I couldn't locate yesterday. She'd taken it. It must've been she who'd rummaged through my luggage. Here I'd thought the culprit was someone affiliated with spy work, and it had been a thieving maid all along.

I moved toward her, ready to confront.

She glanced over the gentleman's shoulder and spotted me. Her eyes widened on a gasp. But I was already close enough to block her retreat.

Finn moved alongside me, but I could see the questions on his face.

"Fröken Blake," the maid sputtered. "I—I can explain." Her petite frame trembled, making it difficult for me to accuse her. Because I'd been in her position. Having worked alongside Mamma cleaning houses of wealthy families, I knew the temptation of luxury. I remembered gaping at fur stoles draped in a closet or wanting to spritz expensive fragrance just so I could experience it. Though I'd never resorted to filching even a button, I understood.

"There's no need," I began but stopped short, eyeing the gentleman beside her. More specifically, his hand.

Because he was missing the end of his pinkie finger.

≡ CHAPTER 15 ≡

Danikan Skar had said the man asking questions at the boatyard was missing the tip of his last finger. Dressed in a faded suit, he was younger than I expected. Perhaps twenty or so. He glanced in my direction and jolted. I moved closer, but he sprinted off, disappearing among the crowd.

Finn stood beside me, observing everything. "Care to tell me what this is all about?"

The maid stepped forward, her head bowing low. "It's my fault, Herr Ristaffason."

"Yes," I spoke before Finn could question her. "I told you not to wear that sweater unless you're certain it won't rain. That's expensive fabric, and rain can ruin it." I made a show of studying the sky. "But I suppose you're safe for now." I reached and smoothed out the collar. "It looks divine on you, just as I said it would."

The maid's jaw dropped.

Finn looked between us.

"I hope you don't mind." I faced him. "But I overpacked and thought this cashmere sweater would fit. . ."—I couldn't remember her name. Had she told me her name?—". . .this darling, since we're close in size."

The maid exhaled, even as her eyes welled with tears. "I can't thank you enough, Fröken Blake."

"Indeed." Finn looked past my shoulder as if he were distracted by something. "Perhaps we should let Hedvig enjoy her morning before returning to work this afternoon."

Ah, Hedvig was her name. Good. I smiled brightly at her. "Will you help me this evening? My gowns are extra fussy and require your help."

She nodded readily. "Anything you want, fröken. I'm at your service."

Hopefully, she'd learned her lesson about thieving. Though I couldn't be sorry about this turn of events. I might have forfeited my favorite cardigan, but I'd possibly gained an ally. I understood more than most that the maids knew and heard everything that went on within an estate. Not only that, but I intended to quiz her about the man she'd been speaking with.

Finn and I resumed walking, but something was off. He was stiff. Well, more so than usual. I opened my mouth to ask him, but he spoke first.

"Hedvig seemed touched by your generosity."

It was more mercy than anything. The woman knew her job, her livelihood, was on the line. "It seemed the right thing to do." Finn wouldn't put up with any staff stealing from his guests. But a thieved cardigan was the least of my concerns. There was stolen atomic research I needed to recover.

Finn escorted me back to the estate then promptly left for a supposed business meeting with a shipping client. After spotting Birgitta Lindgurst in front of the Malmö shops, I hadn't noticed her on the return walk, leading me to assume she was still in town. With Anna away at the local church luncheon and the maids off until the afternoon, the only people within the house were the butler, the head housekeeper, and the cooks. So I grabbed my lockpicks and headed to Finn's office.

With every step toward his study door, the guilt doubled its weight on my conscience. Finn had been kind to me recently. I wouldn't say he was falling head-over-heels for me. How could he when I'd spouted off the most outlandish remarks? But he'd been gracious, and I appreciated his effort. He'd even surprised me with another smile. Though it was more of an apologetic smirk since I'd caught him eating more than his fair share of my candy. Who knew the brooding bachelor had a weakness for salted licorice? Getting the man to soften had become my personal challenge, but I knew I was treading dangerous waters. I couldn't let my heart drift away from my protective clutch.

I needed to search his personal effects, especially the drawer Birgitta Lindgurst had been attempting to wrench open. But still, I was conflicted. With a sigh, I glanced left and right to ensure the halls were empty. I grabbed the hooklike tool on the metal ring holding all the picks, inserted it into the keyhole, and lifted until I heard the soft click of the mechanism release.

Once in the study, I closed the door and drew in a steady breath. The faint scents of leather and coffee enveloped me. Masculine and inviting. Shelves of books framed a large window. Sunlight poured in, warming the furniture, two wingback chairs, a sofa, and footrests.

His desk was the feature of the room, large and commanding. I rushed toward it, skimming the surface. A few fountain pens. A wooden table clock. The blotters I'd glimpsed the other day.

I opened the long drawer just beneath the desktop. Nothing here either. Only paper clips. A silver letter opener. Just boring office supplies. Perhaps there were no secrets to find here. Part of me hoped that to be true.

I crouched in front of the lower left drawer Birgitta had targeted. It was locked as it had been yesterday. I tried several picks without success. The backs of my legs throbbed, so I forewent any modesty and plopped my backside on the floor. I switched to the last pick on the ring. Using extra force, the tool jerked out of my fingers, nicking the wood beside the lock. I cringed at the tiny scrape.

Hopefully, Finn wouldn't notice.

I rallied for one more attempt, wiggling the pick until the sweet click of the lock release made me exhale.

I peeked around the desk at the door. I was still alone. But for how long? I could be intruded upon at any moment. Shifting onto my knees, I eased the drawer open. Letters were stacked in the front beside a pile of folded papers. What appeared to be invoices filled the rest. No ledger book. Or itinerary. And no atomic research by Dr. Niels Bohr.

I picked up the stack of papers and leafed through. Most were receipts. Some were letters of recommendation for employees. A few maintenance requests for his boats. I shook my head, ready to surrender my search, but a name on the last paper caught my eye.

Bruun Enterprises.

A letter, written in English, from my father?

> *Finn,*
>
>   *I agree to your terms. I think the partnership will work splendidly for you. I think it's wise not to mention our agreement with Anna. She's against the idea, but I know you made the right choice.*
>
>   *Erik Bruun*

Partnership? Agreement? With my father? A Nazi sympathizer. The letter wasn't typed. The inky scrawl was untidy, but the message was clear. Herr Bruun and Finn were in business together. My chest tightened. I recalled our conversation hours earlier on our way to town. Finn had said he wouldn't allow Herr Bruun here during my stay. Not that he wouldn't invite the man in my absence. Finn had been concerned about my feelings, but he hadn't openly disapproved of the man.

Now I knew why.

Herr Bruun hadn't pestered Finn during dinner about financing his pursuit of icebreaker vessels. Only me. Because according to this letter, Finn had already partnered with him. Maybe that was why Finn had allowed Herr Bruun to give his spiel. Had Finn been secretly wanting me to invest? I felt sick.

The OSS had suspected Finn had links to a Nazi sympathizer, and they'd been right. I'd known this from the beginning. It was why I'd been sent here. So why did my heart split while reading that letter? Why did I feel the sting that accompanied betrayal?

If Finn held no qualms shipping steel to Nazis for guns and machinery, he'd have no reservations about sending them the atomic research, which held the possibility of creating the most powerful weapon in existence.

I had to find that document.

I searched the rest of the papers, not finding anything else of importance. So why had Fru Lindgurst been interested in this drawer? There were a few invoices with her husband's signature, but I couldn't understand how the purchase of wood and paint would provoke her to break into his desk. Unless. . .she'd suspected her husband had been embezzling and wanted to scour Finn's record books. But I didn't see any financial ledgers.

I closed the drawer and relocked it. My heart thudded a dull beat. I couldn't shake the heaviness. Because the more I was with Finn, the farther down the villain list he'd become. Axel's message pushed to the front of my mind. He'd warned me to keep away from him.

Had Axel known? It didn't matter. Because I wasn't going to hide from Finn. I determined to push closer. If he had that manuscript, I vowed to snatch it from his betraying hands.

———≈———

To my satisfaction, Hedvig arrived in my room considerably early to help me dress. Her porcelain complexion washed pale in her black maid's uniform with a white apron, cinching her tiny waist.

"Here you go, Fröken Blake." With shaking hands, she withdrew my cardigan from the bag she hooked on her elbow. "Thank you for not tattling on me to Herr Ristaffasson."

I twisted on the vanity chair but didn't reach for the sweater. "I meant what I said. Please keep it."

Her auburn brows lowered to almost a straight line on her forehead. She stared at me in question, as if uncertain she'd heard me correctly.

I offered a friendly smile. "Consider it a gift."

"I—I can't. I don't deserve any kindness. It was wrong of me." Her tone grew emphatic and distressed, revealing hints of a rural dialect. "I only meant to borrow it for my meeting with Franc. I hoped to put it back before you noticed. Honest."

Franc. Was that the name of the young man who'd talked with Danikan Skar? I had to find a way to get Hedvig to trust me. To open up. With her trembling chin and glossy eyes, she seemed more likely to flee the room in tears than stay and chat. "Did you know my mamma was a charwoman for many years, then afterward a housemaid? I've done my share of domestic work as well."

The palpable shock on her face almost tugged a laugh from me. "But. . .but you're a cinema star."

"I wasn't always. I can relate to your hardships." To the time when I'd owned only two dresses and one pair of shoes. My stockings had been repeatedly mended because we couldn't afford a new pair. "But I will say, if Franc doesn't like you for who you are, even being draped in mink stoles won't matter."

She sighed and stroked the cashmere with her fingers. "I only wanted him to think. . .I'm pretty." Hedvig had stopped shaking, and her voice had steadied.

I understood her feelings about the drive to be noticed. In Hollywood, it was always a competition: to be the prettiest, to land the starring role, to present yourself as three notches above perfection every time you stepped out in public. It was exhausting.

I opened my mouth to respond, but Hedvig wasn't finished.

"I just don't want him to forget about me. You see, he got a new job—"

"Who did?" I inserted naturally. "The young man you were speaking with when I saw you?"

"Yes, that's Franc. He was bragging about how much money he'll make. And here I am, stretching each krona."

Ah, so Franc got a new job. One that seemingly made money. Interesting. "Let me give you advice that I learned the painful way. Whatever draws Franc to you will be what draws him away from you if the attraction's only skin deep. Keep your heart beautiful, Hedvig. It's the only beauty that lasts."

Brother, I'd not only stepped out of character, I'd leaped out of it. But something told me Hedvig wouldn't leak a word, simply because I had more damaging knowledge about her. Plus, the poor girl needed some guidance.

She nodded, her white ruffled headband bobbing along. "But I don't know if he'll want to see me again."

"Why not?"

Her gaze dropped to the thick carpet. "He's upset I couldn't go with him to Frossa. You see, he gets his first paycheck tonight, and he wanted to celebrate." She gave a heavy sigh. "A girl like me doesn't get asked to go to a ritzy dance palace like that. But I have to work."

"That's disappointing," I commiserated. "Perhaps another time."

She pressed her lips together, unconvinced. "Do you need help dressing this evening?"

By her shuttered expression, I knew our conversation about Franc was finished. "Yes, please." I gestured toward the closet. "Would you like to pick something for me to wear this evening? I can't decide."

She gazed longingly at the hanging dresses, and interest slowly crept into her features, her troubles seemingly forgotten. With gentle movements, she placed the cardigan in her bag and set it down. Her feet took almost reverent steps toward the open closet.

"These are beautiful." Her childlike fascination tugged at my heart, making me wish I could shower her with all my gowns. Perhaps I could discreetly leave some for her when I returned to Stockholm. "Your dresses are much lovelier than Fru Lindgurst's." She made a face as if the woman dressed in potato sacks. Birgitta had worn oversize gowns, but they weren't exactly hideous. Maybe there was another reason behind Hedvig's slight.

Her head tipped left and right as she searched my dresses. I'd only brought seven or eight, but she examined each as if counting the stitches.

I grabbed my hairbrush and pulled it through my curls. "Has Fru Lindgurst required your assistance during her stay?"

"Hmm?" She pulled her attention from the closet and shot me a distracted glance. "Oh no. Thank goodness. I wouldn't want to offend *that* woman."

Understanding dawned. "Is she hard to please?"

That got Hedvig's attention. "No, no. Nothing like that. It's just. . . with all the rumors and all. . .the staff doesn't want to go near her. One of us might disappear like her husbands."

My mouth dropped, and Hedvig's expression turned panicky.

"I'm sorry," she sputtered. "I forget sometimes, and my words run out of my mouth. I shouldn't have said anything. I know better than to gossip. Even if. . ."

I rose and met her. "Even if?"

Her shoulders slumped. "The woman got married twice, and both her husbands vanished. The police found the first one's body. But poor Herr Lindgurst is still missing."

My pulse leaped. What? One talk with the maid, and I discovered in fifteen minutes what I'd yet to ascertain in the three days I'd been staying here. "I didn't know any of this. Thank you for telling me."

She seemed heartened by my gratitude. "Us maids don't like her. She has her sights on Herr Ristaffason. That's how she works. Her first husband was a fisherman, so she tossed him aside for Herr Lindgurst."

"So her first husband died?"

"Boating accident." Her brows arced in skepticism. "But there's been talk, if you get my meaning."

I caught it. But surely Birgitta Lindgurst hadn't killed her first husband, had she?

"He was dead only a few weeks before she remarried." She tsked as she ran a finger over the side ruffle of my blue chiffon gown. "But Herr Lindgurst has more money than her first husband but not as much as my boss." Her tone had sour edges. "And she works fast. She hasn't been married to Herr Lindgurst very long at all. And now he's gone too."

My head was spinning. I'd gotten more than I bargained for with this conversation.

Hedvig shot me a cunning smile. "Maybe we can divert Herr Ristaffason's attention to someone else." Her eyes narrowed with mischief as she reached inside the closet, withdrawing a dress. "And this will help. You'll look so enticing, my boss will forget other women exist."

❙ CHAPTER 16 ❚

The conservatory was dark and shadowed, but it was the only vacant place I could find to collect my thoughts. I always did my best thinking while walking. Hedvig would no doubt gasp at my being here. The greenhouse wasn't exactly filthy, but since I strolled among potted plants and rows of autumn blooms, there was a possibility of my brushing against dirt and grime. The maid had been fussier about my appearance than any wardrobe director on a studio set, selecting this bold dress of scarlet satin. The gold-studded choker collar wasn't comfortable, but the cut of the neckline exposed my shoulders, which proved cooler and breathable. Hedvig had changed my hairstyle slightly, giving me a deeper side part, combing out my curls into tumbling waves.

Though, I wasn't standing in the glass parlor to mull over my appearance but to strategize. How should I proceed? Combining my knowledge from Herr Skar and Hedvig, Franc was the young man who'd visited the docks and asked questions about the briefcase. He'd also landed a job that paid good money. Was Franc's trip to the boatyard linked to the work he'd been hired for? Had he been recruited to recover the briefcase? Or was I grasping at loose ends and hastily tying them together?

Then there was Birgitta Lindgurst. The young woman with lovely features and a secretive behavior had also been at the docks asking questions. Though Herr Skar hadn't specified if she'd inquired about the briefcase, only the rescue her husband had helped with. What about the disappearance of Herr Lindgurst? And her former husband's suspicious accident? Had Birgitta been responsible?

Having often been the victim of malicious rumors, I knew better than to take gossip at face value, but the truth was, both her husbands had left her—one from death, the other to be determined.

Johan Lindgurst could be involved. He'd vanished the day the briefcase had gone ashore. That would suggest he'd already recovered the document and was able to sell it.

So what was my next move? Should I attempt to search for Herr Lindgurst? If only to rule him out of the hunt? But then…there was Finn.

He'd partnered with a man who had unashamed Nazi leanings. What if Finn had offered the use of his docks with the sole purpose of confiscating the manuscript and intended to use those same boats to deliver it to Germany?

"Looks like the party is in here tonight."

Heart lurching, I spun at the masculine voice.

Elias leaned against a pillar, a tease lighting his brown eyes. I almost scowled. This was the second time in as many evenings that I'd been caught unaware of my surroundings. But for some reason, I'd been more comfortable on the beach with Finn than in this spacious greenhouse with Elias. Which was ridiculous, considering what I'd discovered about Finn today. Maybe it was because I hadn't yet grasped Elias' character. One moment he was quiet and contemplative and the next, an extreme flirt. I couldn't predict his responses. At least with Finn, I knew he had two moods—broody and broodier.

"Good evening." I smiled cheerfully. "I thought I was alone." From my understanding, Elias didn't live at the estate, but the man was often here.

He lit a cigarette and shook out the match, keeping his hooded gaze on me. "Disappointed?"

"No. I try not to get disappointed. Frown lines are hard to get rid of." I tapped my forehead in exaggeration. "I was only taking a stroll before dinner."

His gaze swept over me in obvious approval. "You look more fit for dancing than meandering about shrubbery and plants."

Dancing. That was it. I clasped my hands and hugged them under my chin. "Oh, what a wonderful idea." I was getting tired of my flaky voice and overly bright smiles, but it seemed to charm Elias. "Have you heard of Club Frossa?"

"Of course. It's the best one around. They bring in entertainment from all over." He flicked ashes onto the tiled floor. "Are you thinking of visiting in the near future?"

"Very near," I said airily. "Like tonight." I wasn't sure if Franc would still keep his plans to go this evening, despite Hedvig turning him down. Still, it was worth checking into.

He huffed a laugh. "I like you, Amelie. You're spontaneous. A man never knows what to expect from you."

I wasn't naturally impulsive. In my films? Yes. Every role had me daring and fun. Brainlessly reckless. In real life? Never. I planned and prepared. And therein lay the issue. I'd discovered early on some men would be attracted to the image I'd presented in my movies, but once they'd realized I wasn't the spontaneous minx they'd perceived me to be, their interest waned. It seemed I could lump Elias in that group.

"We should make a party of it. You and I can scrape up a few more, like Finn and Birgitta." He tossed his cigarette on the ground and crushed it smoothly with his shoe. "Birgitta needs a night out. She's returning to her lonely cottage tomorrow. Poor kid. I'm heading out of town in the morning, but I'll be back before dinner, and—"

"Oh no. Is Birgitta leaving?" I pressed a hand to my cheek. "She's not staying here any longer?"

He shook his head. "She didn't want to come here in the first place. But you know Finn. He must always have his way." His tone wasn't quite a scold yet not a compliment either.

I took a second to answer. "I feel so sorry for Birgitta. About losing her first husband, and then the second one being away."

He scoffed. "The first one was no loss. The man was a scoundrel."

I blinked at his words.

"He married Birgitta for her beauty, then tired of her." He ran his finger disinterestedly along a leaf from a nearby hanging basket. "The man worked for the boatyard. I knew him fairly well."

My heart sank. Poor Birgitta. I knew what it was like to be valued for only what I could give a man. To be a prize on his arm until he'd gotten what he wanted. I still bore the bruises on my heart from when it had been tossed aside.

"But Johan Lindgurst is a good man," Elias was quick to add.

"What happened to him?"

He shrugged. "Whatever it is must be dire. Because he wouldn't leave Birgitta for anything. He's been crazy about her for a long while.

Even before her first marriage." His head tilted. "And I thought she was in love with him. But you never know what's in a woman's heart."

Why would he say that? Did he assume Birgitta had her sights on Finn too? If Finn and Birgitta had a secret liaison, they'd hidden it well. Finn hardly glanced at the woman, and she him.

He checked his pocket watch. "It's time for dinner. Shall we?"

I nodded, and we began our trek down the webbing of halls toward the dining hall. Once we reached the reception room, I spotted Anna and Birgitta by the mural wall speaking with an older couple who I suspected were from Anna's church. Margit stood there as well but didn't seem inclined to join the conversation. Finn was by the fireplace, his back to the room. The evening temperatures had dropped, warranting a fire. Since the coal supply was limited in Sweden, most houses helped the conservation effort by utilizing their fireplaces rather than their furnace.

As if sensing my presence, Finn turned, and his eyes met mine. Finn's gaze swept my form, but if Hedvig expected her boss to be overcome at my appearance, I feared she'd be disappointed. A taut band stretched between my shoulders. This was the first time I'd seen him since discovering the letter in his study. I shouldn't feel any hurt, but I did.

I might as well admit I'd developed a tiny hope we could be friends. It was foolish. What kind of spy was I? Clandestine agents weren't sent to gain friends but to complete a mission.

I withdrew my hand from Elias' arm to greet the women, but Finn stepped forward, blocking my path. My stomach dipped, and I steeled myself against that awful wave of attraction. I couldn't be drawn to a man who'd acted against everything I believed. We were on two different sides.

He peered down at me, a curious look in his eyes. Could he detect my struggle? How could he? I'd been trained to control my facial expressions, appearing unshaken and composed no matter what my head was screaming.

"Amelie." He dipped his chin in greeting. "I'd like to have a word with you."

This morning I'd been reluctant to don my silly disguise in front of Finn, but now? I was ready to embody the ninny. Only this time, I'd be certain to keep my guard up and my eyes open. "Okay. Which one?" I asked with a forced grin.

His brows shot up. "What do you mean?"

I sighed as if he was a simpleton. "You just said you want *a word* with me. As in one word. And I asked which you'd like to share." I could give the man a single word—traitor.

"You mistake me," he said in a lower voice. "I would like to speak with you in the study after dinner."

The study? Why there? My throat cinched. Had he seen the nick on his desk drawer? If so, how had he concluded it was me? Unless I'd left something behind. Panic swelled, but I mustered a chipper smile. "Oh, certainly." Before he could respond, I brushed past him, moving toward the women.

If he intended to call me out, I needed to be prepared. He could toss me out of his home for snooping. Or worse, turn me over to the enemy. Though. . .he hadn't seemed angry. Well, no less stone-faced than any other time.

Birgitta acknowledged me with a polite half smile, but she appeared pale and weak. I noticed she slightly leaned against the wall for support. Despite my initial dislike of her, I couldn't help but feel for her. The situation with her missing husband distressed her. At least it appeared that way. And I couldn't help but question if her stay here only made things worse on her. If the staff speculated her intentions toward Finn, no doubt others did as well. Perhaps it was best for her to return to her home tomorrow.

Anna introduced me to her guests, who were indeed from her church, Herr and Fru Gutin. Because the ratio of female to male was off-balance, Finn escorted Anna and me, while Elias had Birgitta and Margit on each arm. I took the extra moment to study Finn's profile. If the man was truly furious with me, I should be able to spot one identifying tic. His brow was usually set low in a stern expression, but nothing else about him was out of the ordinary. Maybe he'd invited me to his study for another reason.

Tonight, I was seated by Herr Gutin. I smoothed my napkin over my lap and faced him with a smile. "I hope your meeting went well for the charity," I offered simply. "Anna told me all about it." They'd planned on raising money for the refugees. Of course it made sense why Herr Bruun had specified in the note that Anna would disapprove of their ties. She was obviously an advocate for the Allied effort.

"Yes, yes." His bushy brows seemed like a silver caterpillar on his forehead, worming up and down with the bobbing of his head. "We were without a few members, but we managed all right."

"The committee secretary didn't show." His wife sniffed. "I don't know why she's in that position if she refuses to come to the meetings."

Anna gave a reproving smile. "She has young children to tend to."

"We told her to bring them along. We'd rightly spoil the poor things." She slurped a spoonful of soup. "The three children are from a former marriage, and her husband refuses to help care for them. But then he's gone all the time. Hard to be married to a man that disappears."

"Excuse me." Birgitta pressed her fingertips to her temple. I'd caught that she'd stood to her feet in the middle of the woman's complaints. "I'm not feeling well." And then she moved from the table and out the door.

"I'm sorry." Fru Gutin gaped at the empty doorway Birgitta fled. "That was insensitive of me. I shouldn't have said anything about a disappearing husband."

Maybe I should check on her. Though that might make things worse. Finn's brow lowered, but he didn't say anything. Nor did he go after her.

The main entrée was served, and Birgitta still hadn't returned to the table.

Finn leaned over and whispered, "You're upset with me over something."

No. He wasn't supposed to pick up on that. My breath pinched in my chest. Maybe I wasn't as wonderful an actress as I'd believed. Not exactly a comforting thought. I took a sip of water, needing an extra second to compose myself. I straightened with a smile. "Why do you say that?"

His eyes were on me, searching, as if he held power to peer beyond the surface. "You've barely said anything."

"Ah, ah." I wagged my fork at him. "That's all your fault."

"My fault?"

"Of course it is. You're the one who said you wanted to speak with me *after* dinner." My gentle rebuke made his brows dip. "This is *during* dinner. If you wanted to speak with me now, you should've said so." I stabbed at a dumpling and regarded him with a long-suffering expression. "But you want to talk to me later, so we wait until. . .later." And with that, I took a dainty bite and turned toward Herr Gutin with a satisfied smile.

Dinner concluded, and the guests dispersed. But something troubled me, and I couldn't pinpoint what it was. With a sigh, I made my way toward Finn's study to face my fate. Hedvig came around the corner, scurrying as if behind on her duties.

When she saw me coming, she slowed and offered me a mischievous smile. "Did the dress work? Was Herr Ristaffason besotted all through dinner?"

I almost snorted. Finn hadn't seemed a man to be besotted with anything or anyone. He'd given me looks throughout dinner, but I wouldn't call them ones of admiration. "I need to ask you something." I motioned toward a secluded alcove, and she followed. "When I was in town earlier, there was a dark blue building four or five doors down from where you were speaking to Franc." The very one Birgitta Lindgurst had walked out of today. "It had a bright yellow sign, but I couldn't read it. Do you know what place that is?"

≣ CHAPTER 17 ≣

Loud voices crashed into the hall from inside Finn's study. After I'd spoken with Hedvig, I'd resolved to find Birgitta, but it appeared others had reached her first. Because inside the office were Birgitta, Finn, and another man. I crouched in the shadowed doorway, a shiver creeping up my spine at the thick tension.

"Johan, please!" Birgitta's voice was a fragile plead.

I pinched my lips, trapping a gasp. Herr Johan Lindgurst had returned. Or had he? Because the man standing only a few yards from me contradicted everything I'd heard about Birgitta's husband. Hedvig had claimed him handsome and kind, and Elias had touted his goodness. But this guy? He looked lethal. His dusty brown hair was matted in some spots and stood on end in others. An unkempt beard shadowed his taut jaw. But it was his eyes that alarmed me. They darkened with fury.

"Don't deny it. I have proof." His harsh tone made Birgitta inch behind the wingback chair. With bumbling movements, he reached into his pocket. I hoisted the edge of my skirt, ready to grab my gun if the man flashed a weapon. But he withdrew a letter and fixed his loathing glare on Finn. "See? I found this on your desk before you got a chance to open it."

Confusion bent Finn's brow. He took a step toward Herr Lindgurst, but the wild man slashed his other arm in the air, stalling Finn's approach.

"I–It's not what you think." Birgitta's fingers splayed against her stomach, her face twisting in anguish.

"No?" His head shook fiercely, and he staggered back, clearly drunk.

I braced for him to tumble into the hall, but he slammed against the doorjamb, too close to where I hid.

With a curse, Herr Lindgurst righted himself and moved farther into the room. He shook open the letter and read, "*Finn. I need to see you. I can't let Johan know. I'm scared to tell him. Too afraid of how he might react. But things can't be undone.*" His face crumpled, but his eyes held disgust. "You can have any woman you want, and you take mine."

"There's nothing between Birgitta and me," Finn refuted calmly. Too calmly. If there was ever a time for Finn to be adamant, this was it.

"Don't lie!" Herr Lindgurst's shout echoed off the walls. "I know the truth." He shoved the letter into his trouser pocket. "There's only one way to go from here." He shrugged off his jacket, shoved up his sleeves, and curled his hands into fists. Adopting a boxer's stance, he spat at Finn. "I'm going to enjoy breaking your face."

Birgitta fainted onto the floor.

I abandoned the shadows and barged into the room. "Stop all this," I commanded as I rushed to the young woman. "You've no idea what you're talking about."

I darted a glance at Johan. Thank goodness for the element of surprise, because the man's bluster withered at my sudden appearance.

"Are you. . ." His voice fell to a whisper, and he rubbed his eyes as if he didn't trust his vision.

I grabbed a pillow from the chair and gently placed it beneath Birgitta's head. After seeing to her comfort, I stood and smoothed out my gown. "I'm Amelie Blake, and I'm disappointed in you, Johan." Might as well drop formalities. Nothing about this situation was dignified.

His stunned stare continued. No doubt his drunken stupor magnified his confusion. Finally, he shook his head and pressed a limp hand to his chest. "M–Me?"

"Yes, you." I took a bold step toward him, but he didn't shuffle away, only kept gawking.

"Amelie, maybe you should go get smelling salts." Finn tried to step between me and the drunk man, but I shook my head. It was kind of him to want to protect me, but I knew I could defuse the situation.

"No, you go, Finn." My authoritative tone made him blink. "But don't fetch smelling salts." Birgitta couldn't smell strong fumes in her condition. "Have your cook mix sea salt with eucalyptus oil if she has any. If not, peppermint should work."

Questions filled Finn's eyes, and my stomach dropped.

I hadn't expected to forsake my cover. Would the OSS be disappointed? I bent and smoothed Birgitta's hair from her face, but she didn't stir.

"I'm not leaving you." Finn's voice was emphatic.

"Fine." I stood and moved to the bellpull and tugged it. "Whoever answers this"—I motioned to the corded rope—"tell them to bring the peppermint oil straightaway. Until then, let me handle this."

Johan puffed out his chest, his indignance returning. "I need to thrash him."

"Talk to me first," I ordered. "If you feel the need to pummel Finn afterward, then by all means, I won't stop you." I heard Finn make a noise of dissent from beside me. "But for now, sit here by me."

I didn't have to repeat myself. He claimed the spot beside me on the tufted sofa. His suit was rumpled as if he'd slept in it for days. Maybe weeks, considering the pungent odor rolling off him. I fought to keep from pinching my nose.

Finn stood behind, his hands gripping the top of the sofa, his stance wide as if ready to intervene if needed.

I gave him a nod as if to say "trust me" and turned to Johan. "You've got it all wrong. Your wife is expecting a baby." According to Hedvig, the building Birgitta had exited earlier belonged to the local midwife. Judging by her loose-fitting clothing, her frail appearance, and how she'd repeatedly placed a hand over her abdomen, all signs pointed to Birgitta Lindgurst being pregnant. Those words she'd written to Finn? It wasn't about a secret love affair, but a child.

He shot to his feet. "I'll murder you. Murder you!"

I snatched his shirttail as he tried to spin toward Finn. "Wrong again." I tugged harder, and he fell back onto the sofa. It rocked slightly, making me fear it would topple with the force of his bulk, but Finn clamped his hands on the frame.

"Finn's *not* the pappa, Johan." At least, I hoped Finn wasn't. All I had were strong clues and intelligent speculation.

Stevens, the butler, appeared in the doorway, and Finn obediently went to him, hopefully informing him to hurry back with the oil.

"If the child's mine, why's she afraid to tell me?" Johan's crestfallen countenance was quite the change from his furious expression only seconds ago. "Why would she be scared to tell me if I was the pappa? I'm not a monster."

"But her first husband was," I said. "And she's pregnant with his child." Which accounted for her behavior at the dinner table tonight. Everyone had assumed she'd fled because of the mention of the disappearing husband, but Birgitta had already been standing by that point. She'd risen to her feet the second Fru Gutin had spoken of a husband refusing to take care of another man's baby.

Finn shifted behind me, but I kept my focus on Johan who kept blinking. How much alcohol had he consumed?

I sighed. "When Birgitta's first husband died, she must've been early in her pregnancy. Then you promptly married her. She didn't realize her condition until later, and was frightened to tell you because—"

"I hated Oskar." His voice cracked. "He mistreated her. It's not her fault or the child's."

"But she didn't know how you'd react." Hence the letter to Finn detailing her fears. I'd wager she'd realized how that note could've been misinterpreted and attempted to recover it from Finn's desk drawer.

"Here I thought. . .all this time. . ." He shook his head slowly. "I thought my wife and best friend betrayed me." His eyes glossed over, and I wasn't sure if he was seconds from passing out or sobbing. "I've let her down." His softened gaze slid to his wife, still unconscious on the floor.

He sniffled. "Left when she needed me most." His shoulders shook, followed by heaving breaths, then finally the flood of manly tears.

To my surprise, Finn clapped Johan's shoulder in support. "I wouldn't betray you. You're like a brother to me."

He nodded, pressing the heels of his hands to his leaking eyes. "But that's why I left. I didn't know what to do." His voice broke on a gulp. "How can she forgive me?"

"It's not too late," I said soothingly. "You can give her a thorough apology and raise that child as your own."

"I will," he vowed, which would've made my own eyes glisten if not for his belch that ensued.

The butler returned, and Finn retrieved the oil.

I turned to Johan. "Go with Stevens and clean up. Maybe get some strong coffee in you." I handed him his discarded jacket. "You don't want her to wake up with you still looking like this." I waved a hand at his disheveled appearance. "And for goodness' sake, shave as well."

He shot to his feet and stumbled forward a few steps. "Thank you, Amelie."

Finn skewered me with his probing gaze, but I hadn't time to address anything. Poor Birgitta needed tended to. As Stevens led Johan from the room, I went to Finn for the oil.

"Cook didn't have eucalyptus." He handed me a glass bowl and some balls of cotton. "But she had peppermint."

I nodded and moved across the room toward Birgitta.

I kneeled beside her and dipped the tuft of cotton into the scented oil. "Since she's expecting, strong fumes from smelling salts could have been harmful." Something I wouldn't have considered if not for a fellow actress who'd blamed the tragedy of her recent miscarriage on being exposed to potent chemicals. It could've had nothing to do with her loss, but after seeing the pain my friend had suffered, I didn't want to chance it with Birgitta. I waved the peppermint fragrance beneath her nose, while my other hand rubbed her arm. "Wake up, Birgitta," I said softly. "Everything's all right." At least I hoped it was. I'd jumped to a conclusion without verifying the facts. I could've easily made more of a mess of things.

Her lashes fluttered, and her right index finger twitched.

I repeated the oil treatment, and this time her eyelids drifted open. She groaned. It seemed the moments before her swoon came flooding back because her face twisted with horror even as her hands flew to her stomach in a protective gesture.

"Everything's okay," I soothed.

"Johan?" Her voice was rusty. "Where's Johan?"

"He's getting cleaned up." And, hopefully, sober. "He'll be ready to speak with you soon."

She glanced at Finn.

"He's okay too." I took a deep breath. "Johan knows about Oskar's child."

She sat up. "What? How?"

Relief swept through me at my correct assumption, though panic tightened her features. "I told him. You don't have to be afraid to talk to him. He's the one who's sorry."

Tears gathered in her eyes. "Johan's always hated Oskar. Wouldn't even let me mention him. I was frightened he'd reject. . ."

"I understand." I took her hand. "But there's nothing to worry about now."

"How did you know?"

"I wasn't completely certain." Thank God, I went with my gut. "I saw you leaving the midwife's place earlier, and I coupled that with all your recent reactions. When Johan read your letter to Finn, it all made sense." Plus, there weren't any sparks between Finn and Birgitta. I watched for stolen glances or secret exchanges. Other than the moment she'd cried in his office, nothing indicated any romantic relationship.

"You're quite the detective, Amelie." Her grateful smile matched the warmth in her eyes. "Thank you for all you've done."

I returned her smile as Finn assisted her to her feet.

"I should go find him." Her bloom returned.

Finn watched her leave, his face still registering unbelief. "What just happened?" He held out his hand to me.

I let him help me stand but also raised my guard. The man was blameless in this instance but plenty guilty in other areas. I glanced at the clock on his desk. Elias had planned for us to meet in the foyer at ten o'clock. It was fifteen till.

My muscles were sluggish with fatigue. After all the emotion from the past thirty minutes, I was ready for bed. But this might prove my only chance of meeting Franc. I'd already discarded my disguise in front of Finn. At least I could pursue this angle of this mission.

Finn barred his arms over his chest, eyeing me. He most likely awaited an explanation, but I hadn't the time or strength to provide it. I needed to hunt down Franc. "Please excuse me."

I fled the room.

⟩ CHAPTER 18 ⟨

The mood of the Frossa was surprisingly...American.

My attention swung to the big band orchestra gathered on the corner stage. One enthusiastic trumpeter stood, rocking back and forth as he blared the intro to Glenn Miller's "Kalamazoo."

Cigarette smoke climbed to the rafters, leaving a darkened haze the ceiling lamps fought to push through. A cluster of tables were situated near the entrance. Tall booths lined the left wall. The open middle of the space boasted a large and crowded dance floor. Those not jiving to the swing music huddled around the bar on the right side of the room.

Elias peeled my wrap from my shoulders, his fingers skimming my bare arms. Whether or not his lingering touch was accidental, I didn't have time to weigh his intentions. I needed to find Franc. While Elias handed my things to the coatroom attendant, I searched the space for the lanky gentleman but couldn't see past a flock of guys preying like scavengers on the fringes in hunt for a partner.

"I need to get on that dance floor," I muttered to myself. Being centrally located, it had the best viewpoint.

"Then I'm happy to claim the next song." Elias moved beside me, and I jolted. He had impeccable hearing.

"This place is popular." I raised my voice as we neared the action. "Do you come here a lot?" Now that I'd shed my cover in front of Finn, I struggled keeping up the pretense. But if I held to light conversation, nothing should appear amiss.

He shrugged. "Every once in a while. But I've a feeling tonight's going to be much more interesting. You're already getting looks." His eyes narrowed even as his hand settled on my lower back. "Am I to take on the role of bodyguard?"

Irritation snapped my gaze to his but soon fizzled at the uncertainty on his face. Did he suspect trouble? He seemed to be scanning the crowd just as much as I was. "I'll be fine, Elias."

We joined the couples on the outskirts of the floor. His hand curled around my waist, and my mind drifted back to the dance on the beach with Finn, the confident feel of his arms around me, the beads of water clinging to his hair, the moonlight painting our silhouettes on the sand.

With this area so congested, Elias and I could hardly move a foot in any direction, unlike last night, where Finn had spun me along the shoreline as the tide kissed our heels. I stifled a groan. That was the one drawback to my incredible memory, I could revisit past moments with perfect clarity, almost like watching a film of my life.

But I had a job to do.

Elias' hand shifted on my back, pressing me closer to avoid colliding into a spirited couple. "Are you enjoying your time in Malmö?" His gaze drifted over my shoulder.

"It's a charming place." I wasn't sure if Elias heard my response. He seemed more interested in observing his surroundings than engaging in conversation. "Are you searching for anyone?"

"Hmm?" His eyes shifted, meeting mine. He smiled down at me. "No, I just thought I saw a friend. That's all."

Speaking of friends, my attention snagged on a man I'd thought to be hours away.

Axel.

Dressed in a dark suit, he leaned against the bar, taking in the room. Why was he here? And since he was in Malmö, why hadn't he tried to contact me?

The song ended, and Elias peered down at me. "Care for another dance? I promise not to get distracted." Yet as he'd said those words, he'd fought to keep his gaze trained on me. It was easy to discern he wanted to be elsewhere, which contrasted his hovering behavior only moments ago.

I shot a glance at Axel and feigned surprise. "Oh, there's Herr Eizenburg. I met him in Stockholm." No need hiding my knowing him. After all, we'd made a public appearance at the charity event. "Care if I say hello?"

The taut lines in his face relaxed. "Not at all. I'll be around if you need me." And with that, he disappeared. Odd. For being so concerned about my safety earlier, he held no objections to leaving me now.

I started toward Axel, then paused. Having finally rid myself of a chaperone, wouldn't it be better if I devoted this time to finding Franc? I snaked my way through the dance floor, my gaze searching. A few people spared me curious glances, but no one attempted to seek me out. I casually perused the row of booths. No Franc. Perhaps he wasn't coming tonight. With a sigh, I headed toward the bar.

Axel straightened to full height at my approach, his mouth curling into a slow smile. "Ah, Amelie. I was hoping I might see you."

A gangly man on the barstool beside Axel nursed his drink yet subtly leaned toward our direction, clearly eavesdropping.

I tugged Axel's hand and searched for any open spot to speak with him. A young couple vacated a table, and I rushed to claim it. Once we both were seated, I bent my head toward his. "What are you doing here? Are you following me?" I asked teasingly.

He sighed. "If only I was. It would be a far more interesting assignment than my current one." He jerked his head toward the stage. "See anyone you recognize?"

I waited for a herd of laughing females to pass, and I squinted at the band. My jaw slacked at the sight of the Chilean singer from the Grand Hôtel. "That's Rosita Serrano." The woman who'd participated in the auction had been listed on the OSS watch list. And she was just as lovely as I remembered. Tonight, she wore a bright yellow cocktail dress with her hair piled atop her head.

It appeared Axel had been ordered to keep an eye on her, but I wasn't buying his disinterest. "How trying it must be for you to follow around a beautiful woman."

"If you put it that way, I suppose I have no complaints." He inched closer, keeping his voice low. "So far, she's kept her nose clean."

I studied the young woman as she adjusted her guitar strap, then returned my focus to Axel. "Maybe the rumors about her are false then."

His brow quirked. "There are pictures of her singing in front of a Nazi banner. And German newspapers headlined her as the voice of the Third Reich."

Oh. So much for giving her the benefit of the doubt. But if she was a

Nazi nightingale, why was she in Sweden? More specifically, why was she in Malmö? My stomach clenched. With her status as a performer, she could gain entry to high-profile events. Same as me. Had she also been sent to collect Dr. Bohr's document? I couldn't dismiss the possibility.

His gaze ran over me. "I see you've come armed."

Surely he couldn't see my holster. I glanced down at my hemline, relieved the leather strap was concealed.

His eyes glinted with amusement, and he dipped his head closer. "Who needs firearms when you can tease a man to madness just by wearing that dress?"

I feebly swatted his arm. "Remember what I said about flattery?"

He smirked. "I believe it had something to do with pushing me into the Norrström. Thankfully, we're hours from Stockholm."

"There's always the Öresund." I drummed my fingers on the table along to the music. This place was lively enough but couldn't rival the exhaustion melting into my bones. I was ready to return to Finn's estate. Franc hadn't shown, making me wonder if I might've missed him, considering we'd arrived on the late side. A sigh parted my lips.

"Tough night?"

"I chased a lead here, but nothing's come of it yet." This entire mission had been a swirl of ups and downs. I wasn't much closer to finding that briefcase than when I'd first arrived. At least I could eliminate the Lindgursts from my lists of suspects. Unless their scene in Finn's study was all a performance. One thing about this assignment, there seemed to be an unending line of questions. But with Axel here, I could at least get one answer. "Why did you send me that missive?"

A shapely brunette walked by with a sultry smile aimed at Axel, temporarily diverting his attention.

I rolled my eyes and nudged his foot beneath the table. "The missive. Explain."

He shrugged. "I received a report that Ristaffason sent a lot of money to Erik Bruun."

This wasn't new. I was painfully aware Finn had partnered with my father, though hearing it aloud hit me afresh. Of course the OSS would discover that important detail before I did. The allied intelligence had a wealth of information, yet they didn't seem to have any idea I was related to Erik Bruun. Or did they? "What do you know of that man? Herr Bruun?"

"Let's just say the man's greedy and without morals."

Again. Something I'd already known. "I met him last night. He tried to coax me into investing in icebreaker vessels for the Gulf of Bothnia." For some reason, I withheld the truth of my connection to Herr Bruun. "Of course, I told him no."

Axel nodded, still keeping a vigilant eye on Fröken Serrano. "We heard last spring that he's searching for investors. If he's still asking, he hasn't secured the money yet. That's good news."

I agreed.

"How are things going?" he asked nonchalantly.

"I'm not sure." I scanned the room again. If Franc didn't show, how was I to go forward? I suppose I could talk with Hedvig again to determine if she knew where Franc lived. But I didn't put much hope in that route. No, it seemed my best path would be to stick close to Finn. That was, if he'd let me. After those moments in his study, I wasn't sure where our relationship stood. He could be angry with me for deceiving him.

"Did you come here with anyone?" He moved his chair in to allow a portly fellow to squeeze through the aisle between tables. "I know better than to ask if Ristaffason brought you. He avoids crowds like I skirt angry fathers."

I wouldn't dignify his last comment with a response. "Elias Rickertz escorted me here. Do you know him?"

"I've heard that name before." He tipped his head to the side. "It wasn't Elias though. I believe the man has a brother. Lives in Gotland, I think." He made a face. "And from what I remember, he's a troublemaker."

"I'll keep that in mind." Elias had never mentioned any family, let alone a menacing sibling. Perhaps they weren't on speaking terms.

"How's it going, staying at Ristaffason's estate? Has he kept his paws off you?" He leaned back in his chair. "You have to watch the quiet ones."

"The obnoxious ones aren't any better." Another voice joined our conversation. Finn's.

I swiveled, peering up at the man who'd just been haunting my thoughts. Why was he here? A crowded dance hall would seem the last place Finn would like to be trapped in. I folded my hands in my lap to keep from fidgeting. Had he followed me here to call me out?

Axel tossed an annoyed glance at Finn, and I could tell by the tightness of his jaw that whatever he'd say next wasn't going to be pretty.

So I spoke first. "I didn't know you were coming tonight, Finn."

"It was a last-minute decision." His eyes held mine. "Care to dance?"

At the Grand Hôtel, Finn had led me to the balcony, away from prying eyes. Yet this dance hall was three times as packed. What was his game? Was he purposely trying to unnerve me?

Or was his objective to keep me from Axel? It was apparent the men were rivals, though the history behind their veiled hostility was yet to be discovered.

Either way, I needed to determine where I stood with Finn. And the dance floor seemed as good a place as any. I gave a parting smile to Axel and took Finn's proffered hand.

Finn seemed to remember Axel. "Do you mind if I whisk her away?"

"This wouldn't be the first time." His tone held barbs, but Finn didn't seem the least torn by it.

"What was that about?" I asked when out of Axel's earshot.

He shrugged. "Old grievance." And by his dark look, it was one he didn't care to divulge. I could only speculate from Axel's cutting reply the feud was over a woman.

The orchestra played Duke Ellington's "Sophisticated Lady," and I stepped into Finn's arms for the third time in less than a week.

His hand rested on my back with comfortable ease, and like last evening, he held me close. Though this time, he couldn't blame his nearness on sand mounds. We swayed to the gentle rhythm, the saxophones and clarinets setting the moody tone.

He gazed down at me, his tightened mouth bringing out his dimple. Was it wrong to admire someone's scowl? Yes, it was. I couldn't allow myself to appreciate any part of him, even the small things.

I glanced at our linked hands. "How are the Lindgursts?"

"They're good now, thanks to you."

I wasn't sure how to respond. But I did know there wasn't any point in carrying on my flighty ruse. "I only spoke the truth."

"I'm obliged to you as well."

"More like your handsome face is obliged. Johan was intent on rearranging it."

Something glinted in his eyes. Was it because I'd called him handsome? Or because of my quip? This was the first time I'd allowed myself to respond with any sort of wit. Though I chided myself for complimenting him. Didn't I just determine not to admire him? He shook his head. "I had no idea Birgitta was expecting."

Because Johan had intercepted his wife's letter. I'd suspected Birgitta was under the impression Finn hadn't gotten a chance to read the letter and hoped to retrieve it before he did. Which was why she'd been trying to break into that drawer. I brought my gaze to his. "Yes, well, people are adept at hiding their secrets." I meant this as a jab at him, but he seemed unmoved.

"Speaking of which." He leaned in, murmuring against my temple, "I know your secret, Amelie."

My eyes slid shut. I'd expected him to confront me but not this way. Not with his lips nearly skimming my skin. Or the stroke of his thumb over mine.

I eased back, putting much-needed space between us. "Just one secret?" I shrugged, feigning disinterest. "I suppose that's okay since I have many."

"Most women do." There was a pocket of space around us, and Finn used it to his advantage, spinning me under his arm. But when he brought me back, we were closer than before. I could count the silver flecks in his eyes, watch the dip of his Adam's apple. "But I'm only interested in yours."

I raised a brow, challenging him to reveal what he knew of me.

"You took impressive control of the situation with Johan. It proved you have a quick presence of mind."

"Perhaps I'm just good at dealing with people."

"It's more than that." He shook his head. "I've noticed things here and there. But tonight sealed it. You're cleverer than you've been letting on." He dipped me, his strong arm supporting my arched back. He slowly guided me to standing, his eyes hot on mine. "You've been hiding your brilliance, and I want to know why."

Our faces stood only inches apart. He was awaiting my answer, and I struggled to breathe. Having this man's sole focus, being the target of his heated stare, made concentrating more difficult. "I give the public what they expect."

He didn't seem furious at my deception. If anything, he seemed relieved. "There's nothing wrong with intelligence." His brows bent in expectation. But I refused to offer any more details. Why should I explain my motives when he so clearly masked his?

"It's easier to read others when they assume to know all there is about me. And it's far more effortless to keep people at a distance."

He drew near. "But what happens if someone wants to get close?"

A flashbulb blinded from the left.

Journalists. Wonderful. And the way Finn held me against him, I was certain whatever was captured on film appeared far more intimate than it truly was.

As always, I acted unfazed by my privacy being intruded upon.

So did Finn. "We'll be on the front of the papers tomorrow."

I exhaled. "Giving the impression of something we're decidedly not."

His hand slid up my back. "We can give the press something better to print."

I blinked. Was he. . .flirting with me? I'd expect such a remark from Axel, but from Finn? "If you take liberties and kiss me, I won't be responsible for my actions. What Johan planned for you would be mild in comparison."

His lips twitched, but I was totally serious. Commandant Skilbeck had trained me well. Finn would be on the floor in five seconds, three if my skirt allowed more movement.

He cleared his throat. "I only meant about your decision to help Farmor's recent project." Finn had heard my remarks during dinner? I'd thought I'd voiced them quietly to Anna. He shrugged. "The church is a beloved building. The locals would adore you more than they already do for aiding its restoration."

Oh. I shouldn't have jumped to the rash conclusion.

Finn led me off the dance floor, ignoring the open stares of other couples. "You're donating to a worthy cause. It's commendable."

"A worthy cause." We paused, allowing a group of young men to pass, and I fixed my gaze on him. "Now that's a term with free interpretation. Because what I might deem worthy and what *you* might judge worthy could be completely opposite. By the way, you never told me if you're investing in the icebreaker vessels."

His brows hiked at my boldness. "I know better than to get involved with Herr Bruun."

And just like that he'd lied to me. A chill pulsed through my veins, freezing any regard I'd felt for him. But I couldn't stew over Finn's deceit, because just over my shoulder was Franc.

He was holding a briefcase.

≡ CHAPTER 19 ≡

The band announced a break, and the dance floor emptied. People swarmed by, hemming me in, blocking my view of Franc.

"Excuse me, Finn, I need to freshen up." That excuse should buy me some time. And it wasn't a complete fib, for I intended to visit the powder room once I had the briefcase to check its contents. If I could ever get to the briefcase, considering the mass exodus off the dance floor.

Finn nodded politely, and I shouldered past the flow of couples toward the place I'd glimpsed Franc. I needed to get to him before that briefcase changed hands. The camel-colored case and ivory handle he'd clutched matched the description in my files. It had to be it.

I reached the area he'd stood only moments ago, but. . .he was gone. Heart sinking, I turned in a slow circle. He couldn't have gone far. Sharpening my gaze, I searched the crowd for the dove-gray suit he had on. Unfortunately, it was a popular shade.

He wasn't in any of the booths. Or at the bar. Perhaps he'd gone to the—

There!

He lingered near the cloakroom, but his hands were empty. What? Where was the briefcase? Had the exchange already happened? Panic surged, forcing my feet into action. I skirted an amorous couple and weaved through the tables, refusing to check if Axel was still seated. I had to reach Franc.

I was only twenty feet away, but he'd already procured his hat from the attendant and moved toward the door.

I couldn't let him leave. "Franc!"

He halted his retreat and pivoted on his heel, facing me with a questioning expression.

I expelled an airy laugh. "I'm so happy I caught you."

His gaze dipped over my form in a lazy crawl, pausing on my curves. "I know who you are, but the question is. . .how do you know me?" This morning in town, he'd run from me, but he didn't seem the least skittish now. Rather, the opposite.

"I don't know you but learned about you from a lovely girl." I cupped my mouth as if sharing a secret. "It's a good thing you're popular with the ladies or else I'd never have found out your name."

Surprised pleasure lit his hooded eyes. As much as I disliked flattery, Franc seemed to lap it up. "To what do I owe this honor?"

I refrained from lowering my brow. Other than his blatant leering, he didn't seem to recollect our paths crossing earlier. "It's rather silly." I dipped my chin and peered up at him through my batting lashes. "But I saw you carrying a briefcase."

His open expression shuttered, his mouth flattening into a scowl. "What about it?"

"It perfectly matches a camel-colored suit I own. Just think of how smart I'll look carrying it around." I gave a dreamy sigh. "I want to buy it from you."

"Sorry, fröken. I don't have it anymore."

"Oh no." I pouted and tried not to cringe as he stared at my lips. "I was willing to pay a lot for it. I like getting what I want."

He gave a wicked smile. "I do too."

"We have something in common." I pitched my voice higher in delighted glee. "And since we're good friends now, I would love to know what you carried inside your briefcase?"

He tensed. "Why do you want to know?"

"So I can look as professional as you do."

He huffed a chuckle, the line of his shoulders lowering. "You really want to know?"

"Of course." I beamed at him. "That's why I asked."

Franc ringed my wrist and tugged me to him. I nearly bounced off his chest. He peered down at me, his eyes glinting with what I could only call mischief. "Nothing that would interest a girl like you."

It seemed he took pleasure in toying with me. Not that I could blame him for siding with the world in thinking I was a nitwit. But I'd hoped to get better information out of him than this. "Well, if you don't have the briefcase anymore, can you tell me where it is?" I pressed my flattened palms together in a plea. "I really love that camel color."

He shook his head. "No. It's not a good idea. I shouldn't even be talking to you about it."

"Why?" I pressed a hand to my chest. "Is it a secret?"

"You can say that." He slapped his hat on his head. "And I don't think the people who have it want that secret getting out."

"Oh, I see." I slouched with defeat. "But what if. . ." I straightened with renewed purposed. "What if I paid you to get the briefcase for me? I want it all now. The secrets inside and the pretty case. I'll pay you double what they did."

"All right." He was too quick to agree, which put me on my guard. "How about you give me the money, no less than fifty thousand kronor, and I'll get to work?"

Now I understood his swift readiness. Because he intended to swindle me. No doubt take my money and skip town. There was devilry in his eyes. "I want to see it first before I pay you. Just to be sure it matches my pretty suit. I wouldn't look as smart if I were mismatched."

"Listen, fröken." He dropped all pretenses. "As much as I could use your money, I can't get it for you. Sorry." He gave a clipped goodbye and exited the building.

Maybe I should've abandoned my ditsy attitude. I'd truly felt if I approached him any other way, I'd frighten him off like this morning. But. . .he hadn't even mentioned seeing me near the town square. He'd acted as if tonight had been the first time he'd seen me in person. I needed answers, and he was the only one who had them.

Determination lifting my chin, I followed him out the door.

The night's chill wrapped around me like a frosty cloak. Franc had at least a thirty-second head start on me. I hadn't any clue which direction he'd fled. On a whim, I went left, picking the road that led into town. I hastened my pace and was rewarded. The dim streetlamp carved Franc's outline. To my surprise, he turned right at the corner. I wasn't familiar with that part of Malmö, but I decided to keep trailing him.

Pushing my hair from my face, I took off, my heels clopping against the cobblestone street.

I turned the corner and stumbled to a halt because Franc had planted himself there, and judging by his wide stance and hardened glare, he wasn't thrilled to see me.

"Why are you following me?" He grasped my arm, but I wrenched it away.

"Listen, Franc." I stepped back in case he attempted to grab me again. "I apologize for deceiving you, but I need that briefcase."

A car's motor sounded in the distance, even as Franc shook his head. "What kind of game are you playing?"

"It's not a game." I kept my voice calm. "Can you at least tell me where I can find it?"

He released a scoff. "No chance. I can't tell you a thing. They already threatened me. I know too much." His voice hardened. "Now leave me alone." He sprinted away, his rushed strides easily putting distance between us.

An automobile pulled onto the street, its headlamps blinding. Franc kept running. Was that car his getaway? But then. . .the car's engine roared, and tires squealed, barreling toward him.

Dread gripped me. The driver was intentionally after him. "Franc! Take cover!"

He yelled and dove to the left, but the car swerved, a sickening thud proving it hit its mark. A scream scraped my throat. I pressed my spine against a shadowed doorway.

The car sped past me, and I rushed toward Franc.

Someone had hit him on purpose. Franc's words came back to me. *They already threatened me. I know too much.*

His broken frame writhed in the gutter.

I crouched beside him. "I'll get you help."

"No." He coughed blood. "It's too late. God forgive me, it's too late." His face twisted in agony.

He was at his final moments. I needed information only he seemed to know, but. . .he was about to meet his Maker. I seized his hand. "Franc, you never needed mercy more than you do now. We're going to pray."

"Please," he sputtered, as seeping crimson stained his pale face.

By the time I said *Amen*, he was fading. His eyes drifted shut, his fingers limp in mine.

"Ah...Bruun..." His whispers were barely audible. "Secretary." Then his head lolled to the side, and he slipped away.

⧘CHAPTER 20⧘

I shook violently. My sharp breaths burned my lungs, my heart pounding fiercely. What had just happened? One minute Franc bolted to escape me, and the next, he lay lifeless on the street. I'd been trapped in this scene before. The darkened alley. The fog. The man lying still on the ground. But Franc wasn't playing dead for any camera.

In the studio, I'd longed to be the daring heroine, but in real life, I'd failed. Failed Franc. I'd been armed. I could've shot at the car. At least distracted the driver so Franc could get away, but I'd froze.

Though I hadn't realized the driver's intention until the last second. Still. Could things have been done differently? With a result that didn't include a young man dead in the gutter?

The beige cobblestones darkened beneath his broken form. *Who did this to you, Franc?* Maybe there was a clue about the murderer in his pockets. My stomach churned even as the soles of my shoes stuck to the blood-stained street. I could do this. With a shaky breath, I searched his coat pockets. Nothing.

I skimmed the ones in his trousers and found a wad of kronor.

The payoff? I hadn't time to count it, but I leafed through the bills, holding them up to the dim streetlamps, hunting for any markings or notes tucked within the stack. No luck. With a sigh, I returned the money.

Footsteps sounded. I scrambled to stand, my trembling hand tangling in the layers of my skirt in a sorry attempt to reach my holster.

"Amelie?" Finn's deep voice should have erased my panic, but instead the alarm raged stronger.

This mission had turned deadly, and I didn't know who I could trust anymore. Leaning forward, hand twitching at my side, I readied to grab my pistol if needed.

He jogged down the deserted street. His eyes caught sight of me, and he increased his pace.

"Stop." My voice quivered as I flashed my right palm.

Finn slowed, his confused gaze falling to the crumpled form a few paces from where he stood. "No." He dropped to his knees and grabbed Franc's limp wrist, checking for life. "Come on. Beat." He pressed his ear to the dead man's chest, Finn's own breaths heaving.

A tear rolled down my cheek at his desperate attempts to save him. But while my emotions slipped from my control, my mind sharpened. How had Finn known I was out here? I was almost two streets from the nightclub. Yet he'd found me.

Finn sat back on his haunches, his face bleak. "He's gone." His words made my blood run cold, the hair standing on my arms.

I'd never witnessed anything so horrible. "S–Someone hit him with their car." I shuddered. "On purpose."

He dragged a hand over his crestfallen face, his eyes sliding shut for several long seconds. Then, as if remembering my presence, he launched to his feet and drew near. "Are you okay?" His gaze stretched slowly over my person. "Are you hurt?"

"No." A numbness seeped through me. "I wish I could've helped him." Franc couldn't have been more than twenty. Too early to leave this world.

"Me too." Regret burdened his tone. He stripped off his jacket and wrapped it around me, his warmth pressing into me. "When I couldn't find you, my mind jumped to the worst conclusion. The man at the coat check-in said you left with someone." He held out his closed fist. "Then I found this on the street." He opened his hand, revealing my hair comb.

My fingers went to my wayward locks. No wonder my hair had fallen in my face while chasing Franc. My comb had slipped free.

"I had to find you." He pressed the comb into my palm and curled his hand over mine, a tremor coursing through his fingers.

My suspicious heart weakened at the noticeable hitch in his voice. Either he was the best actor this side of the Atlantic, or he'd truly been sick with concern.

His downcast gaze settled on Franc. "If only I could've prevented it."

Why would Finn bear any blame? He hadn't seemed to know Franc. Yet somehow, he felt responsible for his death? My mind—so clear only a second ago—hazed with confusion. Question piled upon question until I became overwhelmed. "We should alert the authorities."

Finn nodded. "Did you happen to see the car?"

I drew in a ragged breath, knowing what needed to be done. I lowered my lashes and revisited the horror. The bright lights. Franc's silhouette, his arms waving as if hailing the driver to brake. The car, a black menacing beast. I searched the memory, combing over the picture in my mind. But everything was light or darkness. Once the car hit Franc, I'd hid in a doorway until it had passed. I hadn't caught sight of the driver. The car's plate. Or even the model.

Disappointment cut through me. How many times could I fail in one night? "I saw the car but nothing memorable about it." But what *was* memorable were Franc's last words, still spinning in the cyclone of my thoughts. *Bruun's secretary.* What did that mean? Was my father connected to all this? Had Franc admitted who killed him?

We walked toward the Frossa, my chest twisting. I hated leaving Franc in the gutter, but I understood not to move him.

Upon entering the building, Finn spoke with the manager, who showed us to his office to call the police. It occurred to me that the killer had most likely visited the nightclub tonight. Maybe it was the person Franc had delivered the briefcase to. Had the murder been premeditated? What if the killer had every intention of harming Franc? Of course, I'd seen it often in mystery movies—the villain always eliminated the extra persons involved. I sighed and sank onto a wooden chair. It was sad my only knowledge to base these deductions came from pictures. If only I'd been able to witness the briefcase's exchange. Wait. Maybe Axel had seen something. I was heartened by the thought.

Finn ended the call, the muscles in his jaw flexing. "The authorities should be here any minute." His flinty gaze burned into mine. "They'll want to hear your account. But I'd like to hear it first. Why were you out in the dark streets with him?"

Why, indeed. "Hedvig spoke a lot of Franc this afternoon." Poor Hedvig! How would I break the news to her? "And I was interested in meeting him."

"You couldn't talk with him inside the club?"

"He seemed to want fresh air. So we took a stroll." *Separately, and at a very fast pace.*

"I see." A somber silence followed his words.

I couldn't be certain if he'd believed my story, but he seemed more focused on Franc's accident than on my conversation with him.

"I must find out who did this." There was steel in his tone. His expression hardened as if chiseled from granite. But it was the untapped fury darkening his eyes that gave me pause. "I won't be able to rest until I do."

My brow furrowed. "You take a great deal upon yourself."

His eyes held mine with heart-pounding intensity. "Franc was my nephew."

------ ≈ ------

How many shocks could a system absorb before shutting down? Because my brain throbbed attempting to process Finn's words. Franc and Finn were related? Two men from seemingly different worlds?

Finn's grim expression all but confirmed it. "Every family has secrets," he repeated what he'd said earlier. That walk into town had only been this morning, yet it seemed forever ago.

Understanding dawned. "Rolf had a son?"

Finn nodded. "Rolf always carried on with women. Farmor tried her best to shield me from his influence by sending me off to boarding school."

I remembered Rolf had been at least a decade older than Finn. I'd never met the oldest Ristaffason son, but his reputation had often been linked to scandals. The man had indulged his every whim without restraint. Maybe that was why Finn held such a tight leash on his passions.

Finn rounded the manager's desk and claimed the chair beside mine. "A little over twenty years ago, Rolf ran off with a local girl. Farmor didn't know where he was until she received his letter detailing his *situation*."

My lips broke with a soft gasp. "He got her pregnant."

"And refused to marry her."

My heart twinged. A circumstance painfully similar to Mamma's—a rich boy dallying with a young girl too blinded by the moment to see truth.

"Farmor was devastated. She gave a substantial amount to the young woman, who then disappeared. Farmor never got to see the child." His brow lowered. "I was young at the time, only about twelve, but she kept it all from me." He exhaled with a slow shake of his head. "Even after Rolf's death."

"How'd you find out?"

From his tense, large frame to his pain-pinched eyes, everything about Finn was a tight coil of emotion. "Two months ago, Franc barged in while we were having dinner. Said he'd ruin the family name if I didn't give him a share of the Ristaffason wealth."

"He blackmailed you?" It seemed to line up with the minor glimpse I'd gotten of Franc's character. The greed that had burned in his eyes. "I'm sure that was a shock." Not only discovering he had another blood relative in this world but also realizing his nephew had wanted to divest him of his fortune.

"I told him the only way he'd get money was if he worked in the family business alongside me. I promised to teach him, but he refused. Since then, I've been trying to reach out to him, but he's avoided every attempt."

"That was why he ran from you this morning." I'd assumed Franc had fled because of me. Franc probably hadn't even noticed me with his uncle standing close by.

Finn looked away, his hands curling into fists on his lap. "He had my brother's eyes, his bearing. I only wanted to help the kid. Give him the future his father never had." His chin sank. "And now he's dead. A foolish, senseless death. Just like Rolf's."

"This isn't your fault."

"I'll get justice for this. It's the least I owe him," he vowed, more to himself than to me. "I was too young to do anything when Rolf died. But this time, I'll see it through to the end."

I set my hand atop his. "I'll help you."

He jolted at my words as if he'd forgotten my presence.

"I won't put you in harm's way, Amelie." His tone softened. "It's unfair to ask that of you."

Assisting Finn provided a route for me to investigate without exposing my mission. "You didn't ask. I offered." And I was the only one who knew where to start.

⟫ CHAPTER 21 ⟪

It was almost dawn before we returned to Finn's estate, both of us exhausted yet restless. Finn was determined to attend to everything regarding his nephew. He'd revealed his familial ties to Franc with both the police and the press. Claiming his nephew and using the clout behind the Ristaffason name ensured Franc's body wouldn't be buried in some forgotten strip of earth but rather beside Rolf in the family plot. That was, if Franc's mother approved. Finn, not knowing how to contact her, left that task to the police.

It hadn't taken long for word to spread throughout the nightclub. Elias and Axel had sought me out, making certain I was all right. I'd discreetly asked Axel if he'd caught a glimpse of anything. He hadn't. So I was back to following the lead Franc had provided.

My father. Or rather my father's secretary.

Finn walked me to my room as if in a daze. He'd suggested a plan of nabbing a few hours of sleep before rushing into anything. I reluctantly agreed but only for his sake. Franc's death had truly shaken him. His reputation for being cold and unfeeling was as false as Clark Gable's teeth. For the man had clearly cared about his nephew and fought to keep composure.

"Thank you, Amelie." His voice was husky with fatigue. "I need to break the news to Farmor before she hears it elsewhere." The lines bracketing his mouth deepened.

My heart went out to Anna. How much grief she'd known in her lifetime. "I wish there was more I could do."

Finn's hands came to my shoulders, their weight anchoring me to the floor. His head dipped lower. Under any other circumstance, I would imagine he was positioning to kiss me, but surprisingly, his eyes filled with tenderness. "You've done more for me than you know." Then his lips feathered my brow, sending a spike of awareness through me. "I'm grateful you're here."

The unexpected gesture wasn't sensual or romantic by any stretch. It was a kiss born of gratitude, which only added to my confusion. Could someone be both bad and good? It was always my belief a person was either one or the other. Finn was adamant about claiming justice for Franc, yet those same morals bent for an alliance with Herr Bruun?

I gently stepped back, my shoulder blades brushing my bedroom door. "I'll meet you in the library at nine." And at that time, I would confront him.

Three hours wasn't enough rest. My vision dulled at the edges, and my muscles protested every step to the library. But I pushed past the exhaustion. If Finn wanted to find his nephew's killer and I the briefcase, we needed to act.

A part of me debated if we should've gone straight to Lomma from Club Frossa, but I wasn't alone on this venture anymore. I now had to consider Finn. I hoped our decision to take the time and strategize would work in our favor. But it was challenging to devise a plan with a man I didn't wholly trust.

I found Finn pacing alongside the rows of shelves. At my presence, his gaze lifted, his measured strides pausing.

"How's your farmor?" I couldn't even bring myself to utter good morning. General pleasantries seemed out of place, especially since there was nothing *good* about this day.

His shoulders curled forward slightly. "She's heartbroken. She wanted to establish a relationship with Franc, but now. . ."

He didn't have to finish. Because there was now no hope of her connecting with her only great-grandson. Not on this earth, anyway. "Please tell her she's guaranteed a reunion. A heavenly one." Then I told him how I'd prayed with Franc in his final moments.

His eyes glossed, brightening the silver flecks among the blue depths.

I would expect a man of his stature to be ashamed of authentic emotion, but he wasn't. "Truly?" His voice wavered between hope and caution, but I couldn't blame him, considering how Franc had treated him.

I nodded. "I wouldn't offer false comfort."

"Thank you, Amelie." He gazed down at me. "But I've been thinking about your offer to help. As much as I appreciate it, I don't feel it's wise. What kind of man would I be if I put you in harm's way?"

I had a feeling his reservations would return. Which was why I'd purposefully withheld Franc's final words. Though after thinking upon last night, there was another strong motive for me to join Finn in the search. "I understand the danger, but it doesn't seem like you do."

His mouth pulled down.

"Finn, I'm involved in this." More than he knew. "I was in the street when Franc got hit. The killer might think I saw him."

His jaw tightened. "But you didn't."

"But he doesn't know that. He could come after me next." I hadn't meant to appeal to Finn's protective side, but it couldn't be helped. I could be a target. A chilling tremor skittered from my spine to my toes. "I'd rather hunt than be hunted."

Struggle clouded the blues of his eyes, but I was right, and he knew it. After seconds of contemplation, his chin dipped in a resigned nod. "I didn't consider you already being in danger." His mouth pressed tight, causing that dimple to appear. "It would be best if you came along then." He blew out a breath. "Though I don't know where to begin."

"I do, because Franc told me."

His head reared back slightly. "What did he say?"

I took a deep breath, a surge of boldness rushing through me. "I think Erik Bruun is responsible for Franc's death."

I'd intended to shock him with that reveal to gauge his response, but he didn't seem to have one. His face didn't twist in disgust, nor his eyes widen in shock. If anything, he appeared somewhat confused. As if Erik Bruun was the last man on his mind.

"Your father?" he finally asked.

"And your partner."

He jolted. "Who told you that?"

"I saw it somewhere." That *somewhere* being his inner sanctum where I'd peeked at his personal correspondences. But I wasn't about to confess.

"I read that the two of you were in a partnership."

He exhaled a sigh. "Someone has grossly misunderstood."

Another lie? I'd glimpsed the very words in my father's own handwriting. How could I misinterpret what was there in bold letters? "What do you mean?"

"Several years back, I designed a vessel and saw to its building. Erik offered me a considerable sum, and I sold it to him. Only recently, I'd heard he was using the SS *Partner* for running loads of iron ore to Germany. I didn't want my ship, my creation, used in that capacity. So I bought it back. Though it cost me two times what it's worth. Farmor objected because she didn't want me doing business with him, but it was a matter of principle."

So it wasn't a partnership, but a *Partner* ship. Reading so quickly, I'd misunderstood. And Herr Bruun's messy handwriting hadn't helped either.

"The *Partner's* out of port at present, but I can show you when she returns. Or if you don't believe me, you can inquire with Farmor, or even Johan Lindgurst or Danikan Skar. They all know the details of the transaction."

Finn wouldn't suggest my checking with Anna or his business partners if he wasn't speaking the truth. "There's no need. I believe you." Once again, I'd jumped to a faulty conclusion. But I couldn't even be disappointed in myself because I was far too relieved Finn wasn't in cahoots with the awful man. "Unfortunately, we still need to visit Herr Bruun."

"Why? What makes you think he's involved in my nephew's killing?"

I relayed Franc's dying words, and Finn's brow flattened.

"You see?" I offered, trying to explain the connection. "I believe the answer lies with Herr Bruun's secretary."

Finn looked at me squarely. "Erik doesn't employ a secretary."

Oh. This was unexpected. I was hoping we could get to the bottom of this and bring the culprit to justice. "What do you mean he doesn't have a secretary? Especially with a company that large?" I'd never heard of anything so peculiar. No secretary? What kind of operation was he running?

Finn shook his head. "Erik handles all his business affairs directly. Writes out the transactions and receipts. Oversees all the correspondences."

Which made sense thinking of the letter he'd written Finn about the sale of the *Partner.*

"Erik trusts no one." Finn's remark seemed to prove Herr Bruun was up to no good. "He hires a man to check his financial figures, though he doesn't show him any details." He shrugged. "I don't envy how many hours Erik must put in."

I claimed a seat on the sofa. "Surely he has people answer his phone?"

"He takes it all upon himself. He informs his clients when he's in his office and the best time to call."

I sank lower into the cushion, disheartened. "Then what did Franc mean?"

Finn settled beside me, his nearness bringing a measure of comfort. "Are you certain that's what he said?"

I nodded. "So if my father doesn't employ a secretary, Franc could've been referring to another person with the surname Bruun. Can you think of anyone?"

Finn looked thoughtful. "The name is vaguely common. I'm certain there are other Bruuns in the country." Which made the hunt more puzzling.

I moved to the bookshelf. On my first night here, I remembered seeing a digest on various Swedish coat of arms and wealthy families. The book appeared relatively new. Perhaps it would give insight into yet another Bruun.

But then my eyes skipped to the volume beside it, a slight feathering in my brain. Last evening during poor Franc's final moment, he'd clasped his chest while trying to speak. "I might have heard wrong."

"Pardon?" Finn joined me beside the bookshelf.

"I think Franc was trying to speak something before he said Bruun. I thought it was a gasp of pain, but it sounded like the syllable '*ah.*'" Franc's anguished stare had latched onto mine as if trying to communicate. "What if he was trying to form a word?" I folded my arms, my fingers dancing a fast rhythm on my elbows as I thought. "Ah Bruun. Ah bron."

"Aubrund," Finn and I said at the same time.

We glanced at each other in surprise, and I broke into a smile. "Do you think that's it?"

Then as if preplanned, Finn and I reached for the book on Gustavian architecture I'd spied only a second ago, our hands meeting on the spine. He gently brushed my knuckles and lowered his arm, allowing me to do the honors.

I located the page and angled the book so we could both see. "In Sigtuna is the famous 'Aubrund House.' Built in the early 1800s." I met Finn's eyes. "We're not looking for a person at all."

"But a renowned piece of furniture."

The secretary.

⚡CHAPTER 22⚡

Finn and I had scrambled to catch the late morning train toward the capital. Stockholm wasn't our destination but the nearby village of Sigtuna where the Aubrund House was located.

I remembered learning about the Gustavian home in primary school. In those days, I'd absorbed as much knowledge as I could, having been aware that any day my education could be ripped from me. And it had.

As history went, Evelina Aubrund had been the daughter of a wealthy businessman and had fallen in love with one of his apprentices. The father had discovered their relationship and sent the young man away. Evelina had faithfully written to him, storing his return letters in a secret compartment in the massive secretary. At one point, her lover's letters had abruptly stopped, but she'd continued writing him into her old age—until she'd passed. No one knew if Evelina had posted the later letters she'd penned or had hidden them away. The irony was not lost on me that we were traveling to a place famous for lost papers in order to recover a missing document.

Finn and I had arrived at the same assumption of the Aubrund House, but had we guessed Franc's words correctly? What would an old secretary have to do with the briefcase? Was it the destination of the next drop-off? I blankly stared out the train-car window. Leaving this area was a significant risk. If we were wrong, we could lose any chance of finding the killer, or recovering the briefcase. But we had to take a chance.

While my heart rate rivaled the speed of this locomotive, I was at least encouraged by the prospect of seeing Mamma soon. My time spent in Malmö had opened my eyes to all that she'd suffered and overcome. Even though her youth had been seized from her, throughout the years she'd kept a resilient spirit and a strong faith. I hoped one day that could be said of me as well.

I pulled my gaze from the window to catch Finn watching me intently. "What?"

He shook his head. "Nothing, really. I was thinking about chance encounters."

"What about them?" Conversation with Finn was like drawing water from the pump at Morfar's cabin. It had been challenging to prime. My hands and arms had burned from the effort. But the springs it had tapped into were the best around, refreshing and satisfying. So it was with Finn. He needed coaxing into talking, drawing him from his surly shell, but having his sole attention, knowing he was attuned to me, was oddly gratifying.

"Our chance encounter. Meeting you at the Grand Hôtel like I did."

Oh. My breath lodged in my sternum beside a hefty lump of guilt. There was no *chance* about that night. Finn had been the entire reason I'd been at the charity function. How would he respond if he knew the truth? That I'd been charged with getting close to him for the sole purpose of spying on his affairs. The secrets piled in my gut like sharp rocks, heavy and cutting. Though maybe I could dislodge one heavy stone that had sat far too long on the banks of my soul. "But we've met before."

His gaze burned into mine. "I'd remember it."

"Would you?" I challenged. "Because I didn't meet you as Amelie Blake. I met you as Mel Blakstrom at Count Vernalette's Christmas party."

His brow lowered. "You were their guest?"

"I was their help." At that time, I'd been ashamed of my low station, but looking back, those crucial years had shaped my character. I never would've survived stardom without first understanding that humility and kindness trumped wealth and prestige. "Mamma's cleaning service was hired for the party. I somehow heard you were attending." Finn had just turned eighteen. With Rolf's passing, Finn had become the only heir of Ristaffason Enterprises. Needless to say, scores of young ladies had swarmed after him. I'd never stood a chance, but I'd been only thirteen with a head full of romantic delusions, resulting from consuming numerous love stories at the local library. "I was determined to meet you."

He eyed me skeptically. "Does this story end well?"

"Not at all." I laughed, and there was healing in it. This particular instance had been sewn with bitter thread in the fabric of my memories. Tugging it free proved a mending of sorts. I'd thought it would be more painful to relay, but it was surprisingly humorous. "I'm going to draw out this tale and make you feel every mortifying second."

He kicked out his heels, settling more comfortably on the seat. "I probably deserve it."

"You certainly do." I beamed at him and continued, "I was scrubbing the floor by the library and saw you coming down the hall. I remember the scene well. It's like an act straight from a slapstick comedy." I clasped my hands in front of me, being purposefully animated to poke at his prickly exterior. "The servant girl secretly fawns over the moody aristocrat and rallies the courage to speak with him."

"I'm glad you're enjoying this." Despite the firm scowl lining his mouth, Finn's eyes glinted with amusement.

"When I saw you, I climbed to my feet and smoothed out my skirt." I made a fuss of brushing out invisible wrinkles from my suit. "This was my moment. That pivotal time in history when my entire world would change."

Finn groaned.

"I stepped forward but was so engrossed by you that I knocked over the suds bucket. Water went everywhere. I felt humiliated. I threw down all my rags, trying to sop it up. Then the unthinkable happened."

"You slipped and fell into my arms."

"No."

"I slipped and fell into your arms?"

"Definitely not." I laughed. "No one slipped. You just walked by as if I didn't exist." I'd been accustomed to being overlooked and invisible, but that day I'd wanted nothing more than to be seen. If I'd gained approval from a guy like Finn, I'd finally have worth. Now I could see how damaging that reasoning had been. Value was not a trophy to be won from other people's acceptance.

All pleasure leaked from his expression.

"Hold your despair until the end, Finn." I gave a cheeky smile. "Because, at last, you turned and reconsidered. One step toward me. Two." I stood and re-enacted, pausing between my shuffled paces for emphasis. "You gazed deeply into my eyes." So I stared into his, ignoring the subtle shifting of the mood from playful to something else entirely. "Closer and closer." My voice dropped with each inch nearer to his perfect face. "And then you said. . ." I said in a breathy whisper.

His throat spasmed on a hard swallow.

"You missed a spot," I spoke bluntly and straightened. "Then you looked pointedly at a puddle beside my foot." A laugh sputtered from my lips. "Finn Ristaffason, you were, as the Americans say, a colossal jerk."

"Yes, I was." He shook his head as if in a stupor. "You should've dumped the remaining water on my head. Or shoved the dirty rags down my tux."

"I considered it." I claimed the seat next to him instead of returning to my side of the cabin. "I got my revenge that night by spitting in your soup."

His eyes grew wide.

"I'm teasing." I nudged his shoulder. "Though I considered that too."

"I'll remember to keep on your good side." Then all teasing fell from his face. "I'm not surprised by how I acted, but I am sorry for it."

For years, that one memory had slanted my perception of him—and the upper class in general. I'd never imagined telling him of that day, let alone hoped for any apology. But he'd offered it with a humble tone that heightened his attractiveness. "You're forgiven."

"Thank you." He rested his elbows on his knees, regarding me with open curiosity. "So how did you go from scrubbing floors to gracing the silver screen?"

I'd often been asked how I'd gotten my "lucky break" as most would call it. My standard response had always been that I was at the right place at the right time. But in this conversation with Finn, I found myself wanting to be transparent. Well, as transparent as an OSS spy could be. "Mamma's favorite client owned a department store. One of his models canceled at the last minute for a photo shoot for their publicity ad. The man's wife suggested I fill in. The photographer said I was a natural and often recommended me to his colleagues. The extra income helped pay the bills. Mamma didn't have to take on double the work anymore. It felt good to take care of her."

Finn's gaze softened, and I continued. "I got hired as an extra in a short film. It wasn't even a speaking part. But there was an American on set who approached me. The man was surprised I could speak English so fluently. We fell into conversation, and he asked if I'd consider auditioning for his studio. Then he introduced himself as Louis B. Mayer." I'd had no idea I'd been speaking to the head of MGM studios, and I believed that was what had first charmed him.

Finn shook his head. "Talk about chance encounters." He brought that up again, and guilt pinched my heart.

"I told him I hadn't the first idea about acting." I smiled at the memory. "I'll never forget his response. He basically said he never sought talent. All he ever looked for was a face. If a person looked the part, he had people who could help with the rest." I shrugged. "Hollywood sounded intriguing, but my main motivation was to make enough to support Mamma. She had sacrificed so much. I felt that was my chance to give back."

Finn sat silent for a long pause, then met my gaze. "That's admirable."

The following hour passed pleasantly. I peppered Finn with questions to keep him speaking. He told me about working in the shipping business, and how it had been his idea to expand the harbor, create a boatyard, and have a convenient spot for the local fishermen.

I smiled, my eyelids growing heavy.

Shortly after, I felt something shift, causing me to adjust and reclaim my comfortable spot. I wrapped my arm tightly around my pillow, pressing my cheek into its softness. Though it wasn't exactly soft. And my pillow was breathing.

I cracked one eye open, my steady breath catching. I was snuggling with Finn. My head was nuzzled into his shoulder, my arm across his core. Never mind, I was delightfully cozy, and he smelled amazing.

I craned my neck, braving a glance at his face. His eyes were shut, his mouth slightly parted. Phew. Finn was sound asleep. A feathery sigh slipped my lips as I openly studied him. His blond lashes fanned against his upper cheeks. A rogue curl brushed his forehead. I was absolutely certain I hadn't looked this attractive while dozing. In fact, the corners of my mouth were still damp from my sophisticated drooling. I moved to wipe it away only to realize I couldn't budge. His right arm draped over my back, pinning me to his side.

I had no idea how we'd arrived in this position. Had I drifted off first? Had he? I supposed it didn't matter, because the pressing question was, what should I do now? Should I just sit here cuddling? Or dart to my side of the cabin and risk waking him? Thankfully, the train slowed, signifying the approach of the station, helping me decide.

"Finn," I said softly. "We're here."

Though his eyes remained shut, his brow dipped, my fingers tingling to rub the frown away. His head gently rolled toward me, but there was nowhere for me to go. The edge of his lip brushed against my forehead.

His chin blocked any sight of him, but I knew he wakened the second his mouth made contact with my skin because his breathing changed. His fingers gently peeled from my back, and his arm lifted. Free from beneath his hold, I eased away, and my movement made him jolt.

Our eyes met.

Finn appeared slightly flustered. "Forgive me." His voice rumbled low. "I thought you were still asleep."

"It seemed we both needed rest," I offered, hoping to make the situation less awkward. I smoothed my hair back. "I'm sure I look a mess."

His gaze drifted over my face. "Not at all."

Finn wasn't exactly known for his flattery. But I liked him more because of it. I reached over and centered his tie knot. "There." I also smoothed a wrinkle in his collar, which was probably my fault for falling asleep on him. "You look. . .satisfactory." I tossed him the exact compliment he'd given me the other night.

His lips twitched. "I won't let your sweet talk get to my head."

Had he just cracked a joke? I gave a pleased nod of approval at his surprising playfulness but also caught his subtle implication—that his remark the other day hadn't been intended to be taken as disparaging. "You're allowed to smile, you know. It helps a lady know when you're teasing."

He snatched his hat from the corner of the bench and positioned it on his head. "Why are you always concerned with my facial expressions?"

"Correction." I wagged a finger at him. "Your *lack* of facial expressions. Your smile is like an aurora borealis."

"Being a touch dramatic again?" Most men would be flattered to have their face likened to a natural phenomenon, but not Finn. While he humored me, it was as if his analytical brain had no leniency for exaggeration.

"Yes, your smile is like the northern lights." I slid a curl from my face, tucking it behind my ear. "Because I know it exists, but I've yet to see it." I'd caught a ghost of his smile in the library my first night in Malmö, but I wanted to experience it in all its fullness.

His gaze turned curious. "You've never seen the northern lights?"

I shook my head. I'd visited the southern portion of Sweden, but I hadn't traveled much past Stockholm. The capital rarely got traces of the brilliant night display found so easily in the north.

The train eased to a stop, the landing stage coming into view. The area was as crowded as it had been earlier this week when we'd left for Malmö. The scene before me reminded me of the events that had unfolded on that very platform between Finn and the mysterious young man. "Who was he?"

Finn eased closer. "Who was who?"

"Last week. You spoke to a gentleman right there." I pointed to the part of the stage where he had conversed with the stranger.

"Ah, he was a man I hired to search for Johan. Johan has family here in the capital. I had a hunch he might have come here."

"Did Johan explain where he was over the past weeks?"

"I didn't ask." He shrugged. "He already felt guilty for believing the worst about his wife."

"And you," I pointed out.

"I'm used to people believing the worst about me." He peered out the window. "The weather seems mild for our visit to Sigtuna."

I caught his swift change of subject. Did it bother Finn that others thought him heartless? I'd learned to numb myself to rumors and scathing gossip, but I knew that wasn't easy for everyone. Many actresses had left the industry because they couldn't handle the ugly words printed about them. "First, we should see if there's another train to Sigtuna. If not, we hire a car to drive us there." My pulse pounded a wild rhythm as doubts invaded. "I pray we're right." What if the briefcase wasn't at the Aubrund House? Where would we go from there?

We descended off the train and bypassed the luggage claim. We'd been in such a rush to leave his estate that I hadn't had time to pack my things. Not that it mattered, considering I had a residence in Stockholm with everything I'd need. So did Finn.

We approached the ticket agent, and I was pleased to discover a train for Sigtuna would leave within the hour. Our destination was roughly fifty kilometers from Stockholm, which, after the lengthy train ride from Malmö, seemed considerably short.

By late afternoon, we strolled down Stora Gatan, Sigtuna's main street since the Middle Ages. This area was usually a public attraction, considering it was Sweden's oldest town and very first capital dating back to the tenth century. But like most of the country during this time, tourism had taken a hit.

The town centre was colorful with its pastel-painted buildings from the 1800s. Museums and shops lined the main thoroughfare. The ruins of St. Peter, Sweden's first cathedral, noted my country's Christian heritage. In my profession, the number one enemy wasn't overbearing directors or lousy roles. It was age. Because age touched the body with a withering finger, indenting of the forehead, sagging of the jawline, webbing around the eyes. But staring at the beautiful remnants of our first church, I was refreshed. Old age wasn't something to be afraid of but something to attain to. It was the testimony of the goodness of God.

As much as I'd love to browse the ancient streets, we had to reach the Aubrund House.

"There it is." Finn pointed at the wooden-framed structure, which seemed hulking compared to the smaller surrounding buildings.

We reached the entrance gate just as a woman exited the place. She held a set of keys, and with a bag tucked under her arm, I assumed she was the museum curator leaving for the day.

"Quick." I gently prodded Finn. "Stall her before she locks the door."

He wouldn't budge, his scowl firm. "I'm not the actor. You are."

"But you've got what most females find irresistible."

His brows raised in silent inquiry.

"Money. And lots of it." To my credit, I kept a straight face. "Now go tell her all your ships are ocean liners. And for goodness' sake, smile." I pushed on his cheeks until he voluntarily produced a forced grin. I imagined his natural smile to be breathtaking. This one was not. "A real smile. You're supposed to dazzle her, not send her running." Though I supposed that would work too. "Now call out to her."

"Let me go instead. What if the killer's inside?"

I pretended not to hear and ducked beneath the tall hedgerow. I heard Finn's disapproving grunt as I slipped off my heels and hunch-walked to the edge of the bushes.

"Excuse me, fröken?" Finn's voice was forced and woefully impassive. Oh brother, if he was to take on any more of these roles, I needed to give him acting lessons. "Can you spare a moment to help me?"

I glanced back to catch him angling away and dropping his wallet. With the tip of his shoe, he nudged it beneath the manicured brush.

He cleared his throat. Loudly. Which was probably some sort of signal for me to move away. "I believe I dropped my wallet here earlier but can't find it."

"Of course." The lady's voice pitched high. Even with Finn's stiff movements and dull tone, the woman sounded besotted already. "Just let me lock this door and—"

"Please hurry." Finn's voice turned pleading. Somewhat believable. "My only picture of my farmor is inside it, and the damp ground could ruin it forever."

I heard the clanging of keys and the rush of steps. Was she running? I shuddered with guilt for deceiving her, but we needed inside the old house. And I doubted she'd let us poke around an expensive and historically significant piece of furniture without an explanation. Even Finn didn't fully know all the details. He'd assumed we were here based on Franc's final words, which was mostly the truth, just not the whole of it.

I rounded the side, even as the woman approached Finn. With her back toward me, I dashed to the house, keeping a tight hold on my shoes. Thankfully, the door had been left ajar.

Finn's gaze flicked to me before returning to the woman, and they commenced to search for his *lost* wallet. I slipped inside the house and was assaulted by a curious odor of pine oil and mildew. The entryway featured beautifully papered walls and a wooden podium boasting a wire display stand stuffed with pamphlets. I grabbed one, quickly locating a map of the rooms.

According to the rough-hewn drawing, the secretary stood in the library at the back of the house. I skirted the grand staircase and passed the dining room. I found myself in the kitchen. The old cabinetry was a work of art, but I noticed a tall hutch had been shoved in front of the back exit door. It appeared the only way out was the way I'd come in. Good to know.

A questionably skewed archway led into the library.

And there it was.

I dropped my shoes and hurried to the massive secretary in the corner of the room. I pulled open drawers, searching. But there were only tokens of the era. Quill pens. Ink pots. Parchment paper. There was a sign tacked to the wall beside it, pointing to Evelina's secret compartment on the right base, perfectly sized for storing letters. Though not large enough to conceal a briefcase.

But what if the killer had removed the manuscript and discarded the container? With renewed purpose, I pried free the wooden lid and pressed my fingers inside the narrow slot.

Nothing.

With a sigh, I lowered the writing desk, exposing a dozen nooks and crannies great for holding knickknacks, but no documents. I scooted back the cushioned bench and crouched to open the bottom drawers. Empty. I dropped to my hands and knees and crawled beneath the desk, skimming my fingers along the sides for any other secret hideaways.

My heartbeat was having a race with my rapid breaths. I wriggled from under the desk and rounded the left side. Maybe someone had stowed it behind the secretary. There were a fair amount of cobwebs and a lot of dust but no briefcase.

Perhaps the handoff had already happened. The killer had a tremendous head start on us. Unless we completely misinterpreted Franc's words. A likely possibility. Sighing, I grasped the sides of the bench to slide it back but then paused.

What if. . .

I pushed at the bottom edge of the cushion. It lifted!

With both hands, I tugged the well-worn satin cushion from its wooden base.

There was the briefcase.

≡CHAPTER 23≡

The briefcase rested sideways in the nook of the bench in a two-hundred-year-old house. My heart warmed with triumph. I'd fulfilled my promise, aided the war effort, and hadn't even broken a fingernail.

Yet there'd been loss along the way. Poor Franc had made wrong choices that shortened his life, but in the last possible second, when it often mattered most, he'd made the right decision. He'd led me here.

Hopefully, Finn was still distracting the curator. The man wasn't one for prolonged conversation, so I should work fast.

With shaky hands, I tugged the satchel free from its wooden snare. Not wanting to be sloppy, I grabbed the bench cushion and replaced it on the stool, sliding it under the desk.

Plopping on the planked floor, I set the beige briefcase before me. I ran my fingers over the engraved initials *SR*. Stefan Rozental. Dr. Niels Bohr's assistant in atomic research.

Everything in me wanted to savor this moment—for I knew something of this magnitude wouldn't occur again. Soon I'd return to reciting meaningless lines in front of boxy cameras. It had been predicted that my second film—the one I'd won an Academy Award for—would retire as a cinematic legend. But here I sat. Alone. No cheering crowds or flashy fanfare. I'd accomplished a task that would never be recorded in history books, but this moment was mine.

I couldn't linger much longer. The briefcase's presence revealed the blatant fact that the handoff hadn't occurred yet. The killer may be nearby, or the person this case was intended for may appear any second.

With bated breath, I lifted the brass-toned latches and peered inside.

It was empty.

What? Dread pumped my veins.

No. No, no, no. This couldn't be! I hoisted the lid all the way and scoured the felt-lined cavity. But there was absolutely nothing inside. Not even a paper clip.

I'd been wrong.

The pickup *had* already occurred, and whoever had found this brief-case had withdrawn its contents. Which would make sense. For it was far easier to hide a document under one's overcoat than an entire briefcase.

But what now?

I closed the briefcase, taking it with me, slipped on my shoes, and retraced my route to the foyer. With a frustrated groan, I stuffed the pamphlet into the display stand on the podium, my gaze snagging on a ledger beside it. I grabbed the leather-bound register and flipped it open. It was a guest record, filled with pages and pages of names of the museum's visitors. Leafing through, I located today's date. Seven entries had been logged. I doubted the killer would jot his actual name, but I read through the lines carefully, committing them to memory.

Time to leave.

I reached for the door. The knob wouldn't turn. My stomach seized. I was locked inside.

What else could go wrong today? I peeked out one of the oval-shaped windows framing the entrance, my gaze darting to the hedgerow. Finn wasn't there. Neither was the museum lady. I moved to the front parlor, which afforded a better view of the street. It was vacant.

He wouldn't desert me for the pretty curator, so where was he? Panic gripped me. Could he have encountered the killer? Was he in danger? Since the door was locked, I could easily climb out this window. I glanced down and groaned. It was sealed shut. I checked the others on this floor. All the same. Who would nail down an antique sill? Had they no regard for historic preservation? My bodily preservation? Because now I was forced to the second story. I supposed I could break a window and anonymously send a large donation to cover the damages. But shattering the glass pane could draw attention.

I dashed up the staircase leading to all the bedrooms. I wasn't enthused at the idea of scaling the walls of an old house, but I didn't want to spend the evening in this stuffy relic.

The front bedrooms indeed had windows. This time, they opened, but there wasn't any way to climb down safely. Where was a tall oak when I needed it? I blew a noisy breath and entered the master bedroom, crossing the space to the balcony door.

I tested the knob, and to my surprise, it opened. But I wasn't in the clear yet. I leaned over the stone railing. No surrounding trees, but to the left of the balcony was an ivy-wrapped lattice. I eyed the crisscross pattern suspiciously, sincerely hoping it wasn't two-hundred-year-old wood. Since this master was at the back of the house, I at least had privacy.

Better nix the shoes again. I needed to dress more carefully next time. Granted, when I chose my outfit, I hadn't expected I'd be scaling walls of historic homes. I set down the briefcase and peeled off my heels, tossing them over the ledge.

Someone grunted in pain.

I gripped the ledge and peered over, knowing I'd find Finn below. Having been around the man for an entire week, his grunts and growls were as identifiable as his face.

He rubbed at a red mark on his forehead, my navy shoe in his other hand. "A warning would've been nice."

I breathed out relief. "You're. . .okay." He hadn't been in trouble. Hadn't come across a vile killer. The only mishap he'd suffered was a run-in with my heel.

"Thank you for your sympathy," he said dryly.

"I'm sorry about my shoe. I didn't know you'd be there."

His mouth pinched. "Where did you expect me to be?"

I could usually handle his surliness, but my own temper hinged on the edgy side. I flicked an annoyed glance at the briefcase. "I wasn't sure since I didn't see you out the window when I was trying to leave." Which reminded me of another point of frustration. "Why did you let the woman lock me inside?"

A frown darkened his brow. "I tried to stall her."

His definition of *try* and mine seemed vastly different. "You manage a world-renowned business, Finn. I'm sure you could outmaneuver one curator." I huffed. "I could've been locked in this place all night."

He folded his arms. "I recall telling you to let me go into the house, but you ignored me. If you would've listened, I'd be there." He pointed to the balcony. "And you'd be here."

Despite myself, I laughed. It was a romance scene gone awry. The hero was so often portrayed reciting sonnets or serenading the simpering maiden on the stone balcony, but here we were arguing like an old married couple. I blinked at my turn of thoughts. I didn't want to imagine myself married to Finn, or anyone else for that matter. "Well, now I have to climb down this lattice." But I couldn't attempt just yet. I ducked back into the open doorway and hiked my skirt.

"Amelie?"

"Give me a second." Peeling off my stockings took twice as long with a gun holster fastened to my leg. I managed to pull the hose from my limbs and returned to the balcony. I gently wadded them up into a ball, garters and all. "Here. Catch these."

"Your. . .stockings?"

And I did it. I accomplished the impossible. For I had made the impenetrable Finn Ristaffason blush. "Of course. These are silk," I said, a bit cheekily. "And any lady knows these are hard to come by nowadays." I leaned over the ledge. "Ready?"

He mumbled something but stepped forward, positioning directly below me, outstretching his arms. "Ready."

I set them free, and he caught them with ease. "One more thing." I lifted the briefcase, and Finn's eyes widened. "I found this. Franc had this with him last night. I think someone wanted whatever was inside it."

"Do you think that's why they killed him?" He pressed his flattened hand against his forehead, shielding the late sun from his eyes. "Because they wanted the briefcase?"

I nodded. "Why else would it be here?" I wasn't technically lying, but it bothered me not to be entirely truthful with him.

"Did you open it?"

"I did. It was empty." My heart panged. If only I had reached this place sooner. The research couldn't have traveled far. But in which direction? I could only guess it had been taken to Stockholm. Maybe, the German Legation? Their building stood only a few doors down from the American one. The OSS had its own *secret* floor. As in the agents had been staffed as diplomatic officers, passport processors, commercial attachés, etc. By moonlighting under these official titles, they could continue their clandestine work without being detected as spies. If the Americans operated as such, I guaranteed the Germans did as well.

I didn't want to accept failure yet, but what other option did I have?

"It will be okay, Amelie." He seemed to read my doubts. "Toss down the case, and let's get you home."

How did he know the exact words to encourage me? For there was nothing I wanted more than to hug Mamma. With renewed purpose, I dropped the briefcase into Finn's waiting arms and moved to the side of the balcony where the lattice was. "Turn around, Finn."

"No." If anything, he moved closer. "I can't let you fall."

"I won't."

"You can't be certain." He studied the lattice with that signature frown. "This is risky, Amelie. I don't like the idea of you possibly getting hurt."

I made a face. I'd heard those words several times over the years. "You sound like my directors."

"And you sound like you're looking forward to risking your neck."

He was right. My heart pumped fast, but not from fear. If I were filming, this would be the moment the director yelled *Cut!* and shuffled me aside, giving way for my stunt double. I gazed down at him with a growing grin. "Let today be the day..." I lifted my skirt only high enough to preserve modesty and swung my left leg over the side of the ledge, keeping my gun hidden. Then I hoisted my right one and shifted until I sat on the edge of the balcony railing, my bare legs and feet dangling over. "...that Amelie Blake performs her own stunts."

Finn grunted. "I just want *Amelie Blake* to remain in one piece."

"Why, sir, I do believe you care." I pressed a hand dramatically to my chest, earning another scowl from Finn.

"Be careful." His tone was on the gruff side. "Please."

"I will." I grabbed the bright yellow lattice, ready to commit to this task. But there was no way I'd climb down with Finn close enough to see up my skirt. "Back up until you can't see anything."

"Define *anything*."

"Finn!"

"I'm not moving out of helping distance."

"But—"

He released a frustrated sigh. "I promise I'll avert my eyes, and keep my gaze on your..."

I raised my brows.

"...higher portions."

"You'd better," I shot back. "Or you'll get a swift kick to your lower portions."

He didn't appreciate my humor. "I can't have another person harmed while I'm near."

I softened at his words, however untrue they were. Yes, Finn had been nearby when the car had struck Franc, but it wasn't remotely his fault even though he seemed to bear the guilt. "Okay." I nodded. "I'll ask for help if I need it."

I set my foot in one of the diamond spaces and pushed down, making sure the lattice could hold weight before I succumbed to its mercy. It seemed sturdy. Reassured, I grabbed the lattice with my other hand and eased my bulk over.

So far so good.

Ivy and other foliage weaved in and around the woodwork, making me even more cautious as I lowered one step. Then another, repeating until I fell into a rhythm, adjusting my handholds and footholds in tandem.

This was easier than I'd thought. The lattice was secure and—

Something crawled over my hand.

"A spider!" I yelped and almost fell backward.

Finn shouted something, but I couldn't make it out. There was an eight-legged menace inches from my face. I hurried down as fast as I could move. Strong hands gripped my waist, supporting me for the last stretch of steps. The soles of my feet touched the cool earth, and I almost collapsed against Finn.

I proved brave in most things, but spiders brought out the coward in me.

The bodice of my dress had somewhat twisted during my escapade, so I righted the seams and pulled a twig from the narrow spot between my buttons. "I knew I could do it." I brushed another stem from my sleeve.

Finn's expression warmed as his gaze tracked my face, inspecting every contour and plane as if searching for any broken parts. His fingers cupped my jaw, lifting my chin. His eyes narrowed as they trailed the column of my throat. "You've got a small scrape on your neck."

I tried to swallow. "It'll heal."

He nodded, his hand sliding to my shoulder. With gentle movements, he tugged something from beneath my collar. He lifted a leaf, a rare look of tenderness in his eyes. "You missed a spot."

My breath locked in my chest. He had repeated the words he'd said years ago when we'd first met, but this time he'd aided instead of mocked. I lifted on my tiptoes and kissed his cheek. "Thank you, Finn."

Our eyes held for several heart-pounding seconds until Finn broke the connection by reaching down to hand me my shoes. "We better get going. The train leaves in twenty minutes."

I nodded.

He dug in his pocket and handed me my stockings. There was something weirdly intimate about the exchange, but I was too tired to examine my jumbled thoughts. While I escaped behind the bushes to put on my hose, I caught sight of the briefcase lying on the grass. A shudder coursed through me as I thought of all the different people that had held its ivory handle. The person who'd carried the case before me had most likely been the killer.

≡ CHAPTER 24 ≡

Mamma handed me a steaming mug of coffee with a soft smile and lowered beside me on the sofa. I held the cup, savoring its warmth. The sun had gone down as Finn and I boarded the train in Sigtuna, and I'd been fighting a chill ever since. But I couldn't only blame it on the crisp fall evening. There was something about this mission that made me uneasy. It could be the lingering shock of Franc's death. Or the devastation of discovering an empty briefcase. Or maybe it was my puzzling emotions concerning Finn.

I glanced at the front door where he'd said goodbye a few moments ago. He'd urged me to rest and promised to return early tomorrow morning so we could discuss our next move. But the part that troubled me? I'd felt an acute pang at his leaving. It was silly. Unreasonable. And yet, my heart had been slowly favoring his nearness.

I glanced up and found Mamma patiently watching me. "Sorry." I offered an apologetic smile. "I've been getting distracted easily."

"Mm-hmm." She took a sip of coffee. "I would be too if I was your age and in the company of Sweden's most eligible bachelor." Her tone wasn't exactly approving. Her bias against handsome, rich men continued, but now I understood the reason more than before. My heart twisted. I'd already decided not to mention seeing Erik Bruun. There wasn't any point in it. It wasn't as if he'd improved over the decades. If anything, it was the opposite. And it would only fuel Mamma's belief that men in these positions couldn't be trusted. And for some reason, I wanted her to offer Finn an honest chance. Though I doubted she would. She lowered her mug onto the saucer. "So, tell me about your trip to Malmö."

"It was eventful." From dancing on the shores with Finn to crouching beside a dead body, and everything in between. "And seeing the Öresund made me miss Morfar."

Her eyes clouded. "I miss him too."

I reached and clasped her hand. Mamma had always sloughed over conversations about her family, almost as if she'd severed the memories to cut their power to hurt her. But her remark held tangible regret, making me wonder if my trip had given life to those dead feelings. "He'd be proud of us, Mamma. I know he would."

She turned away, but I heard a sniffle. After several long seconds, she faced me again and pressed her hand against my cheek. "That time all those years ago was so painful and scary. I questioned if I'd ever survive the weight of it. But I look at you and remember God breathes light into our darkest moments. That's what you are to me. My brightest light. My greatest joy."

"Oh, Mamma." I set my coffee down and hugged her tightly. "God's got more shining moments for you ahead."

She nodded, which was a step in the right direction. Mamma had erred in holding the notion that her shame disqualified her from any happiness. But mistakes shouldn't define our futures. We should never allow them that power. My heart swelled at the possibility that Mamma was finally kicking down the walls of lies.

"So." Mamma dabbed her eyes. "Did Herr Ristaffason return to Stockholm with you? I thought I heard a male voice outside the door." She glanced at the foyer.

"Yes." I hesitated, unsure of how much I could reveal. "We're on an adventure of sorts." I caught her eyebrows flicker but kept a casual tone. "I don't know where to begin."

"How about with that briefcase?" She pointed to that dratted leather case by the door. "I don't remember you leaving with it."

"It's a long story that doesn't have a happy ending. Not yet, at least." Then I relayed a watered-down version of the past week, excluding my ties to the OSS and the unfortunate interactions with my father. She audibly gasped when I told her about Franc's murder. "And last night Finn revealed Franc was his nephew."

Her eyes widened. "Rolf had a son?"

"Yes." One he'd refused to claim. Something I didn't need to voice. It was painfully obvious, considering everyone knew of Rolf's reputation.

Mamma shifted on the sofa, twisting to face me. "And how exactly are *you* involved?"

I drew in a breath, knowing my next few words wouldn't please her. "I offered to help Finn locate the man responsible."

She stiffened. "The man responsible? That's a very mild way of saying you're hunting a killer." I opened my mouth, but she raised a hand, stilling my protest. "Herr Ristaffason doesn't object to putting my only child in danger?"

"He objected very strongly." I pleaded his case. Mamma already thought ill of Finn. He didn't deserve any more of her ire. "But as you know, I'm stubborn. I forced him to allow me to help."

"Why, Amelie?" She sighed. "Why the risk for a stranger?"

So many reasons. It was a job I'd willfully accepted, knowing the consequences. But just like with Finn, I couldn't divulge everything. Though if I scratched beneath my noble purpose, I'd find traces of guilt. "Because I feel responsible in a way." If Finn had felt any blame, I did even more so. "I met Franc at a club. I kept asking him questions about that briefcase." I rubbed my brow. "We know his murder had something to do with it." More like, what had been inside of it. "What if the killer overheard our conversation and wanted to shut him up before he told anyone what he knew?" My insistent pressing could've been the reason for his death. Because obviously the killer had been at the nightclub, especially if he'd been the other party in the handoff. "I can't fully explain it, Mamma, but I must do this."

"You're stubborn when you've made up your mind." She'd said those exact words after I'd told her Louis Mayer wanted to bring me to the States. It had been one of the hardest decisions, especially since Mamma had refused to join me. But how else could I have provided for her?

"I come by it naturally."

"That you do." She begrudgingly kissed my cheek. "So where do you go from here?"

Good question. "To be honest, I feel like I'm running in circles." I relayed how Franc's dying words had led us to visit Sigtuna. "The briefcase is empty." And I'd only brought it here because I was unsure if the OSS would still want it. Maybe they could dust for prints. I groaned. My fingers had been all over that case. I had to be the world's worst spy.

She seemed to absorb my words slowly. "I see."

I took another long sip of coffee. "I can't help but think. . .what if we stayed in Malmö and talked to people at the club? I'm sure someone heard something, knows something."

"No." She shook her head. "No one will speak up now. Not when there's a killer on the loose. I doubt anyone would surrender any names in fear of being the next target."

Names! That was it! "I'd completely forgotten." I rushed to the kitchen and grabbed a notepad and pen from a drawer. "Can you write the names down as I go?"

"Certainly." She took the pad and flipped open to a fresh page.

I slid my eyes closed and *read* the Aubrund House register from my memory. "The Abbick family. Fru Hilga Frencs. Herr Pontz. Herr Lutz." Pontz and Lutz. That sounded fictitious. A murderer wouldn't voluntarily list his name, but perhaps I could locate the Abbick family or Fru Frencs and ask if they'd toured the house with other guests. Or noticed anything suspicious. It was worth a shot. "And Bengt Ferguson." I opened my eyes just as Mamma was finishing the last name. "That was today's Aubrund House visitor list."

"You still have that amazing memory," she said with a hint of pride, as if it was something I attained.

"But it doesn't help if I don't recognize any names."

She skimmed the list. "The fifth one sounds familiar. Bengt Ferguson." Her face pinched in thoughtfulness. "He's an artist of some sort." She shook her head. "No, that's not the one I'm thinking of, never mind."

"What's odd about that entry is that his name was written by a woman."

I awakened to the indistinct chatter of female voices. Ah, Vilde was here to *clean*. Years ago, I'd hired Mamma a housekeeper to tidy the penthouse three times a week. Mamma had spent decades scrubbing other people's homes, so it was my hope she'd allow someone else to do that service for her. I was absolutely certain Vilde was the highest-paid housekeeper in the country, but I also knew Mamma had never given her the opportunity to prove her capabilities.

Mamma still scoured this place with her own two hands, and Vilde faithfully arrived at the penthouse to perform her duties on an already clean penthouse. Since the two of them had become dear friends, I hadn't minded supporting Vilde in the least. She'd been here when I was several thousand kilometers away. I quickly readied for the day and joined Mamma and her friend in the kitchen for morning fika.

Upon my entrance into the room, Vilde jumped from her seat and wrapped me in an embrace. "I was hoping to see you." She squeezed tight with surprising strength. "Your mamma allowed me to empty all the wastebaskets and launder the drapes."

I patted her shoulder. "It's okay, Vilde. You don't have to report your efforts to me. I know how hard-nosed Mamma can be. Thank you for trying."

"I have my way of doing things," Mamma said simply. "But Vilde is the best cook in all of Scandinavia."

I snatched a pastry from the tray on the table and bit into it with a drawn-out sigh. "You're right, Mamma." The flaky crust, paired with the creamy almond frosting, melted in my mouth. Even as I took another bite, Vilde pressed a second pastry into my hand.

"You're too thin." She tsked. "Don't they feed you in America?"

I laughed and leaned against the counter, much too restless to sit. "Not like this."

Someone knocked at the door, and Vilde moved swiftly to answer it. I heard Finn's voice before I saw him. He greeted our housekeeper, who led him into the kitchen. Mamma casually sipped her coffee, observing him over the brim of her mug.

"Good morning, ladies." He took off his hat, revealing his wavy golden locks, and I could've sworn Vilde sighed. "Fru Blakstrom, I'm glad to see your health has returned."

"My daughter has been telling me of your escapades." Mamma nibbled on a pastry but looked down her nose in disapproval.

"Don't ruin your breakfast with all that scowling, Mamma." I leaned down and whispered in her ear. "Remember Finn just lost his nephew. Can't you summon any kindness?"

She straightened in her seat and lowered her food. "I offer my condolences, Herr Ristaffason."

Finn accepted her sentiments with a nod.

I set my hand upon the back of Mamma's chair. "Besides, our little adventure is stalled until we find something to go on."

Vilde flittered about the room, collecting dishes and providing Finn with a mug of coffee.

Mamma dabbed her mouth with a napkin. "I've been thinking all morning about where I heard the name Bengt Ferguson. It seems like something I should know."

"Bengt Ferguson?" Finn's brows rose as he took the seat opposite Mamma.

"He was one of the names on the list," I supplied.

"What list?"

Oh, I'd forgotten to mention that important detail. I offered an apologetic smile. "The visitor list from the Aubrund House. I didn't steal it. Just memorized the names."

His mouth drew upward. "Of course you did."

My blood warmed at his approval. "Anyway, there was logged a family and a married woman. A pair of gentlemen. And what Mamma had already said, Bengt Ferguson."

"The photographer, Bengt Ferguson?" Vilde paused in wiping down the counter. "My brother follows his work. I went with him to one of Herr Ferguson's exhibits. I think he has a studio outside of Sigtuna."

Something in me twisted. This could all be a coincidence—a professional photographer visiting the same day a briefcase with highly sensitive material had dropped. Though unlikely.

Why would a photographer be of any use in this scheme, unless to transfer the research onto film? Film negatives were smaller to conceal than a bulky manuscript. But worse yet, far more disastrous. With the physical pages of the research, there'd been only one copy. With film? Numerous copies could be developed. Hundreds, even. It had been difficult chasing a single document, but tracking down multitudes of prints would be impossible.

"So, back to Sigtuna today?" Finn's words yanked me from my despairing thoughts.

I pasted on a smile, hoping to camouflage the rising panic. I was the only one in the room aware of the catastrophic possibilities. Maybe we could locate this man and intercept the film *and* manuscript before it changed ownership. Or better yet, discover my fears were false and the photographer had nothing to do with this sinister scheme. If that was the case, we could question him about the Aubrund House and inquire if anyone else had been touring the museum during his visit.

I nodded. "Yes, back to Sigtuna."

Even though Finn had driven us in his Volvo, rather than wasting time waiting for the train, we'd decided Sigtuna's central station would be the best place to glean information. But so far, we hadn't succeeded in finding this mysterious photographer. The several different people we'd asked had known who Bengt Ferguson was but hadn't been able to tell us where he could be found.

That was, until we spoke to the ticket agent. He was a personal friend of Herr Ferguson's, and he'd generously provided directions to his studio.

"Thank you." I shot the man behind the counter a gracious smile, and we returned to Finn's car.

Finn was quiet for the first few minutes of the drive, a severe expression darkening his features.

I couldn't take his surly silence any longer. "Why are you scowling differently?"

He flicked a glance at me. "I always scowl."

"Yes, but your dimple's not showing."

His brows disappeared under his hat. "What's that supposed to mean?"

I sighed. "You have several frowns for each mood. When you're mildly annoyed, you scowl and sniff at the same time. Like this." I demonstrated. "When you're bored and would rather be somewhere else, you scowl and dart glances about the room. My favorite is when you're exasperated, because you press your lips together, and a dimple pokes your cheek."

He slowed for a stop sign and looked at me. "I didn't realize my expressions were so definable."

"It's my job to study your body." Oh, that came out wrong. "I mean, body language. It's important to study body language in my profession."

His lips twitched, and I wanted to melt into the seat. "I see."

"But this last scowl, I've never seen before. Because this time, your eyes crinkled at the edges and your nostrils flared."

He expelled a sigh at my nonsense. "You realize Bengt Ferguson could be a killer. Or at least working with one. Do you expect to just show up? Or do you have a plan?"

Ah, so his frown had been one of concern. "He's a photographer. I'm an actress," I said breezily. "I'll go under the guise of wanting my photo taken by a local professional, and his name was recommended to me."

He rolled his eyes. "So he's going to believe you flew all the way to Sweden from America during a war just to get your picture snapped?"

"No." It was my turn to scowl. "But since I'm in the country, why shouldn't I get my picture taken? Remember, I'm a dim-witted, spoiled starlet."

He shook his head. "That wasn't your best role."

I gasped dramatically. "What? I play the brainless blond perfectly." Though I was aware I'd slipped out of character several times since arriving in Sweden. It was humbling to realize I wasn't the masterful actress I'd believed myself to be. "I think the next turn will take us to Ferguson's place." I tried to divert the conversation, but Finn wasn't having it.

"I spied it first when we danced at the Grand Hôtel, but I've seen it repeatedly during your stay at the estate."

"Seen what?"

"Intelligence in your eyes."

Why those words warmed me, I couldn't say. Maybe because I'd always been complimented for shallow things—like the color of my eyes, how I did my hair, how I filled out a gown—but never for my wit. "Which is usually undetected by the casual observer, which you apparently are not."

He turned the wheel, pulling the car onto the road leading to the studio. "I pay attention to what intrigues me."

His words shot a bolt of pleasure through me. I intrigued him? Though I couldn't pick apart his staggering remark because Herr Ferguson's studio came into view.

And it was on fire.

≡CHAPTER 25≡

I jumped out of the slowing car before Finn braked to a full stop.

"Amelie!" His alarmed voice scraped my ears as I sprinted toward the studio. Plumes of smoke twisted into the sky, the hissing flames striking against the front of the building like serpents' tongues.

But the back of the studio appeared untouched. At least from where I stood. I rounded to the rear of the building, my heels sinking into the soft ground with each determined step. What if someone was inside?

Even at a safe distance, waves of heat prickled my skin. The windows at the front of the studio had already been blown out, but not the ones back here. I carefully approached, peeking inside.

I was right. The fire hadn't yet spread to this part, which appeared to be an office. Smoke seeped into the room, meaning the flames would soon lick through the walls.

I spotted a large desk. Could there be a clue somewhere amongst the clutter? In one of the drawers? The urge to find out clawed at me, but I couldn't just rush into a burning building. It could explode. The roof could collapse. Everything screamed foolish risk.

But then. . .I inched closer to the glass panes. A man lay facedown on the floor, unconscious. Or perhaps dead. My conscience niggled. I couldn't just leave him there. I couldn't help Franc, but maybe I could save this man.

I tested the back door. Locked. I frantically scanned the area, my sights landing on a metal garbage bin nearby.

Finn's shouts echoed loudly. He was undoubtedly looking for me, but I couldn't waste any more precious seconds. I picked up the trash can and rammed it through the window.

Glass shattered. I swiped the lid over the jagged sill, attempting to clear the excess shards. Filling my lungs with air, I climbed into the room, my skirt catching on a spiky spot on the ledge. But I was inside.

"Amelie!" Finn appeared in the broken window. "You're mad! Get back out here."

"I can't leave him." I rushed toward the man, pressing my fingers to his pulse. There was a dull thud. "He's alive." Only the left side of his face was visible, but it swelled with fresh bruising. I gently skimmed a hand over his head, searching for any serious wound.

The haze burned into my eyes, coating my throat. I coughed and buried my nose under the collar of my dress, a poor barrier. I didn't have time to assess injuries. We both needed to get out of here. I grabbed his legs, planning to drag him to the window, but he didn't budge.

"Let me." Finn appeared at my side. "Now go."

I scanned the room for something to cover the glass-strewn windowsill and spotted a discarded jacket tossed on a chair by the desk. I moved to grab it, my gaze hitching on the untidy desktop. Old newspapers, blank envelopes, and sketch paper cluttered the surface. Nothing jumped out as important. I snatched the jacket, draped it over the broken window, and scampered out. My lungs heaved, begging for clean air.

Finn was only seconds behind, gripping the man beneath his arms, staggering with the effort. Finn's hands were. . .bloody.

I gasped. The stranger's coat and shirt were stained red, something I hadn't caught since he'd been lying on his stomach.

Finn turned sideways, maneuvering the man through the window, but he lost his footing, and the injured fellow tumbled out, landing in a heap on the ground. Finn bounded out, taking a quick glance at me as if ensuring I was okay.

He reclaimed his hold on the man and hoisted him a safe distance from the blazing building. I followed, keeping an eye on the fire. Surely someone would see the billowing smoke and come. Then again, maybe not. This place was seven kilometers from the main road.

Finn set his human bundle gently on the damp grass, then knelt beside the bleeding form. I moved next to him.

With shaky hands, I peeled back the left side of the man's suitcoat. My heart lurched at the gash found beneath.

"Stabbed," Finn assumed. He delicately raised the man's lapel opposite his injury, pulling the jacket away, revealing an empty gun holster. Finn and I exchanged a look. Why had this man been armed? And what happened to his weapon? Thankfully, there were no other visible wounds.

Finn lifted the man's shirt and looked closer at the laceration. "Not too deep. He'll need stitched up, but I don't think it's life-threatening."

I glanced at the blazing studio. The entire building was engulfed in flames. This stranger's injuries might not have killed him, but the fire surely would have.

Relief swept through me, but I didn't want to take any chances. "We should try to stop the bleeding." I climbed to my feet, and while Finn was occupied searching the man's pockets, I shimmied off my slip. I folded it into a rumply square and pressed it on the cut. Finn arched a brow, but it was the only absorbent thing I had.

"He has no identification." Finn exhaled, his narrowed gaze on our patient. "Do you recognize him?"

I glanced down at his bruised face with its pronounced brow ridge and lean cheeks shadowed with stubble. "No. I've never seen him before." I switched hands, placing more pressure on the wound.

A groan parted the mystery man's lips. Finn took over holding the compress and gestured for me to move away. I did as he bade.

"Who are you?" Finn's voice was chillingly stern. Understandable, considering he could be addressing a murderer.

Another moan, then his dark lashes fluttered. Hazy green eyes peered at me. "Gyllene," he muttered.

My code name.

Commander Skilbeck had said I could trust the select few who'd been given my code name, but I wasn't ready to hand over my loyalty yet. Finn gave me a questioning look, to which I only shrugged. Let him believe the man was delirious.

I leaned forward. "Sir, you've been stabbed and need help. We're going to take you to a medical facility." The closest was Stockholm.

"No." He sputtered a cough. "No hospitals. Too many questions."

"What's your name?" Finn demanded. "Are you Bengt Ferguson?"

He flinched as if unaware of Finn's hulking presence beside him. "Ferguson's gone. He went with him."

"Went with who?" I shot back, but we'd have to wait for the answer because the gentleman seemed to pass out again.

Finn eyed him for a second, then shot to his feet. "He might be out for a bit. I'll bring the car around."

I nodded, my gaze pinned to the blazing studio. Beams crashed. The roof collapsed. There was no saving it. Who'd done this? And when? At our arrival, the flames hadn't yet spread throughout the building, making me think it hadn't been going for long. I didn't recall passing another car on our way here. Perhaps there was another back road.

What if the fire wasn't intentional? It could possibly be the result of an accident. Because why would Bengt Ferguson torch his own studio?

"No hospital," he mumbled again, making me jolt.

I'd thought the man had slipped into unconsciousness, but his pain-pinched gaze was on me. Why was he refusing to go to the public clinics? Was he a criminal? If that was the case, how did he know my code name? Unless it had gotten leaked. If he wouldn't go to the clinic, I had an idea of where we could take him, but I needed answers first. "Where'd you learn my code name?"

His head lolled to the side, his hooded eyes drifting closed. "Wolf. . .told me."

Axel. "Who are you?"

"Agent Modve." He groaned. "Security Service."

This man was from the secret police.

———— ≈ ————

"What's happened?" Mamma cried as Finn and I helped Agent Modve through the penthouse door. The policeman's arms draped our shoulders, but I was certain Finn supported him more than I.

"He's wounded," I said between breaths. "Can you take a look at him?"

My request snapped Mamma from her stupor. "Let me put an old blanket on the sofa, and you can set him there." She'd been studying medicine for as long as I could remember and volunteering at the local centers for the past decade. She was more than capable of tending to Agent Modve.

Finn and I did as we were told and stepped out of the way, letting Mamma tend him. Over the next hour, she examined the wound, cleaned it—much to the officer's displeasure—and stitched the gash with strong thread. Agent Modve had a few lapses of awareness in which he muttered a handful of cusses.

When Mamma's patient fell into a deep rest, she turned her clinical gaze on us. "Herr Ristaffason, you're covered in blood. Is it yours or his?" She gestured to the snoring agent.

"His," he answered solemnly.

"I see." She turned to me. "And you, Amelie, you've a cut on your leg."

I did? I glanced at my limbs and sure enough, there was a scrape below my right knee. I scowled at my torn stockings. "It's nothing. I can't even feel it." I weakly smiled at her narrowed glare. "I can explain." Partly. "This man was unconscious in Herr Ferguson's studio."

"Which was on fire," Finn not-so-helpfully added.

"Herr Ristaffason." Mamma pointed a finger at him. He, to his credit, didn't cower at her intimidating glower. "You're supposed to protect my daughter, yet you let her go inside—"

"Finn's not to blame," I spoke up. "I ran inside the building. He couldn't stop me."

Her scolding gaze bounced between us, then, with an exasperated sigh, her arms wilted to her side. "No one's ever been able to stop you from doing what you choose."

Finn nodded his agreement. "It's maddening."

My elbow dug into his side, even as Agent Modve made a noise and squirmed, distracting Mamma.

While she fussed over her patient, I turned toward Finn. "What you call maddening," I said tartly, "I call swift thinking. We saved his life."

"And this soot on your face is a reminder of how careless you are with your own life." He swiped his thumb over the curve of my jaw.

I tugged his hand away, ignoring the spike of pleasure from his touch. "You don't have to clean me like a mother cat to her kitten."

"And you don't have to save the world."

But I did. Failure gripped my heart with icy claws. The bad guys had gotten away again. "Isn't that why we're here? To find Franc's killer?"

He peered down at me. "I've known you only a week, and so far, you've dodged a murderous car, scaled an old house, and dashed into a burning building. What's next? Shall I come with you to America so we can walk across the Grand Canyon on a tightrope?"

I snorted at his absurdity but then sobered, my brows pulling low. "No one's ever come with me to America." I know he'd said it in jest, but the realization hit harder than I was prepared for. When I would board the plane to the States, I'd return by myself to my large but empty home.

Finn softened. "It must be hard being apart from your only family."

I nodded. Providing for Mamma had been the only reason I'd gone. Then the war had happened. I'd hated our separation and had missed Sweden. Maybe after I finished the two movies I'd already promised to film, I could retire Amelie Blake and become a Blakstrom again. I peered up at Finn, who watched me closely. "I think leaving this time will be more difficult."

He swallowed and opened his mouth to speak, but a knock sounded at the door.

"That must be Herr Eizenburg." Mamma said, her sharp gaze on me. Had she been listening to Finn and me? "He phoned earlier saying he'd be stopping by at noon."

Questions filled Finn's eyes, and I could only imagine the thoughts running through his head. But I only adopted a warm smile and grabbed an extra washcloth from Mamma's supplies, holding it out to him. "Why don't you get cleaned up." I gestured toward the bathroom. "The mother cat is just as dirty as her kitten."

"You're a boon for my masculine pride." His words were muttered dryly, but his hand lingered on mine as he accepted the cloth.

I teasingly patted his cheek and moved to answer the door. My fellow agent stood before me, his brows rising. "Ah, you're actually here." He gave a wry smile. "You've got a habit of not staying in one place."

I motioned him inside. "I'm sorry about not checking with you. I'm not used to giving accounts of my whereabouts."

"Spoken like a truly independent woman." He stepped into the entryway and removed his hat.

Mamma would soon be in a fit of annoyance. Two utterly handsome men in her domain? For shame!

He sniffed. "Why do you reek of smoke?"

"I found the briefcase." I bent and grabbed it, presenting it to Axel with a sad smile.

His eyes widened as he took ownership. "At the Aubrund House?" What? How did he know? "Yes. It was in the secretary bench."

He examined it, then turned serious eyes on me. "Amelie, we need to take this to the legation. You should've done that by now."

I didn't appreciate his condescending tone. "It's empty. See for yourself."

He opened the case and cussed under his breath.

"I didn't know if the OSS wanted it. If they could run fingerprints or other kinds of tests." I bit my lip. "Though I warn you, I hadn't thought to wear gloves. My prints are all over it." I hated the sinking feeling of failure.

He tucked it under his arm. "I'll have the boys take a look. Who knows, there might be a secret compartment. Or something in the lining."

It was a valiant thought, but even I knew an entire manuscript wasn't hidden in the folds of felt. Though maybe they could find something else to help the mission. "How did you know it was at the Aubrund House?"

"Someone left an anonymous tip at the legation last night. Said the briefcase would be at the museum. I went there this morning looking for it."

Talk about bad timing. If only the legation had received that tip earlier, we would have the document in our possession rather than chasing it all over Sweden. "There's something else. Whoever has the research also has an expert photographer in their clutches."

His jaw tightened. "If they make film copies, it'll be impossible to recover them all."

I nodded.

"Who's the photographer?"

"Bengt Ferguson." I watched him tense. He seemed to be familiar with the name. "His studio was on fire this morning. We dragged Agent Modve from the building. He's been stabbed."

He gripped my shoulder. "Where's Modve now? I assigned him to patrol Ferguson's movements."

"In the living room." I waved a hand that direction. "He forbade us to take him to a clinic. So Mamma nursed his wounds. He's currently sound asleep."

"Then let's go wake him. Perhaps he knows something useful." He moved to walk past, but I pressed a hand to his elbow, stilling him.

"Finn's here too."

He pinched the bridge of his nose with a drawn-out exhale. "I'm not surprised. The man's desperate to keep you in his sight."

I shook my head. "No, it's not like that."

Axel gave a disbelieving snort.

"He only wants to find his nephew's killers."

Axel barred his arms, his jaw tight. "He should leave that to the police. To us."

"Finn's decision to chase the killer has been a convenient cover for me." Plus, I could admit that I was grateful to have him around. I retracted my hand from Axel's sleeve, but his fingers swept up mine.

"You did well, thinking on your feet." His voice was soft, his thumb stroking my knuckles. "Now we need to get rid of Ristaffason."

"Get rid of me?" Finn stepped into the foyer. "I'm not sure I like what that implies."

My gut sank. He'd no doubt been eavesdropping. His gaze dropped to my hand, still captive in Axel's, and then to the man himself. "I think there's a lot more going on here. And you two are going to tell me."

⫷CHAPTER 26⫸

Axel's expression hardened. "How much did you hear, Ristaffason?"

It was the battle of the scowls, but Axel's proved weak compared to Finn's. For the man's entire body exuded displeasure—his stern set of his brow, jutted chest, and widened stance. It was as if he readied for a tussle. "Enough to know this goes deeper than a briefcase theft." His cool gaze snapped to me. "Have you been lying to me all this time?"

Axel stepped between us, as if shielding me from Finn's wrath. "She doesn't answer to you."

"And she does to you?" His jaw worked.

I stepped aside and placed a hand on Axel's arm, his muscle tense beneath my fingertips. "It's okay. We should tell him."

He jerked from my touch. "You're not allowed."

I barely stifled an eye roll. "I was given permission to disclose whatever needed to secure the recovery of the briefcase." But Donovan had advised against it, saying only to divulge if absolutely necessary. I'd been carefully avoiding exposing my cover, but it appeared there was no other option. I hated the traces of disappointment in Finn's expression. He'd hid it behind aggravation, but I saw it nonetheless. "Finn can help us."

"How?"

I closed my eyes, and something flashed. Like a snapshot flickering before me then disappearing before I could focus. It was an image of Bengt Ferguson's desk. I'd scanned the clutter but hadn't focused on anything. Things only lingered in my memory when I set my attention on it. And I hadn't then. It was only a passing glance.

I'd missed something. Something big. And I had no idea what it was. "Agent Modve is, thankfully, alive." I resumed my case for Finn. "But now you're down a man. He can't walk at present, let alone chase killers." Axel huffed, but I continued. "Finn wants justice for his nephew. We want the document. We can work together." I hadn't missed Finn's brows rise at my mention of the research.

Axel straightened and so did Finn. Were we now to have a posturing match?

I let out an exasperated sigh. "Gentlemen, I don't know what caused a rift between you, but it's officially on pause." I flattened my palms on their chests and gave them a decided thwack. "Let's work together. When this is over, you two can return to loathing each other."

Finn's scowl didn't budge, but he stuck out his hand to Axel. Axel glanced at me, the hardness still in his eyes, but he exhaled and secured the handshake.

"Good." I smiled at them both. "Now let's all play nice."

Mamma had errands to run, which worked out perfectly. Even though I'd chosen to reveal the mission to Finn, I didn't want Mamma more involved than she already was. If she feared for my safety now, she'd lock me in my room and toss the key away if she discovered I was chasing a killer with possible ties to the Gestapo.

With a kiss to her cheek and a promise to keep an eye on Agent Modve, I saw her out the door and returned to the living room. Agent Modve was still sprawled on the sofa, Axel pouting on the seat beside him, and Finn leaning against the mantel. I claimed the only chair left, placing me in closer proximity to Finn.

As I slipped by him, I leaned in and whispered, "I'm sorry."

Our eyes met, and he nodded.

I lowered onto the chair, and Axel began the questioning.

"Okay, Modve." Axel reclined in his chair and dug out his cigarette case. "Tell us what happened."

I took the security officer's measure, knowing that counterspies were something to be wary about. His face was shadowed with stubble, making me wonder just how long he'd been trailing Ferguson without a break. He was handsome in a Walter Pidgeon sort of way with a long face and wide forehead. I'd place him in his mid-to-late forties.

Agent Modve shifted and winced. "I trailed him this past week as ordered. At first, he kept to himself at his studio, but two nights ago he had a visitor. A man entered the studio and left a half hour later in a black coupe. This same car picked up Ferguson yesterday morning, and they went to the Aubrund House museum."

My heart skipped. They *were* the ones who'd been there.

Modve continued, "The men exited the museum only fifteen minutes later and returned to the studio."

No doubt with the research. We'd been a few hours too late.

Axel lit his cigarette and took a drag. "Amelie says she found you inside the burning studio. Explain how that happened."

He muttered something, then sighed. "I went in for a closer look this morning and was spotted. Ferguson dragged me inside, and we had a scrape. I thought I had bested him until he pulled a knife. I don't remember much of the rest." His gruff voice softened as he looked at me. "Thank you for saving my life."

I smiled warmly.

"Did you see anything at all?" Axel steered conversation back on track. "Hear anything?"

"I couldn't get a good description on the man with Ferguson. His hat was drawn low and his collar pulled high. But I did catch a couple things they said before I got discovered. I heard them talking about a harbor."

Axel nodded. "There've been underground whispers. We're guessing Norrköping Harbor. It's our last chance to recover the document before it sails to Germany. We must not let it leave port."

Our last chance? My chest deflated. I'd failed all the other ones. But at least we had an inkling of where the final exchange would be. Norrköping was about 160 kilometers south of here.

"But I wonder. . ."—Axel rubbed his jaw in thought—". . .at how easy it's been to get the locations. Almost *too easy*, if you catch my meaning. When we got the tip for Club Frossa, I thought—"

I jolted. "What? You told me you were only at the nightclub because of Rosita Serrano."

He looked abashed. "I know. But I was honestly there because my contacts heard rumors of the briefcase drop. It was a coincidence about Rosita performing that night. I used her presence there as my excuse."

What? He'd lied to me? Now I knew exactly how Finn felt, and my guilt tripled. "Why didn't you tell me the reason? Axel, you—"

"Because this isn't your line of work, Amelie. You're an actress. The rumors of the drop were so easily attained, I was nervous it would be a decoy or a trap."

"But it wasn't. Franc *did* deliver the briefcase." Why didn't Axel want me to know? And if he knew about the briefcase, why hadn't he been paying attention to Franc? Or maybe he had been all along.

He offered no apology. "I did it to protect you. If it was some sort of trap, things could've turned dangerous."

Yet they had. Franc had died, and I was only a few yards behind him. I could've been injured. Killed. Where had Axel, my so-called stalwart protector, been at *that* time?

"And the second thing," Agent Modve continued, no doubt to cut the tension between Axel and me. "Ferguson asked the other fellow if he was able to find Isak Jessvurn. There's a hit on him."

Finn stiffened. "Danikan Skar had trouble with a man by that name. He was one of the refugees who came over on the same boat as the Rozental's missing. . ." His eyes widened. "Missing briefcase." He let out a humorless laugh. "I should've put it all together. Here I thought those were two unrelated instances." He turned his gaze on me. "But you've been hunting for the same briefcase as that Rozental gentleman."

I nodded. "It has Dr. Bohr's atomic research inside." I didn't have to explain to him the magnitude of that document.

Axel sniffed, obviously perturbed I'd told Finn about the manuscript, but Finn was already carrying his weight with helping. He had identified Isak Jessvurn. Isak must've been the one who'd initially stolen the briefcase and sold it to Franc. And from what Agent Modve had said, these killers were out to murder Isak Jessvurn. Why? They already had possession of the research.

I turned to Axel. "Is there any paperwork about the refugees? Where they went after reaching Sweden?"

He scratched his cheek. "Some. Trying to process eight thousand Danes in such a little amount of time was an insurmountable task. When they arrived, many stayed at the local churches and town assembly buildings. Then host families took them in."

There had to be some kind of documentation. "Suppose we narrow down the day and time of the rescue. From what Finn says, Jessvurn was on the boat when the briefcase had been sent over."

Axel shook his head. "Our concern is finding the research. Not saving some thief's life."

"But you heard him." I pointed at Agent Modve. "There's a mark on the man. Someone should warn him."

"That's not our job."

"So you're going to let the man die?" Unbelievable. My heart pounded so hard I feared it would detonate in my chest. I needed to change tactics for Axel to see reason. "If those killers mentioned Isak Jessvurn, they're probably the ones hunting him. Find them, and we find the research."

If Axel shook his head one more time at me, I was going to become unhinged. "These men are going to be focused on the drop. Because that's their payday." He took another puff on his cigarette, all casual if you please, as if we weren't discussing matters of murder. "Most likely they'll send someone else to take care of him."

How could Axel be so blasé about a human life? "Please, Axel. Just check and see if there's any information on him." I leaned forward and continued my plea. "We could, at the very least, send a message warning the man. Please, check for me."

Axel's face softened. "I don't know a man who could tell you no."

He just had—several times in a span of thirty seconds—but I wasn't about to contradict him. "Thank you."

"I can check." He flicked ashes onto the carpet, which I was glad Mamma was not here to witness. "But we'll have to prepare ourselves for looking into another route. If it's too time-consuming, you abandon the search because Dr. Bohr's research takes precedence."

I dejectedly nodded.

"So what's the next course of action here?" This from Finn.

"I'll drop off the briefcase at the legation and check what records we have. See if there's any information on the whereabouts of this man." He gave me a tight smile as if he was only doing this to appease me.

"I can return to the Aubrund House Museum." Finn glanced at the wall clock. "There's still time to get there before closing. I can ask the curator about the man who visited with Bengt Ferguson."

I blinked. It was unlike Finn to volunteer such a thing. Small talk wasn't in his conversational repertoire. Maybe he was eager to speak with the pretty young lady again. But that didn't sound like him either. I held in a sigh. Just when I thought I had the man figured out.

Axel agreed to Finn's plan. "Amelie?"

I glanced at Agent Modve. "I promised Mamma I would stay and monitor our injured patient." Though now I regretted it. I'd much rather go play chaperone with Finn and his sudden interest in the curator.

Modve huffed at my insinuation. "Don't need coddling."

I ignored him and leveled my gaze on the blond gentlemen. "Both of you speak with me this evening. I want to hear your progress."

Axel winked and Finn gave a serious nod.

I shooed them out the door, then returned to Agent Modve. As much as he didn't want to be coddled, his pillow was about to slip onto the floor, and I noticed his every movement made his face twist. "I'm going to gently tuck this pillow back under you," I warned. "Then I get to play nursemaid and give you something to eat so you can take your medicine." I carefully slid the pillow into place, only to realize how insensitive I was being. "Agent Modve, is there someone I should call? I'd hate to think a loved one is worried about you."

He grunted. "No, ma'am. I'm a loner."

Something in his voice tugged at my heart, as if he wasn't so by choice. "Well, for now you're staying here. And you're not to move until my mamma says so."

"Are you always this bossy?" His mouth pressed into a straight line, but there was a twinkle in his eye.

"Yes. Now get some rest." I should probably change my clothes and wash up a bit. But I remembered an earlier question that had gone unanswered. "Agent Modve, why were you following Bengt Ferguson in the first place? Did you know he was involved in the research scheme?"

"No." He grimaced. "I was trailing him because he has other talents than photography."

My brows raised. "Such as?"

"Bengt Ferguson is suspected of creating fake visas so people can travel in and out of the country. The man's a forger."

☰CHAPTER 27☰

I stared at the pile—no, piles—of papers. All were filled with information regarding the thousands of Danish refugees. This would take me weeks to sort through. But I hadn't that luxury.

"I'm taking a risk removing these files from the office. I need them back in the morning," Axel had said firmly when he'd stopped by late this afternoon.

There was no way I'd be able to examine each page in ten hours. And that was if I didn't sleep. Axel knew this. This had to be his way of proving his point—that Isak Jessvurn's life wasn't worth saving.

I disagreed.

So after I'd bathed, scrubbing away any trace of smoke from my person, I'd dressed in my nightgown and robe and set out to scan the papers in search of Isak's whereabouts. It was only a little after seven p.m., but I'd already decided I'd lose a night's rest so Isak wouldn't lose his life.

Mamma had retired early for the night with the latest Agatha Christie novel, and so I oversaw tending to Agent Modve. I'd turned on the radio news hours, but judging from the soft snores coming from the living room, he'd drifted to sleep.

A slight tap sounded at the door. I moved quickly from the dining room toward the entrance so the knocking wouldn't disturb the dozing security officer.

"Amelie, it's me." Finn.

My hand tightened around the doorknob. I hadn't heard from him since his unexpected announcement to visit the Aubrund House, more specifically the lady curator. But I hadn't any claim on him. I wasn't even certain if Finn had forgiven me for how I'd treated him.

I opened the door. "Hello."

His gaze swept over me, at my hair falling in unruly waves, my face scrubbed clean of cosmetics. The other night on the beach, I'd been in my robe but hadn't removed my makeup yet.

While I favored my blond eyelashes and spray of freckles, that wasn't the image the public had of me. So I shouldn't be surprised Finn gaped as if I had three eyeballs.

"Did you need something?"

He snapped from his inspection of my face. "I promised to report to you."

I stepped aside, letting him enter. "You could've called." I shut the door behind him.

"I didn't want to." He removed his hat but kept his eyes on mine.

Was he implying he'd wanted to see me instead? Or was I reading too much into his words? I waited for him to expound, but he didn't seem inclined to. I led him into the dining room where the stacks of papers had been spread across the table. "What did you discover?"

"Nothing." His lips flattened. "A foolish waste of gasoline ration. She only remembers Bengt Ferguson because he's a local. He didn't sign the register, so she logged his name for him."

Ah, that explained the feminine script. I'd assumed a woman had written his name, and now I knew why.

"From the sound of it, she seemed to have had aspirations for the man."

I glanced at his collar, my brow arching. "Looks like those affections shifted." I tugged his lapel. "There's powder right here."

"She tried to kiss me."

"Of course she did." I didn't know why it annoyed me. Finn could cuddle any woman he chose. And the burning pinch in my gut was *only* because he continued eyeing me strangely and was delaying me from my task.

"I did it for you."

So he'd lip-locked the curator on my account? As far as excuses went, that one was a stretch. "I don't recall asking you to kiss anyone." I wasn't satisfied with the dim lighting, so I moved to turn on the lamp I'd hauled in here earlier.

"No, I went to see her because of you. I know it means a lot to you to find Isak Jessvurn. I went to Sigtuna to see if I could find any more information for you."

Axel, the flirty playboy, hadn't cared about my feelings, but Finn had. Even after discovering how I'd treated him. My heart skipped. "Thank you." I moved close and brushed the powder from his collar. "But next time, you don't have to be so. . .thorough."

He caught my hand before I pulled away. "I didn't let her." His gaze was intent on mine, as if it was important to him that I understood they hadn't kissed.

Our eyes held, and a soft smile lifted my mouth. "I'm glad to hear it."

He dipped his head, his thumb running over my palm sending waves of heat through me. "Are you?"

I nodded, my breath thinning. A hunger, burning as white-hot embers, lit his eyes. Finn Ristaffason, a man notorious for his cold bearing, was the same man who'd held me and danced with me on the shores to soothe my fragile heart. He'd been labeled indifferent to others yet had followed me into a blazing building to rescue a stranger. There were brilliant depths to this man who, for some reason, refused to unveil them to the world. Yet he'd gifted glimpses to me. Why?

He swallowed, and stepped back, his touch drifting away. "She wasn't pleased at my refusal."

I bit back my own disappointment. "I imagine not."

"At least this time I didn't get a black eye," he muttered to himself, but I caught it.

"A woman punched you?"

His gaze snapped to mine. "No, her fiancé did." The way he'd uttered the word *fiancé* clued me in.

"Axel?"

He exhaled with a grave nod and pulled out a chair for me to sit. I smiled my thanks, and he claimed the seat beside mine.

His hand swept over the table. "What's this?"

"Tonight's work." I sighed. "Now about Axel. Let me guess. You stole a woman away from him."

"No, he stole her from me."

My gaze swung to his grimacing profile. What? I'd thought it would be the reverse, considering the animosity Axel had. "But he seems to have a vendetta against you. What happened?"

"The answer isn't pretty." He sighed. "Ellinor and I were together six months before Axel charmed her away. Two months later, they were engaged."

Ellinor. I remember reading her name in Finn's file. "That seems soon."

He shrugged as if it hadn't mattered to him in the least. "I avoided them until a party at Count Odette's estate." He fixed his gaze on a spot on the table. "You know how I feel about crowds, so I ducked into the library for a moment. Ellinor found me there."

Ah, I could see where this was going.

"She said she'd made a mistake leaving me for Axel and wanted me back. She threw herself at me seconds before Axel entered the room and planted his fist in my face."

I gasped. "But she advanced upon you."

"I'm sure it didn't appear that way to Axel."

Probably not.

"Ellinor invented some story that she was in the library first, and that I had pursued her."

"Axel must not have trusted her story completely." Seeing how he wasn't with her anymore. "But if things were different. If Axel hadn't barged in. Would you have taken her back?"

"No." His answer was immediate. "I saw her true character."

I idly thumbed a stack of papers, my heart picking up pace. "But it still hurt, didn't it?" I met his gaze. "At least it did for me. Especially when my broken engagement was smeared everywhere from radio to magazine."

His head reared. "You were engaged?"

His candor brought a smile to my lips. My breakup had been so widely publicized, I'd assumed everyone knew. But Finn, the man the OSS had claimed was my biggest fan, was completely oblivious about my life. And it was refreshing. For I had the rare opportunity of telling my own story and not one spun to the twisted advantage of the press. "Yes, to another actor. William Graham. He had a supporting role in my third film. He was handsome, seemed kind, and had this way of looking at me as if I was the only woman who ever existed." When really, he'd charmed me with his flattery.

Finn kept his eyes on mine, listening.

"He used me," I admitted. "I didn't realize it at first, but I began to notice he only took me to high-profile restaurants. He wanted me on his arm for all the award events. Everything seemed all for show."

"He was using you to get famous."

I nodded. "Then after we got engaged, he began to pick at my appearance before we stepped out in public. He believed if I didn't look or act perfect, it had a direct effect on him and his career."

Finn tensed.

"So I ended things." And as painful as it was to recap my relationship, I could see a direct parallel that brought me shame. "Finn, I apologize for using you to get to the briefcase. I truly wasn't supposed to tell a soul. Even Mamma doesn't fully know. But if I hurt you, I'm sorry."

He was quiet for several seconds. "I understand, Amelie."

My breath caught. "You're not angry?"

"No." That lone word, spoken in his deep voice, was enough to swell my chest with hope. "As for your ex-fiancé, he's an idiot."

I sputtered a laugh. "I do adore your bluntness."

"I don't claim to understand the workings of Hollywood. I've never watched your movies and probably won't. Though I don't think I'm missing out, because—"

"Never mind." I playfully slapped his arm. "Your bluntness is tedious."

"*Because*," he continued as if I hadn't interrupted, "I feel I've gotten to see the real you: an intelligent, daring woman. And I've yet to see you more beautiful than you are right now."

I blinked. Then blinked again. Finn's words rolled slowly through my mind. I'd misread him once more. Judging by his open staring, I'd thought he'd been disappointed by my appearance. "You surprise me. This is out of character for you."

"Not at all."

"But you're never one to compliment or flatter."

"You're right." He placed his thumb under my chin, lifting my jaw until I met his tender gaze. "But I am one to tell the truth."

"Thank you." And why my eyes stung with emotion, I wasn't sure. Maybe because this was the real me. No evening gown. Only a wrinkled bathrobe. No makeup. Jewelry. Or any touch of glamour. Yet this was what had caught Finn's eye.

"So what needs done here?" Leave it to him to interrupt my pleasurable pondering of his newfound niceness.

I blew out a breath. "These are the refugee forms. Axel only gave me until tomorrow morning to find any information on Isak Jessvurn."

Finn's raised brow wasn't exactly encouraging.

Determination sparked. "I'll find it."

"Then I'll help." He shed his jacket and loosened his tie.

"This may take a while." I handed him a stack of government pages. "We may be up all night."

Finn nodded, accepting the challenge, and a spike of energy ran through me. Maybe, just maybe, we could do this.

The papers included log sheets of who'd been rescued and their intended destination during their stay in Sweden. Minutes turned to hours as midnight approached. We'd narrowed the stacks down to the day of Jessvurn's evacuation from Denmark and now hunted for the specific files from Finn's boatyard.

I offered Finn another cup of coffee, which he waved off. My vision grew blurrier with each page I pored over.

"Maybe we should call it quits." Stifling a yawn, I rubbed my eyes, and it happened again. An image flashed in my mind. Earlier today, it had been Bengt Ferguson's desk. But now? It was Finn's desk. What was wrong with me? Was my brain playing tricks? How was Finn's desk drawer linked to Ferguson's studio?

"Is something the matter?"

I lifted my lashes and found Finn's concerned gaze. "Nothing." I couldn't tell him about my snooping in his desk. Or maybe I should. "Finn, the other day—"

"I think I found it." He sat straighter, all signs of drowsiness vanishing. "Here. Look. That's Danikan's handwriting." He handed me a page filled with masculine scrawl. "Fourth name from the bottom."

"Isak Jessvurn." Beside his name was listed the date and time he'd arrived on Swedish shores. I read aloud the lodging information. "It says his host family wasn't available until October 15th."

Finn nodded. "So he was most likely bunking at one of the local shelters in Malmö. Which also explains how Franc was able to locate him so easily."

I nodded and read on. "Nausträsk." My gaze met Finn's. "He went all the way to Lapland?" Nausträsk was located in the Lapland region of northern Sweden.

Finn didn't look surprised. "The government asked for help for housing refugees. People volunteered from all over the country."

My mouth pinched. There was a lot of open country in the Lapland, and I wasn't certain I'd be able to get a message to Jessvurn. Nausträsk was a tiny town near the Malmberget mine and was at least ten hours away—a full day's drive. "Axel won't allow me to go there." But could I simply do nothing? "He thinks alerting Jessvurn is a waste of time."

Finn nudged my shoulder. "Then we just don't tell him."

⟩CHAPTER 28⟨

With six hours of sleep coupled with my long nap from yesterday afternoon, I'd felt good. Though I couldn't be certain how much rest Finn had gotten. We'd both decided it was best to leave early, hoping to reach this man before the killer did.

I'd left a note for Mamma instructing her to give Axel the files when he arrived. I felt mildly guilty about not informing him, but I knew he'd disapprove. Was I forsaking my mission by warning Jessvurn? Was there truly a hit on him? It was possible Agent Modve had misheard. I pondered over everything repeatedly, but something still seemed off.

"Care to share what you're frowning about?" Finn glanced over from behind the wheel.

I'd been so certain yesterday this was the right choice to make, but now the doubts echoed louder. "If what we assume is right and Jessvurn sold the briefcase to Franc, then from all standpoints, Franc was the only one Jessvurn interacted with."

He nodded. "Seems so."

I needed to be sensitive how I worded the next question. "Since the killer took out Franc, why would he need to kill Jessvurn too? Jessvurn never came in contact with the murderer. He only did business with Franc."

"We aren't certain about anything. It's all speculation."

"But it's the only way that makes sense." Jessvurn had sold the case to Franc, who'd turned it over to the killer at the nightclub. The killer had then gotten rid of Franc and taken the briefcase to Sigtuna for the next drop. "And there's something else that bothers me."

"I'm listening."

"Whoever killed Franc must be different from the man at Ferguson's studio. Agent Modve said the guy visited Ferguson's studio around midnight on *Tuesday*. Which was twenty minutes after Franc was killed. He couldn't get from Malmö to the outskirts of Sigtuna in less than twenty minutes." That was nearly a nine-hour drive.

"No, that's impossible."

"So we're dealing with more than one killer. The person who murdered Franc and the men who tried to kill Agent Modve."

"Cheery thought."

"Then there are the inconsistencies with the handoffs. The first one was in a public place and in person, but the drop in the Aubrund House was more hidden. The museum isn't exactly teeming with people. The person that hid the briefcase in the secretary bench probably didn't meet with whoever picked it up."

"Maybe it was a timing issue?" He sat thoughtful for a minute. "Also, if you consider, Club Frossa was crowded. With that many people, one face blends into the next. A handoff could easily go unnoticed."

True. I'd had tremendous difficulty singling out Franc, and I'd been intent on my search. Others had been there solely for a good time. I could see how a transaction could be made in the open, and yet no one had caught it.

"Maybe I'm looking too much into it." I sighed. "I feel like I'm missing something. Something crucial."

"Perhaps we should use this time to discuss a plan for when we reach Nausträsk. I'm counting on your intelligence to keep me from getting stabbed like Agent Modve."

"Women love men with a scar."

His brow raised, but he said nothing.

I turned my attention to the last blush of fall outside my window. The spruce trees in the distance, with leaves of reds, golds, and bronzes, clustered together in an autumnal bouquet. The warm daylight bathed my face, causing me to want to nod off after a while, but I wouldn't allow myself to fall into a deep slumber. If Finn had to remain awake, I would too. We stopped at a café for a meal and ordered sandwiches to take with us. Once we advanced deep into the country, places to stop were few and far between. After I phoned Mamma to check in, we continued our journey, arriving in Nausträsk well after the sun went down.

The main street—if one could call it that—consisted of a drugstore, a post office, a diner, and a pool hall. Unfortunately, only the last one was open. I grabbed the car door handle, but Finn placed a hand on my knee, stilling my exit.

"No." His tone was firm. "You're not going inside."

"Why not?"

"Because a pool parlor isn't any place for a lady."

I pressed my cheek to his shoulder in playful affection. "It's sweet how you're trying to protect me."

But what I meant as a teasing gesture, he didn't follow suit. He rolled his head my direction, placing only inches between our faces, mirroring the position from the train. Only this time we both were fully awake.

"I know what you're doing."

His breath stirred the hair on my temple. "Which is?"

I'd once assumed that Finn had no idea how to use the moonlight to his advantage. I was wrong. For right now the soft glow touched the sharp angles and defined slopes on his face, as if spotlighting his allure. "You're trying to—"

"Make you see reason?"

"Use your handsomeness to win me over."

"No one's ever accused me of such a thing." He gave a light scoff. "Amelie, they are miners. Rough men. They'll take one look at you and...forget their manners."

I cozied up to him. "I'd rather stay by your side than be left alone to wait."

He gave me an exasperated look, but I caught amusement in his eyes. "Now who's using their charm to get their way? Still, it's not a good idea."

Had he forgotten my upbringing? I was raised among fishermen. Fishermen and miners weren't much different. One plunged into deep waters, and the other pitted the depths of the mountain, but both excavated the fruit thereof. These men toiled hard, tireless hours. A person only needed to know how to speak their language.

But I'd humor him. For now. "Fine. I'll stay out of *sight* unless you need help."

He searched my face. Then, as if realizing that was the only cooperation he'd get from me, he expelled a sigh and got out of the car. Once he entered the pool parlor, I quietly opened the passenger door and stepped onto the gravelly lot. Finn didn't understand how he'd appear, barging into their domain in his perfectly tailored suit and austere expression.

The entrance to the building had been propped open with a brick, and the odor of cigarette smoke and sweat was enough to make my nose wrinkle.

I leaned against the doorframe in time to catch a snarly voice. "Someone's asking after Jessvurn, fellas."

That didn't bode well. I could practically see these men holding their cue sticks like spears, ready to gouge the nosy rich boy.

"I only need information." Finn's voice cut through the jeers. "I can pay any amount."

I winced. Wrong move.

"You think you can wave your money around?" Another voice, decidedly younger but more intense. "We may not have as much as you, but we work for our right to be here."

I stepped into the doorway. "Then how about you earn it?"

I was pretty proud of myself for not stumbling on the uneven floorboards. Though I remained poised, despite my left heel sinking in a wad of chewing tobacco. All heads whipped my direction. I heard a few vulgar slurs. A couple catcalls. And one grunt from a very irritated Finn.

The man standing beside Finn raised his hand, quieting his comrades, then clapped in mock applause. "Amelie Blake. Now that's an entrance." His voice matched the one that had spoken right before I'd come in. It also dripped with sarcasm. "Things just got interesting."

I adopted a bored expression. "Not from my standpoint."

Heckles erupted.

The man, whom I guessed to be around my age, approached. Finn started toward me, but I shook my head, stopping his advance, though he clearly was displeased about it.

I remembered what Morfar had once said. *Never show fear.* So I didn't. "You have information we need. We want to know where Isak Jessvurn is. We must speak to him." I swept my gaze around the room. "And so I'm prepared to work for this." Of course, this was followed by some vulgar propositions. Most of these men had more alcohol in their veins than in their cups.

"Amelie," Finn warned.

The man who'd been creating all the stir eyed me close. "Just what kind of work are you willing to do?"

"More like a wager." I grabbed a cue stick from the rack behind me. This drew some laughs but also some cheers. "I win, you tell me what I need to know."

He rubbed his square jaw. "What happens if you lose?"

I laughed. "The winner gets to keep his dignity. In your case, there isn't much left, so it's worth preserving."

Another round of slaps on the tables and booming laughs.

Finn's wariness made me smile. I knew how to handle these guys. Most already had dulled senses, their eyes glazed and speech slurred. Pool was a game of coordination, but more than that, sharpness of mind. "What do you say?" I popped a hand on my hip. "Who's your best player?"

The ringleader nodded. "You're looking at him. Let's go."

Finn's fingers wrapped my elbow. "What are you doing?"

I tugged my arm away and chalked the end of my cue stick. "Playing pool."

"Do you think they will just let you walk out of here if you lose?"

"Yes, I think they will. Besides"—I leveled him a look—"who says I'm going to lose?"

I breathed deeply and pictured myself in the cozy billiard room in my Beverly Hills home. A place I'd spent most of my evenings after my breakup with William. If I could survive those months of heart-ache, plus tabloid hounds, without any family to comfort me, I was certain I could overcome the next several minutes in a pool hall in the Swedish Lapland.

A coin was tossed. He won and chose to break. I smothered a frown. The break determined the layout of the table and the position of the cue ball. As a person who preferred being in control, I didn't like starting out at a disadvantage, but that was how the game went.

The man shot me a wink, then racked the pool balls. The room went silent as he struck the cue ball for a direct hit into the ball at the apex of the triangle, the topspin driving through the pack. It was a legal break. The 2-ball and the 1-ball sank into pockets, giving him another turn.

His squinted gaze took in the spread, and he nodded. "Four-ball in the corner pocket," he called his shot and, to my dismay, potted it. He repeated the process, calling his move and subsequently sinking it.

He only needed to pot four more solids plus the 8-ball to win. With a smirk, he called his next shot but applied too much force in his hit. He missed.

I rubbed my palms on my tweed skirt, making sure my hands weren't slick. The cue ball lay in a perfect spot to sink the 10-ball. But I didn't aim for that one. "Twelve-ball. Side pocket."

Murmurs rippled through the room, which almost broke my concentration. I closed my eyes and imagined this particular shot—the bend of my legs, the angle of my lean, and the power behind my stroke. I reopened my eyes and, with a steady breath, took the shot—potting the ball. I fell into the rhythm, relying on muscle memory more than anything else. I sank my next three, taking the lead.

"Fifteen-ball. Corner pocket." But when I moved to make the shot the image of Ferguson's studio desk popped into my brain, tightening my joints, locking my arms. I awkwardly hit the cue ball, missing my intended mark.

My opponent realized his chance to get ahead, and he seized it. We went back and forth until he only needed to sink the 8-ball, me trailing with my 9-ball still on the table.

He was going to win. The shot was basic. And I wasn't just losing a pool game but also the opportunity to discover more about Isak Jessvurn. I hid my disappointment as my competitor paraded around the table, collecting hearty slaps on the shoulder from his boisterous friends.

Finn pointed at me and lifted his chin. I realized I'd already accepted defeat, and he was encouraging me. It was kind of him to support me, but there was nothing more I could do.

"This is for my dignity." My rival blew me an exaggerated kiss, prompting another round of laughs.

I resisted the urge to grumble as he leaned to take the final shot. He tried to show off and used a side spin, changing the point of contact. The 8-ball stopped just shy of the pocket.

He cussed, and there was a collective groan around the room.

My air whooshed out. I needed to pot both shots to win, and the balls were on opposite sides of the table, but at least I'd been granted another chance.

Finn moved behind me, warmth from his large body pressing into mine.

I craned my neck, looking back into his face. "Any encouraging words for me?"

"How about our own wager?"

"On the shots?"

He nodded. "If you sink these next two, I promise to buy you a truckload of salmiak."

I grinned at him. "Deal." And I grabbed the chalk and worked it over the cue tip. I called the shot. Potting the 9-ball was relatively easy.

The room fell eerily quiet. The men were in stunned silence—or maybe had passed out from their overindulgence—but I was too focused to glance about.

Sinking the last ball would be difficult. But I'd done this shot before, almost eleven months ago, on a November evening. I slipped back into that moment, feeling the press of the table into my side, but something was different. My holster. I couldn't replicate the stance because of the bulky leather strap. Panic climbed my throat. I'd been hopeful that my photographic brain would see me through the shot, but my entire aim and posture were different.

I glanced over at Finn, and he nodded.

Fine. I'd just create a new memory. One where I refused to cower to the suffocating doubts. I called the pocket and eased back the cue, taking a few pre-shots to determine my angle. With a steadying breath, I brought the stick forward and watched the cue ball smack the 8-ball, sending it into the intended pot.

It sank!

The room was stunned for a full two seconds before breaking into cheers and laughs.

I propped my pool stick against the table and flung my arms around Finn. He tensed at my sudden embrace, but soon his hands pressed my back, holding me against him. "Well done," he murmured against my temple. "You must really like bitter candy."

I laughed, easing back, sliding my hands to rest upon his broad chest. "If you haven't noticed, I'm very fond of what's considered sour."

His eyes flashed, telling me he'd caught the undertone of my words, and then it happened. Finn Ristaffason laughed. It was a deep rumble of pleasure, sending a thousand shivers through me. While most threw around their smiles, he reserved his, which made this moment all worth the earning, stealing the very breath from me. I took it all in. The flicker of silver in his eyes. The curved dimple edged against his grinning lips. The delicious urge to press my mouth to his traveled through me, but I restrained myself. Barely.

"You're the only woman I know"—his voice held faded remnants of his chuckle—"who can compliment yet insult me in the same breath."

I beamed at him. "Your pride can stand being knocked down a peg or two." Then I gazed around the room, realizing I hadn't only been victorious in a pool game but I'd also won over the crowd. Even my opponent was laughing and taking the loss in stride.

I broke apart from Finn as the man approached. The previous predatory glint was now replaced with respect. "You earned it." He guided me by the elbow to the bar, Finn following close.

A tall glass of schnapps was set in front of me. Probably more whiskey than fruit juice, but I wasn't going to drink it. I smiled at the bartender and tossed some kronor on the table.

"Your money isn't good here." Unlike everyone else, this man's face was void of a smile. "You better be leaving."

"Ah, Jessvurn." My former competitor grinned. "Fröken earned a conversation with you. Let her reap her winnings."

My own smile faltered, and I exchanged a glance with Finn. "You're Isak Jessvurn?"

He gave a solemn nod and commenced wiping down the counter. Everyone else went about their business, leaving us to chat.

I leaned toward the man whose life hung in the balance. "We came to warn you."

His hand stilled midswipe. "About what?"

"People are after you because of the briefcase you sold. They will try—"

His laughter cut me off. "Fröken, nobody's going to kill me over that silly case."

Silly? "Franc—the man you sold it to—they murdered him." I'd assumed he was the one who procured the briefcase in the first place, and Isak's haughty grin crimping into a deep frown confirmed it.

He rubbed his furrowed brow. "He was just a lad."

I nodded, conscious of Finn's feelings, and slipped my hand in his. "Someone hit him with their car on purpose."

He muttered a cuss. "Why?"

"I was hoping you'd tell me what you know."

He tossed the cloth down and shrugged. "There's nothing more to tell."

"Please," Finn spoke up from my side. "Any information will help."

"That's what I'm trying to tell you." He sighed. "I sold the briefcase to the lad. That's it."

Why was he being so difficult? "I know you sold it to him. But it's more about what's inside the case. That's what people are killing for."

"Fröken, the briefcase was empty."

≣CHAPTER 29≣

No. It couldn't be.

Finn pressed a supporting hand to my back and asked Isak, "Will you start from the beginning? How did you get possession of the briefcase?"

Isak fidgeted with the edges of the washrag, his gaze flitting everywhere but on Finn and me. "The case was left on the shore, so I took it." He had no shame confessing the theft. "I thought there might be something valuable inside, but it was only a stack of scribbled papers. I tossed them in the nearest burn barrel and tried to pawn the case. But Franc was the only one who wanted it."

I gasped. "You *burned* the papers?"

His mouth turned down. "It was just a bunch of gibberish."

Dr. Bohr's work. A genius in atomic theory. Information that could turn the entire tide of the war had been used for kindling. "So you sold Franc an empty briefcase?"

He looked at me as if I were a few trees short of a forest. "It's good leather. Only a fool would turn down the kronor he offered for it."

When I'd discovered the briefcase at the Aubrund House museum, it had already been divested of its contents. We'd been chasing an empty case from the start.

I sank onto the barstool, my surroundings blurring. My mission. The entire reason I'd been sent here had gone up in smoke. Literally. There was no chance of recovering the research now. Though at least there was no possibility of the Nazis possessing it. I took great comfort in that aspect.

But then. . .why all this fuss over an empty briefcase? Why all the fanfare about the scheduled drops? Why had they killed Franc and placed Isak next on their list?

Someone on the opposite end of the counter yelled for a refill, and Isak held up a finger, signaling him to wait. His dark gaze fell on us. "Is that all you need to talk about? Because I have work to do."

I nodded. "Be on the lookout. Men are after you."

His gaze roamed the room, as if taking in all his compatriots. "I'll be all right."

Isak Jessvurn hadn't only gotten a host family but a host town. Though they had sold him out over a game of pool. But I hardly posed a threat. I suspected if the men Agent Modve spoke of walked through the door, these fellows wouldn't betray their friend. Loyalties ran deep in a group like this. I'd come here and done my job.

And now it seemed like it was over.

Finn wrapped a steady arm around my waist and gently guided me out the door.

"It was empty," I whispered, my mind still struggling to accept it. "The manuscript is destroyed." Questions swirled with each step toward Finn's car, all answers pointing to the fact that we'd hit a dead end. But then why did my gut claw at me, as if urging me to move forward?

Finn opened my door, and I lowered onto the car's bench. As if in a daze, I watched him round the car and settle beside me. He proceeded to drive to the nearest hotel. We both were lost in our thoughts, trying to grapple with this new information.

We arrived at the hotel, a white-siding, two-story building.

Finn glanced at me. "I'll get us checked in. It's probably best if you wait here."

I nodded. One thing about my status, I couldn't give a fake name. It would appear scandalous for me to check in to a hotel with Finn, despite us booking separate rooms. But after learning about my failed mission, I didn't want to go inside any public place. I had no energy for being around people. I wanted to go home, but I knew that wasn't an option. I closed my eyes, trying to ease the headache worming between my temples. The images flashed again. The one of Finn's office drawer and also of Ferguson's desk. But did it even matter now? Wasn't my assignment over? Though maybe, these clues were pieces to a different puzzle.

What am I missing, God?

I felt like it was right there, skating along the delicate fringe of my mind, just out of reach.

The door opened, and I startled.

Finn slid behind the wheel, his scowl deeper than usual. "Bad news."

"There's only one room?"

He shook his head. "No rooms. They're all filled."

It wasn't surprising since the hotel was on the smaller side. Was it wrong that a part of me breathed relief? I doubted we'd be able to sneak into the hotel undetected, and my mood was too fragile to interact with strangers. Though it seemed I wasn't the only one. Waves of frustration seemed to roll off Finn. His jaw was tight, eyes blazing.

I might have failed at recovering the document, but Finn undoubtedly felt he'd failed his nephew. I reached across and grabbed his hand, which was balled into a fist. He responded to my touch, turning over his palm and threading his fingers through mine.

"We won't give up, Finn." My voice was thick with emotion. "We'll get justice for Franc."

He nodded gravely. "I called Axel. Thought he should know what we found."

I darted a glance at the hotel. "You didn't talk long." Finn could only have been inside a handful of minutes. Though the man wasn't known for his extensive conversation, and that was with people he liked. With Axel, I didn't have to imagine their clipped exchange.

"He wasn't in." Finn's tone was gruff. "Did you tell him where we were going today?"

My brows lowered. Where did that question come from? "No, we agreed not to say anything."

Still holding my hand, he shifted to face me, my breath tightening at his dark expression. "You left the papers for Axel to collect with Elsa. Did you tell her where we were headed?"

"Mamma? I don't remember if I said—"

"You need to think, Amelie. It's important."

He made no sense. "Why does it matter if Mamma knows?"

"Because Axel could've charmed it out of her."

"Who cares if he's mad that we left? I think he'll be angrier to find out we've been swindled about the briefcase."

He lightly squeezed my fingers as if trying to get my attention. "Not if he's the one who's behind it."

Finn's words hit me with the force of a gut punch. "Y–You think he might be a counterspy?" My gaze drifted through the windshield, not really seeing anything. Finn's theory shuffled through my mind, redirecting my memory over the past few days. "He was at Club Frossa the night Franc got killed."

"And in Sigtuna yesterday morning."

"But he still couldn't be in two places at once. He would've been in Malmö the night Agent Modve saw the gentleman enter Ferguson's studio. Though that doesn't mean he couldn't have caught up with them yesterday morning." I shook my head. "Agent Modve would've recognized his boss. And Modve said the men left. He distinctly mentioned that Ferguson left with the other man before he passed out. If Axel had joined their ranks, it would've been three men altogether. Not two, like Modve said."

Finn agreed. "Yet somehow the studio catches on fire afterward?"

I sucked in a breath. Could Axel have been the one who started it? Why? "He's also the only person who's had all the information about the drops."

"He probably planted it. And conveniently a day late for the Sigtuna handoff."

This was crazy. Axel Eizenburg? A double agent? "He gave me a difficult time about wanting to alert Isak Jessvurn. I thought it was because he wanted me to focus on my mission, but—"

"Maybe he didn't want you interfering with his plans to kill him."

No, no. This couldn't be. I felt blindsided like I was with the briefcase. Everything was spiraling out of control. "But he doesn't know where Jessvurn is."

"Unless you told Elsa."

I thought back to my conversation with Mamma. I'd told her I was leaving with Finn and would return the following day. She'd given me grief about spending the night with him, and I'd reassured her we'd get separate rooms wherever we stayed. Then I'd given her instructions to give the papers to Axel. That had been all. "No, I didn't tell her."

The hard lines framing his eyes softened. "Are you certain? What about when you called to check in with her at the café?"

"No, I didn't say anything." It all came flooding back to me. "But wait. We're fussing over nothing. When I last talked to her, Mamma said Axel never showed. He didn't pick up the papers." I shook my head. "But he was stubborn about those files, saying he could get in trouble for taking them from the office."

"Yet he didn't come to retrieve them?"

I trembled all over. "I just. . .can't believe it. Axel." The first day we met, I heard traces of a German accent. He'd told me his family hailed from Austria, and I hadn't even questioned him. How I'd boasted I could see through men's charm and flattery, yet I wasn't the least suspicious of him. "I'm the worst spy."

"No, Amelie." He caught up my other hand and now gripped them both with an adamance I wasn't prepared for. "Don't buy that lie. You discovered the briefcase and went with your gut to hunt down Jessvurn. We would've never known about this false chase if not for you."

"What do we do now?" Who did we even approach with our assumptions about Axel? I teetered on the brink of tears. Something Finn must have realized, for he gathered me in his arms, holding me tight. "I don't have anything left in me."

"You're stronger than you think." His warm lips skimmed my forehead. "And you'll feel better after a night's sleep. I know of a place where you'll be safe."

I drew back and peered up at him. "What kind of place?"

"I own a house in Luleå."

Luleå stood on the eastern edge of Sweden, directly on the Gulf of Bothnia. The town wasn't exactly close—probably an hour and a half away—but it sure beat the thirteen-hour stretch to Stockholm. We wouldn't have enough gasoline or the stamina to return to the capital now. I disentangled from his arms. "I'm guessing you have a harbor there." Why else would he own a home in Luleå?

He nodded.

Finn owned docks on the Gulf of Bothnia. The very place Erik Bruun had wanted to purchase icebreakers to keep his harbor in business throughout the winter.

"It's closed now. But it hasn't always been."

I caught his meaning. Mostly because I knew there was a railway line from the Kiruna and Gallivare mines to Luleå for the sole purpose of transporting iron ore. "Did you ship steel to the Germans?"

"No." He blew a heavy breath, even as he drove off the hotel lot. "Not to say I wasn't pressured to."

With Germany in control of the surrounding waters, many Swedish companies wouldn't survive without trading with the enemy. And with Sweden's neutrality stance, they had free rein to transact with anyone. But did that make it right? I was thankful Finn hadn't thought so. He'd chosen the moral side, though his finances must've taken a hit.

"Every now and then, I'd arrange for the docks to take a domestic shipment from southern Sweden. But I assure you, nothing to or from the Nazis." His tone was emphatic. "I know I'm not the easiest to get along with, but I am honest."

That, he was. In the States, I'd been surrounded by people who seemed to only tell me what they'd thought I'd like to hear. They'd flattered to no end. Finn didn't simper or sweet talk, but I preferred him that way. I swiveled my gaze out the window. Thick forests lined both sides of the road, the jagged treetops scratching the sky. Stars dotted above like pinpricks in a purple velvet cloth. "Speaking of honesty, do you think Isak Jessvurn told the truth?"

"Sadly, yes."

I had to agree. "But why?" I slid my eyes closed. Blocking out my surroundings helped me concentrate. "Assuming Axel is involved, why go through all the hassle with the briefcase to make it appear like it contained the research?"

"There's a war going on. Even in Sweden. It's a battle of information and misinformation." His words were similar to Henrik's.

"You think it was all posed on purpose?" And how were Ferguson and the other man involved?

"You're the actress. If anyone should detect something's being staged, it's you."

"What would be the point in creating a fake chase? To lead the OSS and the Swedish secret police on a rabbit trail?" I pinched my eyes even tighter, wishing something would just pop into my brain. "Maybe it's to distract us. Keep our focus on the briefcase while trying to accomplish something else."

Finn slowed the car to a stop.

My eyelids shot open. "What's the matter?"
"I can't have you miss this." His voice held notes of. . .excitement?
"Miss what?"
"Your aurora borealis."

⧛CHAPTER 30⧚

Finn jumped out of the car and jogged to my door. My gaze flew to the sky, and I gasped. I'd blocked out everything for the past few minutes and almost missed the beauty before me.

"Come on." He held out his hand. "It's even better out here."

I slipped my fingers in his and stepped out to see the glories. And. . .oh!

Curls of green and purple glided along the sky as if in a celestial dance. Whimsical and radiant, they filled my soul with their glowing beauty. The surrounding stars studded the sky with wisps of vibrant red, and I took it all in. My mind would display this scene again and again, but it couldn't replicate the feel of this moment—awe unfurling through me, the pressing of warmth from Finn's side against mine. The skies stretched, so vivid and textured before me, like I could reach into the heavens and swirl the colors.

"Is it as breathtaking as you hoped?" Finn's tone was hushed as if any volume would extinguish the lights.

I twined my fingers in his. "More so."

We stood silent, taking in the brilliance, our soft breathing and the hum of my pulse the only sounds.

"Morfar said the northern lights were once called Bifrost because people thought it was the bridge between Asgard and Earth. That the gods were close." I shook my head. "I've never believed in Norse mythology. But in a moment like this, it feels like the one true God is close, even more than we realize." As if the Creator had painted the sky as a reminder of His majesty. If He could ignite the heavens, I could trust him to impart light into my darkness.

Finn nodded, keeping his gaze upward.

This day had been one of desolation, my plans and goals destroyed. But there was beauty among the ruins. We only needed to keep our eyes open or we'd miss it. And I almost had. "I was so focused on the problems with this mission that I didn't look up."

"Maybe that's the best place for our focus. Keeping our eyes on Him."

My heart stirred, shaking loose the debris of discouragement and dashed hope. I turned to Finn. The look in his eyes was different. It could be the splendor of the heavens reflecting in their depths, but somehow, I believed it was more the mirroring of his heart. He'd never looked as sincere and tender as now, in the middle of nowhere, under miraculous skies.

I wrapped my arms around him and pressed my cheek to his shoulder. "Thank you for stopping. I needed this."

His hands hooked on my waist, drawing me to him. "You're welcome."

I inched my chin higher and had an amazing view of Finn's handsome face as well as the dancing lights. I breathed deep, and it seemed like Finn supported most of my weight, as if sensing my need to be lighter, freer.

For years, I'd been surrounded by people who only cared for what I could give them. A flawless movie. A dazzling photo session. The press had stolen pictures of me in public without my permission. Journalists plastered my name to attract readers. My fiancé had taken advantage of my heart to boost his career. Take. Take. Take.

With Finn, it was different.

"I won't take anything from you that you're not willing to give," Finn had said at his estate, and I hadn't realized the grace in his words. But even more so, his actions. He'd provided comfort the night I met my father, offered forgiveness when I hurt him, given me hope when I felt like a failure.

I hugged him closer, and he feathered a kiss on the crown of my head, the gesture so chaste, gentle. My eyes pricking with tears, I gazed up at him. "Finn?"

"Yes?"

I ran my thumb along his lower lip, slowly. "You missed a spot."

His eyes flashed, and he pulled me to him with delicious urgency. I melted against his strong form, bracing my hands on his chest, and felt the rapid beat of his heart thundering against my palm.

I expected his lips to fervently claim mine, but he paused. His gaze rapt upon my face, his eyes taking me in with tender fascination as if I was ethereal like the skies above. I should've never believed him incapable of emotions, for I now felt the unleashed force of them and my breath shallowed. He lifted his hand, cupping my face with reverence, as if holding the stars themselves.

He dipped his head, eyes on mine with heated intent. His hand slid to the curve of my neck, gently drawing me until our lips met. His late-day stubble brushed against my jaw, igniting my every nerve. I kissed him with equal fervor, bunching his lapel, pulling him flush against me.

We broke apart to sneak a breath. He nuzzled my cheek, sinking his hands into my hair. He tilted my head and pressed a fiery trail of kisses along my jawline, on the pulse point of my throat. Burning shivers raced over me. In this moment, Finn Ristaffason revealed a tenderness he'd hidden from the world, and I savored the delicious pressure of his lips upon my skin. His mouth reclaimed mine and explored its contours, thoroughly, deeply.

Finn slowly ended the kiss and rested his forehead on mine, his blue eyes pleasurably hazed. We brushed noses, and I burned to resume where he'd left off, but he seemed content to gaze at me as if I'd been the one who'd given him a gift. A treasure. And not the other way around.

I looked heavenward. "The brilliance is dimming."

"No," he said with a soft smile he'd deny later. "Things like this don't fade." He lifted our joined hands.

I couldn't help it. I kissed him again.

After several delightful moments, he pulled away, his breath ragged. "We'd better return to the car."

Once inside Finn's Volvo, we resumed our trek toward Luleå in peaceful silence. I looked up at the sky through my window and smiled. "You know," I teased, "that could be considered theatrical on your part."

"What could?"

"Kissing me like you did."

"Are you complaining?" Amusement riddled his tone.

"Not at all." I snuggled into his arm, pleased that I could. "You were very thorough in your delivery. Just a touch on the melodramatic side by kissing me under the northern lights."

He shrugged. "I'd kiss you anywhere."

I peered over at his handsome profile. "I hope you aim to back up that remark."

He groaned good-naturedly. "As if I'm not tempted enough. Which is why, after I get you settled in the main house, I'm spending the night in the apartment over the boathouse." He lifted my hand and pressed a kiss to the inside of my wrist.

I smiled at his show of respect. But then, I hadn't been the most respectful toward him. Or rather, his property. It took me several moments to work up the courage. "I have to tell you something. It might be shocking."

He grunted. "More alarming than you being a pool parlor hustler?" He shook his head, almost in wonder. "Do you realize you made your fifth shot with your eyes closed?"

"I wasn't showing off." Had I not explained to him about my mind? "I was seeing myself make the shot like I'd done in my own home. Sometimes I rely on my memory more than I do my senses."

"Is that what you wanted to tell me?"

"No." I straightened and took a deep breath. "I broke into your desk drawer. The one with all your invoices."

"I see." He was quiet for several long, uncomfortable seconds. "You could've asked me. I would've shown you."

His honesty only made me feel worse. "But this was before you knew about me. You would've had questions."

"Undoubtedly."

"My mind keeps flashing back to something in that drawer." I continued despite his lowered brow. "I feel this mission is tied to you in some way."

"How?"

"I don't know. I keep seeing two images. One is your drawer, and the other is Ferguson's studio. I quickly skimmed his desk for the manuscript, but I feel I saw something that links this all together." I huffed the hair from my forehead. "I just don't know what it all means."

"Didn't you just say you relied on your memory more than other senses?"

I sighed. "I do. But this is different. I was intentionally searching for the manuscript. My brain was hyperfocused on that. I rushed over everything else." Did that even make any sense?

"Then do what you did in the pool game. Slowly retrace the memory."

"It doesn't work like that. I only recall that which I purpose to retain." I tapped the seat bench. "Maybe we should go back to the beginning. Perhaps there's a clue we missed. The night of the rescue when Jessvurn took the briefcase, Danikan implied you were nowhere to be found. Did he mean you weren't at the harbor?"

His face grew hard. He didn't want to answer me.

Oh. "Were you with a woman?"

Finn muttered something under his breath. "It was a secret appointment but *not* with a woman. I was needed at my other loading port in Lysekil." He flicked a hesitant glance at me. "The British acquired some motor gunboats. Blockade Busters, they call them. The idea is to sail through German waters at night and reach the port in the early hours for a load." He shrugged. "For ball bearings and specialty steel."

He was working for the Allies. No wonder the OSS had been conflicted about Finn's loyalties. They'd recruited him for service only to discover he'd given a large sum of money to Erik Bruun. Though now, I understood Finn had only been repurchasing his boat. "So that's where you were." I breathed relief. "You were loading British boats."

"Yes and no. I was in Lysekil, but the operation got postponed."

"Anyone know about this?"

He gave me a look. "Not unless they riffled through my private papers."

"I'm sorry for invading your personal affairs."

He shook his head, slowing the car as we approached a stop sign, the city of Luleå coming into view. "You did what you felt needed to be done."

"So you forgive me?"

He braked at the sign, leaned over, and kissed me. "Yes."

"Thank you." I smiled up at him. "Are we almost there?"

He pulled himself away and resumed driving. "Nearly. The Ristaffason docks are on the edge line of the main marinas. More private but still easily accessible. The main house is a few blocks down." He pointed out all the different harbors and explained who owned them. Boats bobbed in the water, their outlines like hulking beasts. Stevedores milled about. I didn't expect anyone to be working this time of night, but Finn told me ships move in and out of the harbor at all hours, their arrival time depending on the weather and rise of water.

"Since you own several loading docks, how do you keep everything separated?"

"Each harbor has its own insignia to avoid confusion. For every load that's imported and exported, the harbormaster stamps the paperwork with the designated emblem."

Emblem. My mind sparked. "That's it."

"That's what?"

"I remember now. I saw an invoice in your drawer with a certain design at the top of the paper."

"Most likely." He nodded. "They're all stamped."

I closed my eyes and caught it. "But when I searched Ferguson's studio, I saw a page on his desk with an identical emblem."

He shot me a look. "Why would a photographer have my harbor emblem?"

It was sifting through me, piece by piece. "Because he's a forger."

Finn exhaled loudly. "What emblem was it? Describe it to me."

I didn't have to because it hung before us on a large sign just off the road. "That one." I pointed at it.

"That's my harbor." But something else caught his attention, for he killed the headlamps and pulled over. "We may run into trouble."

I rubbed my eyes and peered at the docks. It was a good stretch away from the road, but I spotted a ship docked there. "I thought you said it was closed."

"It is." Anger gripped his tone. "That's the SS *Partner*."

The merchant ship he'd bought back from Erik Bruun. "What's it doing here?"

"That's a good question." Apparently one he intended to find an answer to. He pressed a hand to the door, but I reached and grasped his arm.

"I don't think it's a good idea to approach whoever it is alone in the dead of night. We should call someone."

"Who, Amelie? We believe Axel's a counterspy, and everyone else is in Malmö." His gaze swiveled. "Or so I thought."

"What do you mean?" I followed Finn's glare, catching sight of a masculine profile.

His body tensed. "That's Elias."

≣ CHAPTER 31 ≣

I squinted at the man's silhouette, unable to make any distinction. But Finn would know his friend and assistant. Or possible betrayer. "It may not be what you think," I said, even as Finn pulled the car away from the harbor entrance. "What are you doing?"

"Placing you out of the line of sight. If I'm going to confront Elias, I don't want him near you." He braked and killed the motor.

"But are you sure it's—"

"It's him. I send Elias here to supervise loads. But I haven't approved any for months." His voice held an edge. "Which means he's using my harbor *and* ship for a load I didn't authorize."

"Finn?" I laid my hand on his arm, my mind straining to thread the frayed pieces together. "Do you think this is a coincidence? What if everything that's happened over these past weeks was meant as a distraction? To keep you occupied?"

He jolted. "What do you mean?"

"Think about it. The man hired to recover the briefcase was *your* nephew. Bengt Ferguson forged *your* harbor emblem. Harbor! Remember Agent Modve overheard the men speaking of a harbor? Axel assumed Norrköping, but what if they meant yours? Finn, all this could be a clever plot to keep the OSS, the secret police, and you distracted while they carry out something else beneath our noses."

He didn't look convinced. "That's quite a theory."

"Can you think of a better one?" I challenged. "Before you told the papers Franc was your nephew, who else knew?"

His brow furrowed. "Franc interrupted a dinner party a couple months ago."

"Was Elias there?"

He nodded.

"If Elias is the killer, he could've chosen Franc for the job because he's your nephew. Knowing you'd be blinded by his death. Elias was also at Club Frossa. I lost sight of him after he and I danced." Elias could easily have slipped away to nab the briefcase. My mind traveled back to my conversation with Franc inside the nightclub. "Nothing that would interest you," I whispered.

"What?" Finn's deep voice almost broke my concentration.

"Franc said that to me. I asked him what was inside the briefcase, and he said, 'Nothing that would interest you.' I could envision his sly smirk, hear his smug tone. "It might be my imagination, but I could've sworn he emphasized the word *nothing*. Looking back, I see that was his toying way of telling me the briefcase was empty."

"It's possible. But why does that matter?"

I tapped the edge of the bench, my mind swirling with this new information. "Because they didn't murder Franc because he knew the whereabouts of the manuscript, but because he knew there *wasn't* a manuscript." Finn made a grunt of assent. "Same with Jessvurn. He could also break the news that the case was empty. That the document was burned. So that explains the hit placed on him. Someone didn't want us knowing the research had already been destroyed."

Finn shook his head. "Just an hour ago, we accused Axel as the mastermind."

"He could still be part of it." I darted a glance out the window. "But we know your harbor's somehow involved, considering Ferguson forged its emblem."

His gaze narrowed. "That means whatever is on the *Partner...*"

"Might be worth killing for."

"I need to find out. Stay here. Keep low."

"Wait." I seized his sleeve.

"Amelie, I can't let them get away."

"I know." I tightened my hold when he tried to tug from my grip. "But what are you going to do? Are you armed?"

"I'm going to discreetly investigate what's going on." He let out a frustrated breath. "And I'm not scared of Elias. I'm bigger than him."

I didn't like the idea of Finn running full force into a swarm of killers. "Bullets are faster than a fist." I lifted the hem of my skirt, revealing my holster. "At least take this."

A choking noise rattled Finn's throat. "Have you had a gun on your leg all this time?"

I gently eased the pistol from its home on my thigh. "Yes." I held it out to him.

He shook his head, reaching inside his sports coat and withdrawing a revolver similar to mine. "And here I thought I was protecting you."

"Be careful." My voice hitched, and I hated it. Hated that Finn would be in danger. "Please return to me without a scratch."

The tense lines framing his eyes softened. He stroked my cheek with his knuckle. "I thought women love a man with a scar."

I caught his face in my hands. "I'm not just any woman. I'm yours." I wasn't planning on declaring such a thing, but Finn responded with his mouth hot on mine, kissing me quick and hard.

He pulled away. "I promise to be careful." He put his hand on the door. "Please stay here." Before I could say another word, he was gone.

I prayed for his safety and sank lower in the seat, feeling vulnerable. I was in Finn's car, for goodness' sake. If that truly was Elias, wouldn't he recognize it? I knew Finn had parked a fair distance away. So much so, he'd squinted to see Elias. But I still felt exposed, even though I was armed.

I slightly raised my head, peering out the windshield. I wished Finn and I had devised a better plan than him impulsively running toward Elias and whoever else invaded his harbor. Should I go for help? Though how would I know who was trustworthy or not? Especially if Elias was known around here more than Finn.

I flinched at every noise. A distant shout. The screech of a cargo crane. A bird's caw. How many minutes had passed? Ten? Twenty? Sitting in this heightened state of senses, I'd no judgment of time.

Each passing second, dread dripped into me. What if Finn had been captured or worse? He could be injured, while I sat stranded in his car, watching the fog climb from the ground like ghostly fingers.

I was through waiting.

With quiet movements, I stepped out of the car and onto the dark road, gun in hand. Thankfully, the stretch of ports was loud, offsetting the light tapping of my heels. My gaze darted all directions. The SS *Partner* came into view, but its owner was nowhere to be found.

Finn wouldn't just approach the ship, would he? Because if that was the case—

A hand slapped over my mouth. Hard. I jumped, dropping my gun as a sharp tip poked my neck.

"Be quiet." A deep voice seethed in my ear. Elias? I couldn't get a look at him. He held me firmly to his body. "Or I'll slice your pretty throat."

He moved to grab my fallen weapon, slightly lowering the knife. This was my chance. With all my strength, I threw a sharp elbow to his groin. He grunted. I stabbed my heel in his ankle. Jerking from his grasp, I reached for my gun. He kicked it. The pistol skidded across the cement, into the shadows. I feared it sank into a sewer drain. Gone.

My legs scrambled forward in escape, but the brute was too quick. He yanked me by the hair, pulling me roughly against him. He grazed the blade along my neck. My blood iced over.

"Cooperate." His spittle ran down my cheek. "Another move, and you're dead."

Fear's tentacles wrapped around my chest, squeezing the breath from me.

His fingers bit into my arm. He jerked me along with him toward the harbor, locking me tightly against his solid build. I couldn't turn my head or even jolt lest the knife sink into my skin. We reached a timber building. He kicked open the door and tossed me inside. My legs flew out from underneath me, and I fell onto a coil of thick roping.

A low lantern shed enough light to glimpse the cement block walls. No windows. Piles of lumber to my left. A small makeshift desk to my right. The only escape was the door my abductor blocked.

"How charming our paths crossed again, Amelie." Elias stood in the shadows. The knife glinted in his right hand. "Seems strange for a movie star to be traipsing around a harbor at midnight. Why are you here?" He lifted the blade, eyeing it with interest as if taunting me.

I pinched my lips tight, climbing to my feet.

My refusal to answer drew him a step forward into the light. "No response?" He tsked. "I thought we were friends." The lantern glowed upon his face, and I saw it. Or rather, *didn't* see it.

"I've never met you."

His eye twitched. "Don't be coy."

"I know you aren't Elias." It was slight, but the real Elias had a freckle dotting his left lobe. This man had no such marking. But he did have a faded scar on the edge of his eyebrow, whereas Elias didn't. Axel had said Elias had a brother, one deep in mischief. But he hadn't mentioned they were twins. Or that they were nearly identical. Perhaps Axel hadn't known. Or. . .he was in on the scheme.

His derisive laugh echoed off the shallow ceiling. "Someone told me you were an idiot."

Who would've told him that? Elias? Axel? "Someone was wrong." I discreetly scanned my surroundings, searching for anything that could be used as a weapon. Sadly, the only thing within reach was a rough-hewn desk. I doubted I could assault the man with office supplies.

"How is my charming brother faring? I haven't spoken to him in weeks."

I kept quiet, my mind grappling for a way to escape.

"Not one for conversation, are you? Well, Elias wasn't one for my schemes, but he can't keep me from using his identity."

I gave him a sharp look, to which he grinned, appearing even more like Elias. It was uncanny how similar they were.

"I know." He lifted his free hand with a shrug. "The evil twin brother is an overdone cliché. But it works in this instance."

"To give you access to the Ristaffason harbor?"

He didn't answer, but he didn't have to. Why else would he impersonate his brother? Elias held authority here. And since the siblings were identical, the harbormaster and dockworkers wouldn't suspect anything was amiss. "Now let's get back to my question, shall we?" He wagged the knife at me. "Why are you here?"

I decided to play dumb concerning the document. "I'm looking for Niels Bohr's research."

"You're in the wrong place." Displeasure twisted his handsome features. "You're supposed to be in Gothenburg."

Ah, they'd dropped another tip. Either late last evening or this morning. Clever. Since Gothenburg was fifteen hours away from here. Maybe that was why Axel hadn't shown up to collect the papers. Had he been scrambling to get to the other side of Sweden to search for the nonexistent manuscript? "Well then"—I shrugged casually—"I best be on my way."

He didn't budge. Nor was he amused by my humor. "Come now." He took a bold step closer. "You know it's a bogus search. That's why you're here." His lips peeled from his teeth in a snarl. "Eizenburg followed all our tips like an eager hound on the trail, but not you."

Wait. So Axel wasn't a part of this after all. This man had confessed to stringing Axel along with false plants. With Axel and Elias clear of any blame, who was left?

He watched me with a predatory gaze. "Let me guess, no one else believed you." Another stride forward. "Which is why you're all alone."

I shuffled back. "You admit it was a hoax."

"How easily tricked people are. A few hints here and there. A flaunting of the briefcase." His jaw hardened. "That's the interesting thing about truth. It can be manipulated. Distorted."

"No, *information* can be twisted." I lifted my chin. "But truth? Truth will always rise from lies."

His eyes glinted. "The starlet's a preacher."

"No, I'm a cautioner. Because while your little ruse fooled us at the beginning, it's over now. You're surrounded." I had to latch on to something for survival. Sadly, no one was here. I didn't even know where Finn was. Or what was happening on the *Partner*. It must be illegal or else the man wouldn't be threatening me with a knife. "You should escape while you can."

His eyes flickered with doubt, but then his expression tightened. "Brilliant performance. You almost had me." He closed the distance, brandishing his blade, his gaze hardening with wicked intent. "No man would allow pretty bait like you to set a trap." His fingers trailed along my jaw, and I bit the inside of my cheek. "But I've always had a weakness for beauty. Maybe I could convince you to join my side."

"The Nazi side?"

He leaned in, nuzzling my hair, whispering in dark tones, "The side where the money is."

I slid my eyes closed, hating his greedy touch. But maybe I could get information out of him if I played along. "What's in it for me if I do?"

He straightened with a shrug. "You get to live."

Okay, so no monologue of hidden motives. Movie scripts weren't ever true to real life. "What's on the *Partner*? Iron ore for Germany?"

He smiled wickedly. "You don't get to ask questions."

A light knock sounded at the door. "Lukas. Open up." A rushed voice bled through the door.

Lukas, apparently his name, flicked a warning glance at me. "Don't move."

While his back was turned, I scrambled to find something useful on the desk. A sharp letter opener? A heavy paperweight? No such luck.

Lukas flung open the door. It was Bengt Ferguson standing opposite him, the photographer and forger. I recognized him from a picture I'd seen in his studio.

Lukas eyed him with annoyance. "What is it?"

"The crew hasn't come yet."

He pulled out his pocket watch. "They'll be here at one. It's early yet."

"What if they found out what's in the cargo?" Ferguson peeked over at me beyond Lukas' shoulder, his eyes widening. "What's going on here?"

More questions surfaced. If Bengt Ferguson and Lukas were part of this scheme, who was their contact in Malmö? The one who killed Franc?

Lukas looked back at me and winked. "She's my companion for the evening." He closed the door on Ferguson's disgruntled face. My captor turned on his heel, centering me in his preying gaze. "There's no way for you to escape." He licked his lips. "I'll take whatever I want from you."

Oh God. Please let this work.

My fingers lifted the fountain pen like a dagger.

A laugh, hollow and obnoxious, ripped from Lukas' mouth. "What are you going to do with that? Sign me an autograph?"

"No." I made a show of pressing my thumb on the cartridge. "I intend to shoot cyanide at you." I raised it higher, aiming at him.

He halted his advance. "You expect me to believe that?"

"Doesn't matter if you believe it or not. The proof will come when I squirt your face and your skin burns off. The boys at the lab told me it can kill a person within thirty seconds."

We glared at each other.

He let out an exaggerated sigh. "There goes my plan for any enjoyment." He moved toward the exit. "I'll fetch my gun and shoot you from a distance." He yanked open the door.

A bright light flashed beyond the entrance.

The building shook.

Lukas fell backward but launched to his feet, shouting curses. He sprinted out, slamming the door behind him. I held my spot for a second, then tossed the pen back onto the desk and hurried toward the exit. Locked.

Shouts crashed outside. Something had exploded. For all I knew this very building could be on fire.

The doorknob rattled, and I lurched away. With quick movements, I hoisted the chair from behind the desk, intending to break it over Lukas' arrogant head.

The door flew open.

Finn stepped through. My heart pressed against my chest at the sight of him unscathed.

His gaze combed over my frame, his face full of concern. "Are you okay?" He rushed to me as I lowered the chair. "We have to get you out of here."

"What's going on?"

He wrapped my hand, leading me outside. Bright orange flames seared my vision. Men scrambled trying to douse the fire. It was the *Partner*! "Your ship is sinking!"

Finn tugged at my fingers, urging me forward. "I shot a flare gun at the fuel tank."

He sabotaged his own vessel? We ran from view, ducking behind a high stack of wooden pallets. My lungs squeezed, and the backs of my legs burned with exhaustion. A large man raced toward us. I sucked in a breath, seizing Finn's arm.

"It's okay, Amelie." He waved the burly guy over and set a hand to his thick shoulder. "Everything set?"

"They're all here, boss." The man towered above Finn, the breadth of his chest intimidatingly wide. "And ready."

Ready? I glanced at Finn, but my question was answered as a group of brawny fishermen and dockhands emerged from the fog-laden harbor. That must've been what Finn had been doing all this while, rallying men to our aid.

"Amelie." He pulled his gun from his waistband. "My boathouse is about a hundred yards down the docks." His free hand pointed the direction. "Go inside, lock the door, and wait for me."

I opened my mouth to protest, but I wasn't needed here. I'd only get in the way. "Be careful." I quickly pecked his lips. "I'll be praying."

Finn nodded, then he and his ragtag army marched to battle.

Forcing my legs into motion, I ran as fast as I could while keeping to the shadows. The farther I went, the fewer the docks. I remembered Finn had said his personal property was more secluded. I reached the building and barricaded myself inside. Wet wood and turpentine invaded my nose. It was no use searching for a phone to call for help. This place didn't seem wired for electricity.

Moonlight streamed through windows on the far right. I rounded a large, overturned sailboat and weaved through benches laden with tools and paint cans, stepping over ropes and anchors. I peered out the glass panes but was too far from the main harbors to see anything. Though at least I should be able to spot Finn after they subdued Lukas and his bunch.

Lukas. Tonight had been full of surprises but also mysteries. Lukas had said he hadn't spoken to his brother in weeks. So how did Lukas know I'd met Elias? Or had even visited at the Ristaffason estate? Unless he had someone else on the inside. Lukas had confessed to deceiving Axel with the false tips, indicating that Axel had not been involved in any of this either.

A rustling noise made me flinch. No doubt mice scurried about. I shivered at the thought. But I couldn't let rodents destroy my concentration. I closed my eyes, trying to recall what Axel had said about Lukas at Club Frossa. Something about Elias' brother always being up to no good. But Axel had also mentioned where he was from. I'd only been half listening because I'd been preoccupied with searching for Franc. Lukas hailed from one of Sweden's islands. I groaned. Sweden had thousands of them. But, wait. It was one of the larger islands. Öland? No. Not that.

Another scraping noise sounded, but I ignored it, regaining my focus. The name lingered on the fringes of my mind. I'd heard it a couple times over the past week. Both mentions had been in Malmö. That was significant. If I got...got? That was it. Gotland! Lukas was from Gotland.

But so was another person. *Someone on the inside.* When I'd first arrived at Finn's estate, Anna had introduced me to her secretary and revealed she'd lived in a small village. . .in Gotland. "Margit."

"Well done, Amelie."

I swirled around at the feminine voice.

⚏CHAPTER 32⚏

Only a few yards away, and aiming a pistol at my heart, stood Margit Lastrand.

Or was it?

Dressed in a stylish dress suit with her platinum-blond hair in loose waves framing her cosmetic-painted face, Margit resembled more the sultry Jean Harlow than the quiet, plain girl I'd met in Malmö. I almost didn't recognize her if not for her wide-set eyes pinning me in her hazel glare.

A million questions burned on my lips, but staring down a gun barrel made me hesitant to voice the accusing ones. "How did you get in here?" I glanced at the door on the other side of the building.

Her face crumpled in irritation and disappointment as if I'd let her down by my basic inquiry. "The door was locked. So, I was resourceful." She raised her other hand, revealing the metal ring holding my picks. "I believe these belong to you."

Had that been the scratching I'd heard? She must've raided my luggage. I hadn't seen them since the afternoon I'd opened Finn's desk drawer. But her petty theft was nothing compared to the other crimes I assumed she'd committed. "So Lukas charmed you into doing his bidding."

Her throaty laugh had a chill in it. "You're not as clever as you think." She took a step forward, chin raised, narrowed shoulders squared as if she were my superior. "Lukas works for me. He's nothing in this operation except a dispensable pawn." Her lips bowed in a smile. "Just like Franc."

"It was you." My brain made the connections too late. Much too late. "You killed him."

She shrugged as if his life meant nothing. "After he gave me the case at Club Frossa, I saw him talking to you. Men turn stupid around a pretty face. I couldn't have him ruining what I worked for. So really, it was your nosiness that killed him."

"No." If this was her twisted way of passing blame, I refused to take it. "You planned on killing him before he even handed you the briefcase." Because like Elias, she would've also been at the dinner party Franc had intruded upon. "You picked him as your pawn on purpose, knowing he's Finn's nephew."

"Perhaps." She rolled her eyes. "We had to keep Ristaffason occupied. He was mumbling about needing to take a trip to Luleå. I couldn't have him visiting the docks at the time of my shipment." Her smile built, slow and cruel. "Though admit it. I outsmarted everyone, even you. Don't think I didn't know what you were up to the second you walked into the estate. You and your silly remarks." In an exaggerated movement, she tossed her hair over her shoulder in mock imitation. "It was cleverly done but not clever enough. Because you, Ristaffason, and that idiot from the OSS were all scrambling after something that doesn't exist anymore."

While Lukas hardly leaked a word, Margit was a flowing faucet. But there was a wildness in her eyes, growing more untamed the longer she spoke. Wise or not, I determined to keep her talking, if only to stall whatever plans she had for me and that pistol she clutched. "So you planted the empty briefcase in the Aubrund House Museum."

"You think you have it all figured out?" She blew out a long-suffering breath, as if speaking to me was tedious. "The briefcase wasn't entirely empty. I put the stolen papers from Ristaffason's office in it. Ferguson needed samples of his handwriting to forge a letter to the harbormaster about the *Partner*'s arrival. So, I left it in the secretary and dropped a tip to the American Legation. Like I said, I outsmarted you."

"I wouldn't call it that." Hopefully, my provoking tone would keep her chatting. "Seems a lot of effort for a dumb ship that could've docked in this harbor undetected anyways."

"Dumb ship?" She sniffed, her nose wrinkling as if smelling

something rotten. "It's filled with Nazi gold and jewels. We couldn't take that risk."

Nazi gold. As if the Germans had attained the treasure honestly. It was no secret they'd stolen it. Valuables that had once belonged to the Jews. My stomach twisted. The Nazis had raided Jewish communities, seizing anything of worth, looting their jewelry, heirlooms, wedding bands, going as far as stripping the crowns from their teeth.

"But it doesn't matter now, does it?" Her voice snapped. "Because the *Partner* is sunk, and it's your fault." She pulled back the gun's hammer.

Dread sluiced my veins. I stepped back, something coarse and bristly brushing my legs. Rope? "How is your botched scheme my fault?"

"I risked everything for this. I got hired as that old lady's secretary. I discovered the *Partner* would port in Oxelösund. Gave favors so the captain would pick up my load in Germany and run it here to Luleå." She went on wildly, and the hair stood on the back of my neck. "I planned the drops. Killed. And now because of you, the treasure is on the bottom of the gulf."

At first, I thought she divulged her scheme because she twistedly loved the sound of her own voice, but there was more to this. Was she giving herself a reason to kill me? By confessing all the details of her operation, she sealed my fate. There was no way she'd let me walk out of here alive. "Why are you telling me this?"

Her eyes narrowed, slits of dark ice. "Because it's only fair for you to know the crimes you'll be framed for."

I sucked in a breath. She couldn't mean. . . "You can't pin this on me."

"No?" Her syrupy tone made my stomach drop. "You were at Club Frossa and the only one in the streets when Franc was killed. Too bad I was an eyewitness that saw *you* murder him." She dramatically pressed a hand to her chest and pitched her voice higher. "I was so frightened when I saw you run over that poor man. But I must speak up and let justice prevail." She advanced a step. "It was you, Amelie, who was behind everything. A deceiving double agent who fooled both the OSS and Ristaffason into trusting you."

"No." I wrenched the fear from my voice. "Finn won't believe you."

"Of course, once you're dead, the authorities will find letters from high-ranking Nazis in your pocket. But who would expect anything less from Erik Bruun's daughter?"

My hands curled into fists, and her mouth slowly curled into a sadistic smile.

"You shouldn't have private conversations in the breakfast room with Anna." Her brow arched high, her tone a jeering scold. "Anyone can overhear."

No, no, no. Finn had been the one listening at the door that day. But. . .there was the staff entrance. My heart squeezed. Margit had eavesdropped and now held the power to reveal my connection to that monster. And Mamma would suffer. I had to survive this.

"I came here to intervene. As a friend, I wanted to get you help. Begged you, even." Give this woman an Academy because her perverse recitation of lies was alarmingly convincing. "But you refused and tried to kill me. There was a struggle." Her face twisted, and she tore the tulle accents on her dress. "But in the end, you got shot dead with your own gun."

"That's not my. . ." I squinted at the revolver in her hand. My heart stopped. It *was* my pistol. I thought it had fallen into the sewer drain.

"I spotted you tiptoeing around earlier." Her tone was one of triumph. "I told Lukas to hold you in the office, but not before I caught your heroic scene where you dropped your gun." She eyed it with wicked glee. "Turned out well for this instance."

I subtly shifted, dipping my fingers into the pile of corded rope behind me.

"Such a drastic plot twist. The Queen of Diamonds is actually the Empress of Evil." She raised the gun steadily, aiming at my chest. "Take your final bow, Fröken Blake."

"Amelie!" Finn pounded on the door. "Open up."

Margit's gaze swung at the noise. I grabbed the netting and hurled it at her. The rope smacked her in the face and arms. I tackled her. She dropped the gun. It fired. She writhed under my weight, her legs tangling in the netting. Her fist came at me, knocking my chin. I pressed my elbow into her throat, pinning her.

The door burst open.

Finn and his compatriots filed in.

"Grab the gun." I jerked my head toward the weapon.

Finn seized it.

Harbor police crouched beside me, taking over, allowing me to roll off her. I couldn't control my trembling. Even my teeth chattered.

Finn helped me stand, his eyes furiously running over me, as if ensuring I wasn't injured. He shed his jacket, wrapping it around my shoulders. "Are you okay?" He rubbed his hands up and down my arms, trying to lessen the chill. His concerned gaze dropped to my quivering chin, and he pulled me against him, pressing me to his warm body.

I nodded against his chest.

"Rickertz, Ferguson, and their crew are in custody." His large hands spanned my back. "Say something, Amelie. I need to know you're all right."

"I'm okay." My voice shook.

The authorities had difficulty restraining Margit as she thrashed about. I pressed closer to Finn, reminding myself she couldn't hurt me anymore. The men finally subdued her and escorted her out.

For a long moment, I stared blankly at the empty doorway. "Margit confessed to killing Franc. She orchestrated all of it."

"And Lukas Rickertz?" he asked.

"Just a pawn in her plan." I looked up at him, and he kissed my temple. "You sank your own boat."

"I saw that man take you inside the building. I've never been more scared in my life." He gently tightened his hold around me. "I used their own tactic against them. I distracted them so I could get to you." His expression broke. "I sent you here, thinking you'd be safe." He rested his forehead against mine, just like under the northern lights. "I'm sorry, Amelie. I don't know what I'd do if something happened to you."

"Why, sir, I do believe you care," I teasingly repeated my words from the balcony at the Aubrund House.

"Are you trying to pull a confession out of me?" He kissed me soundly, letting me know in no uncertain terms his true feelings on the matter.

I smiled against his lips. "I won't take anything from you that you're not willing to give."

"Liar." He eased back, his eyes alight. "You took my heart that night on my beach in Malmö." The evening we danced the hambo. I'd accidentally let my mask slip, and he'd glimpsed the true me.

"Just as easily as you've stolen mine." I pressed my cheek against his solid chest. I'd faced death more this past week than in all my years, but I'd also tasted life. I gripped him closer, not wanting to let him go.

But soon, I'd have to.

⊒CHAPTER 33⊑

Finn and I were led to an office, crammed into a back hallway of the American Legation. The sign on the door read COMMERCIAL ATTACHÉ, but the man inside this narrow room was no more an economic officer than I was Katharine Hepburn. We knew the job title was a facade, just as we knew we sat opposite of Bill Carlson, the head of the counterespionage division of the United States Intelligence Agency.

"Our operatives heard whispers of possible gold smuggling and even that our *neighbors* are trying to sell stolen diamonds." He motioned in the direction of the German Legation, which was only a few buildings away. "We'll send divers into the Gulf of Bothnia to recover the loot." He gave Finn an approving nod. "That was quick thinking, Herr Ristaffason. If the gold and jewels would've been removed from the *Partner*, they most likely wouldn't be recovered."

"I only thought of Amelie." He placed his hand on mine, and my heart rolled over in my chest. Who'd have thought I'd ever find his bluntness endearing? "But I'm glad for the Allies that it worked out."

"More than worked out." He shoved a stack of papers into a file. "We're launching an investigation into Nazi gold. We suspect Germany has been purchasing Swedish iron ore with stolen Jewish valuables."

I leaned forward, intrigued. "How can you prove it?"

Herr Carlson's gaze met mine. "Something will turn up. It always does." Determination marked his features. "I congratulate you as well, Fröken Blake. You acted on your gut, seeking out Isak Jessvurn and discovering the briefcase no longer held Dr. Bohr's research. We'll further investigate his claim, but I feel strongly, like you, that the manuscript was destroyed." He gave me a nod of approval. "Rickertz is hardly saying a word, but his comrade, Ferguson, is singing like a canary. He told us Margit Lastrand has a Nazi uncle who's a leader in the Third Reich. He's her contact in Germany."

"I have one question." I cut a quick glance to Finn, then back at Herr Carlson. "Finn tells me Margit has lived at the estate for over two months. That's a few weeks before the briefcase hit Swedish shores. How does everything fit together?" Margit couldn't have possibly predicted that Stefan Rozental would lose the briefcase.

He dipped his chin. "The plan has always been about smuggling the loot into Sweden. Lukas Rickertz must've told Fröken Lastrand about his brother's position at Ristaffason's harbors, and she took over from there. Getting hired on as secretary and gaining information along the way." His attention moved to Finn. "Did you discuss the missing briefcase at all?"

Finn nodded. "My business partner, Danikan Skar, came to the estate and told me about its disappearance and that it belonged to Stefan Rozental, Dr. Bohr's assistant."

"And Margit eavesdropped." I put it together. She'd admitted to purposefully listening to my and Anna's conversation about Erik Bruun. "And she hired Franc to recover it."

Carlson nodded. "She took advantage of the opportunity to use the briefcase as a diversion, and if it so happened to contain Dr. Bohr's research, then I'm certain she would've only been too glad to sell it to the Germans. But since it was empty, she continued with her ploy to use it as bait."

It all made sense. Then she'd hired her crew of henchmen to carry out her morbid plot, such as Bengt Ferguson to forge letters to the harbormaster under Finn's name so the load would be accepted in Luleå. Lukas had posed as Elias, fooling the dockworkers and harbor police. "Margit said she discovered the *Partner* was scheduled to stop in Oxelösund and used her *charms* on the captain to go to Germany and pick up the loot to run to Luleå."

"It was a genius plot." Bill Carlson plucked the pencil from behind his ear and tossed it on the desk. "But one that failed because of you. Your first assignment was a success, Fröken Blake."

"First?" I blinked. I'd been under the assumption this was my only assignment.

He leaned back in his chair, casual and confident, as if his words hadn't just sent a jolt of trepidation down my spine. Or maybe it was excitement. I was too exhausted to sort through my jumbled emotions. Either way, the OSS agent grinned at me as if I'd won the Spy of the Year award. "Bill Donovan wants you to report to him when you return to the States."

It was at that moment I realized I'd do anything to help bring an end to this war.

Herr Carlson looked at Finn. "And you have your own work in Lysekil."

Lysekil. That was the mission Finn had mentioned about the blockade busters and ball bearing shipments to the UK.

"I'll be there," Finn promised, and then we were excused.

We stepped into the hall just as Axel exited from another office. He approached us with a cautious gait. "Amelie. Finn." He nodded at us, even as his gaze flickered to our entwined fingers. "I congratulate you on a successful mission. I apologize, Amelie, for not taking your concerns about Jessvurn seriously. It turns out you were right to follow that lead."

"Thank you." I offered a friendly smile.

His mouth crimped as he acknowledged Finn. "Please don't mention any of this to Elias until we decide how to proceed with his brother. And your farmor as well, concerning Margit Lastrand. I never would've guessed a lady was the mastermind." His gaze met mine, notes of admiration swirling in his gray eyes. "It took one intelligent woman to foil another." He glanced at a file in his hands. "Amelie, may I have a moment with you?"

Finn released my fingers with an understanding nod, and I followed Axel into a side office.

"Here's the folder containing the information about your departure." He handed me an itinerary, and I tried not to let my gut sink.

I knew I had to return, but now I wanted more time.

"You will see your flight is scheduled to leave Bromma airstrip in one week. That should give you time to say. . .your goodbyes." He stepped toward me, his expression unusually hesitant. "So are you and Ristaffason together?"

"Yes."

He shoved his hands into his pockets and averted his gaze. "It seems I always turn up second when it comes to Finn. But I wish you all the happiness." He finally met my eyes. "You deserve it."

"Thank you, Axel." I exited the office and was glad to find Finn standing by the stairwell.

I reached for his hand, memorizing the feel of it against mine. "I wasn't sure if you would wait for me."

"I'll always wait for you." His tone was adamant, and I caught his meaning. "As long as it takes."

The war had brought us together, and now we were to be separated. I had several responsibilities back in the States. And he had to fulfill his obligation on the other side of Sweden. We hadn't foreknowledge of when the fighting would end; it could be anywhere from ten days to ten years. I only prayed our blossoming relationship would survive.

———— ≈ ————

December 18, 1945

Camilla, my beauty operator, powdered my face for the last shot of the ending scene of my final film. I sat in a canvas chair with my name printed in white paint. Well, my soon-to-be-retired last name. Hopefully, I would be getting a new one in the near future.

After I'd left Sweden, Finn had returned to his port in Lysekil for another attempt at loading Allied motor gunboats with supplies. Only one of the five vessels dispatched from Britain had reached his harbor. When it had returned with forty tons of cargo, the Allies had counted it a success. Whatever questions the OSS once had about his loyalty were long forgotten as he poured his all into the war effort.

Sadly, this information had been siphoned from my director and spy recruiter Henrik Zoltan since Finn couldn't write such sensitive information in his letters, which was the only way we'd corresponded. All during our separation, I'd fought the fear of becoming a modern-day Evelina Aubrund, penning my heart onto paper, sending my love across an ocean with the very real possibility his own letters could stop. I wasn't naive. I understood the delicacy of our bond. We were thousands of miles apart and had begun our relationship in the middle of a global war.

The days had stretched into months, and this past October had marked two years since I'd gazed into Finn's Baltic-blue eyes and felt his lips upon mine. I'd remained busy serving the Allied cause in between filming. The OSS had sent me overseas under the guise of performing in USO tours while I delivered top-secret documents to generals and commanders.

But now the war was over.

With V-E and V-J Days behind us, our soldiers should return home any time. Yet while the fighting might have ceased, I had a feeling it would be a long season before the battle scars faded, if they ever would. Humanity had experienced undiluted evil, stared into the eyes of hatred, yet good had triumphed.

"Is there any way I can convince you?" Henrik Zoltan approached with a cigar pinched between his teeth. "You're quitting in your prime, Amelie. Throwing your career away. Any decent producer would advise against it."

Camilla finished her dusting job on my forehead and moved on to the next actor.

I smiled up at Henrik. We'd had this conversation several times, and despite his complaints, I knew he supported my decision. "I'll only miss your excessive reminders to smile without using my teeth." I flashed a full grin. "Which I still think is absurd."

"No, it's sultry. You want every man to fall in love with you, not think you're a walking dental ad."

I laughed. "I only want one man's love."

"Hmm." Henrik lowered onto his director's chair beside mine. "Last time we spoke, you said you hadn't received a letter from him in weeks. Has that changed?"

I tried to keep my expression from crumbling. With the war being over, I had thought I'd hear more from Finn, not less, especially with Christmas approaching. "It doesn't matter. In January, I'll be in Sweden."

"And if you find you've given up everything for a man who doesn't return your affections?"

I lifted my chin. Finn wasn't the most expressive regarding his emotions, but I truly felt he cared for me. Loved me. But two years was a long time to be apart. "I'm making the right choice, Henrik." And of course,

I'd always have Mamma. Though now I had to share her with Sebastian Modve. Who would've thought when I'd brought him to the penthouse the day we'd pulled him from the fire that I'd introduced him to his future wife? They were blissfully happy, and I was thankful Mamma had found someone who cherished her.

Henrik shifted in his seat, his critical gaze upon me. "Amelie, I don't like that hat for the final scene." He took a drag on his cigar. "Go tell Mae I want something less flashy."

I glanced at the set. Everyone was preparing for the shoot. "It looks like they're ready to film."

He harrumphed. "They'll film when I say so. And right now, I'm saying go change your hat."

I rolled my eyes and climbed to my feet. "Fine. Fine." Henrik was never overly picky about my wardrobe, but I understood the pressure of a final scene. All aspects must be perfect in order to leave a lasting impression on the audience. I located Mae taking a smoke break behind a rolling rack of costumes. After several choice words and a few mild threats to Henrik's well-being, she fitted me into a new hat, sleek and stylish.

By the time I returned to the set, everyone was in place, the cameras ready to roll.

"Very nice." Henrik gave his approval. "Now make this your most convincing performance, Amelie."

I arched a brow at him. There wasn't much to this scene. I only had one line and then the ending. But I wouldn't argue. I wanted the final moments of my career to be memorable. With a smile and a nod, I walked onto the set, stepping inside my *home*, which was only the appearance of a living room and foyer.

The studio quieted. The camera aimed at me but would switch angles after the doorbell rang. I sat on the sofa and lifted my teacup.

Henrik called, "Action."

I adopted a forlorn expression. As the script went, my fiancé had headed west with a promise to return for me. But my character hadn't heard from him in months. I didn't need to put much effort into making this believable. My heart ached for Finn.

I moved to take a fake sip from the empty teacup, but something grazed my lips. I lowered the prop and spotted. . .a piece of salmiak? Why was salted licorice in there? I was to appear listless, so I returned my tea to the tray and went about adjusting the knickknacks on the mantel. Centered the lamp on the three-legged table. Moved to lower the lid on the gramophone, but my gaze snagged on the record on the turntable. Traditional Swedish songs? It was an album Swedes would dance the hambo to. What was going on? There was only one person who understood the importance of that dance. My mind moved to the gentle sway of the memory—the stars a silent witness as our bodies spun as one across the shoreline. Finn's arms curled around me. His breath stirring against my temple. I stared at the record, longing coursing through me like the current of rapid waters. Could Finn have arranged all this? As a reminder he'd not forgotten me? I knew he'd exchanged some letters with Henrik. Or was this Henrik's idea of a joke?

I kept my gaze from straying to the Hungarian director. Henrik had once told me he didn't play pranks, but this certainly felt like one.

The door buzzed, pulling me from my stupor, prompting the scene transition. I crossed the carpeted floor into the staged foyer and set my hand on the brass knob, pausing for dramatic effect. Of course, I knew Phillip Gregory, the other lead, would greet me on the other side. But everything in me did not want to pretend to be in love with another man. Not when my lips tingled with the ghostly touch of Finn's kiss. The scene only called for an embrace, but. . .I wanted Finn.

I opened the door, and my hand pressed against my parted mouth.

Because there he was.

Not Phillip. But the man who'd changed my life with his broody face and golden heart.

The man I loved so desperately.

The camera angle had switched to behind his head, catching my full reaction. My heart leaped in my chest. Finn was only a touch away. But I was afraid to move, lest he disappear, and I'd discover it was only my vivid imagination that conjured him. Finn didn't have such reservations.

His hands were on my face, his gaze drinking me in like a man parched of the only thing he'd ever craved. His eyes. Those eyes! How could I have gone over two years without peering into their heart-stirring depths?

A tear slipped, nestling in the crook between his thumb and my cheek until he tenderly brushed it away. My line. I had a line. What was it? It didn't matter because no silly movie would overtake this moment. So I spoke the breathy words drifting through my heart. "You came for me." My thoughts traveled to the day in my penthouse when I'd confessed to Finn that no one came to America. Yet he was here. For me.

He responded to my heart's pull with his mouth on mine. I'd believed Finn wasn't a man of emotions, but I was wrong. His arm curled around my waist as his other hand slid to the back of my neck, anchoring me to him as he devastated me with his fervent kiss, pouring into me as if unleashing the intensified pressure of his feelings. I tasted it all. Desperation in the fervent rise and fall of his chest against mine. Hope in the tangling of our breaths. Love in his tender embrace, as I melded into him, as if we both vowed never to separate again.

"Cut!" Henrik's brogue seemed to sound from somewhere in the distance.

Movement spun around us, but we clung to each other. My hands gripped his lapels tightly as I kissed him back with equal intensity.

We finally broke apart, and my gaze lingered on his face, committing everything to memory.

"I never believed I'd see the day." I pressed my cheek into his solid shoulder. "Finn Ristaffason, an actor."

His chest rumbled with low laughter. "That's a bit of a stretch." With him being similar in size and shade of hair to Phillip, the world would never know of the switch, but to me, there couldn't be a better finale to my career.

"Why didn't you tell me you were coming?" I tipped my chin back to look into his handsome face. "I was starting to worry we were drifting apart."

He tightened his hold. "No. I was busy pooling all my resources to get a flight here. I needed to see you. I'm a patient man in most things but not about you. This separation." His eyes pinched as if it pained him to think of it. "I was slowly losing my mind."

I smiled at his frankness. "How long are you planning to stay?"

"At least through Christmas. Maybe the new year. But I'm going to use every form of persuasion to convince you to return with me."

"I'm invested in the idea. Let's go back to Sweden together." I laughed at his stunned expression. No doubt he'd been prepared to sway me. I hadn't had the chance to inform him in my letters of my plans to return home. With the war just ending, I'd scrambled to get all my business and accounts in order to make the move seamlessly. "But I still would love for you to persuade me." I pecked his lips.

Finn did not have a dramatic bone in his large body, so when he expelled a lengthy sigh of relief, I laughed. He drew me closer. Our noses brushed, a prelude to a kiss.

But instead of claiming my lips, he gazed at me with depths of affection. "I love you, Amelie. I never want to be apart again." Then his mouth met mine, sealing his declaration.

Over the past decade, I'd had many roles, but God had called me to go off script. To be the leading lady in the story He'd written for me. I peered at the man who'd just pledged his love. Never again would I recite lines for a worldwide audience, but I intended to follow the cues from the Director of my heart. For He'd led me to Finn, to this moment.

In the movies, this would be the time when two very important words flash upon the silver screen in giant bold letters. THE END. I could only smile. Because for Finn and me, it was only the beginning.

AUTHOR'S NOTES

For those who've read my previous books, you know I love inserting as many historical truths into my stories as I can. Actual people, events, places, etc. So to say *The Starlet Spy* has by far the most historical elements than my other stories is truly something. This book is loaded with historical truths! And here is where I get to list them all. You ready?

Let's start with the briefcase and discuss what parts are true and what are fiction. In September 1943, Dr. Niels Bohr gave his assistant Stefan Rozental his research to carry over the Öresund, or the Sound, into Sweden. Rozental gave an account of the incident, and here are his own words:

"Bohr called me to his home at Carlsberg," Rozental said. "He told me what I must do to escape to England and gave me all his papers on charged particles through matter, a manuscript that must not fall into Nazi hands. He gave me money and said we should meet again soon. He also gave me messages for King Christian's sister and the King of Sweden."

Rozental endured nine stormy hours in a rowboat borrowed from a Danish city park. According to Rozental, the briefcase was left on the shore that night. It never made it into the boat with him. The Danish resistance found the briefcase and sent it to Sweden with another refugee, but it never turned up. To this day, the research has never been found. So I took creative license and made a story of the missing document, which if in fact had fallen into Nazi hands could have proven disastrous.

The entire premise of this story is patterned after many rumors of Greta Garbo being a spy. According to the widespread gossip, Greta was approached by Hungarian producer and director, Alexander Korda. Korda was lauded for his contribution in the war effort as he worked closely with Winston Churchill. It's believed that the Prime Minister of Britain wrote some motivational speeches in Korda's movies. Propaganda was important during wartime, and many movies were filmed to inspire patriotism. (I patterned the fictional director Zoltan after Korda.) He supposedly asked Greta to spy on a wealthy Swedish businessman who seemed to be pro-Nazi. It's also a long-believed rumor that Greta placed a phone call to the King of Sweden, pleading with him to receive the Danish refugees. And that was how Amelie Blake was born!

The Danish rescue actually happened and is considered one of the most successful Jewish rescues of the entire war. It's said that 90% of the Jews in Denmark survived the Holocaust. Denmark is the only nation in Western Europe that saved most of its Jewish population from the Nazis with over seven thousand Danes fleeing to Sweden. The popular passage was from Copenhagen to Malmö, which was why I placed Finn's harbor there.

Speaking of Malmö, let's talk about Sweden! Sweden's stance during the global wars has always been neutral. But that didn't always mean they played fair. In March 1943, a pro-Nazi newspaper declared that Stockholm was the center of international espionage. In fact, the Swedish government allowed German troops passage to Norway during the German occupancy. They'd also allowed the Nazis to use the Swedish railways to move troops and supplies. Also, they'd sold iron ore to Germany. Over nine million tons of Swedish steel was sold to the Nazis annually during the war until 1944. It has also been argued that the Swedish export helped prolong the war.

But it can also be argued that if Sweden hadn't agreed to provide Germany the iron ore, the Nazis would've invaded the country. Kiruna mine in Sweden is the largest iron ore mine in the entire world, and Germany took advantage. There was indeed a railway that transported the iron ore from the mines to Luleå ports. The iron ore would then get shipped out through the Gulf of Bothnia which flowed into the Baltic Sea—Nazi-controlled waters during WWII. The Gulf of Bothnia would freeze in November, and so the iron ore would then travel out through Norway.

Sweden realized the Germans were losing the war, and by November 1944, all Swedish trade with Germany halted completely.

Leslie Howard, beloved actor in *Gone with the Wind*, was in a civilian airplane traveling between neutral countries. His plane was attacked by the Luftwaffe, and many historians believe Howard was involved with Allied Intelligence.

Bill Donovan was the head of the Office of Strategic Services in the United States. So it was fun to incorporate him into the story.

Camp X, otherwise known as the Farm, was a 275-acre training camp in Canada, located on the shore of Lake Ontario only fifty kilometers from the US border. This camp was originally built by William Stephenson to help train US recruits into the clandestine operations. It had to be located in Canada because at the time it was built, the United States hadn't entered the war yet. Lieutenant-Colonel (Commandant) Cuthbert Skilbeck was the third and final Commandant of Special Training School. In the story when Bill Donovan was giving Amelie a tour of Camp X, or the Farm, I found a research site with old footage that gave a rough sketch of the layout of the spy facility.

The route that Amelie took into Sweden was the exact route one would take into Sweden during WWII from America. There was, indeed, a small airport in Bromma where pilot Brent Balchen ran an air transport service. The planes he'd flown were unmarked military planes painted dark green. He was instrumental in operations that helped safely evacuate thousands of Norwegians from the Nazis. Unarmed B-24s were painted dark green, almost black, with military insignia removed.

Rosita Serrano was a Chilean dancer who had spent a good deal of time in Germany during the Nazi Empire. She entertained high-ranking leaders such as Hermann Göring. There are pictures of her singing beneath Nazi banners and newspaper headlines heralding her as the Voice of the Third Reich. She gained stardom in Germany but left to tour Sweden in 1943. This also coincided with my fictional time line, which made me one happy author. Serrano toured the country and remained on the OSS watchlist. She'd performed at a benefit in which the proceeds went to aid Jewish evacuees. The Nazi leaders had gotten wind of it and declared Serrano a traitor and a spy. She wasn't welcomed back in Germany or she'd get arrested.

The hambo is a real Swedish traditional dance, dating back 350 years ago. I really wanted to infuse some of the Scandinavian culture into this story and loved the idea of Finn and Amelie swirling about, creating memories.

Sigtuna is a real town just under fifty kilometers from Stockholm. It was founded in the tenth century and was Sweden's very first capital. In the charming medieval town, there are ruins from St. Peter's cathedral, Sweden's first church. The Aubrund House and history are entirely from my imagination, but since the Stora Gatan (Sigtuna's Main Street) features buildings from the nineteenth century, I figured an 1800s house would fit right in.

I inserted hints of Scandinavian and Norse mythology. According to the myth, the Näck was a shapeshifter that would turn into any form to lure its prey into the water. To overcome it, a person must throw an iron cross into the water. I really enjoyed creating the analogy of the German U-boats being like the Näck and Amelie clinging to the cross for protection. Also I talked about the northern lights. According to Norse mythology, the northern lights were to represent a bridge from Asgard to Middle Earth. Again, I loved having Amelie make the connection to God bridging a way to be close to her.

The mission that I had Finn participate in at the Lysekil harbor truly happened. The Allies needed the Swedish ball bearings and steel, but to get to Sweden they had to break through German-infested waters. On September 23, 1943, the Allies attempted a run using motor gunboats (MGB), but the operation had gotten postponed because of an engine bearing problem. This timing worked out perfectly in the story because it could plausibly coincide with the day Stefan Rozental lost the briefcase. I love it when it works out this way! On October 26, 1943, the British dispatched five MGBs to Sweden, but only one made it to Lysekil. And it returned with forty tons of cargo.

Bill Carlson was the head of the OSS department in Sweden and did indeed moonlight as a commercial attaché. The German and American legation were close in proximity to each other, and there were actual rumors that the German Legation was trying to smuggle in and sell looted diamonds.

The Nazi heist is considered history's biggest robbery. It's believed the Nazis captured nearly $600 million worth of gold. The Germans demanded that Jewish communities surrender their gold—taking everything from their jewelry to their heirlooms, and even the crowns upon their teeth. This gold was used to fund the Nazi war machine. The gold then was smuggled in and melted and recast, erasing Nazi markers. The Allies put pressure on Sweden to refuse Nazi gold as payment. By the time the war was over, Sweden received nearly 75,000 pounds of gold from Germany. Most of it had been stolen from the Jews. After the war, the Swedish government tried to return the gold to Jewish communities, but declassified files state that many tons are still unaccounted for to this day.

ACKNOWLEDGMENTS

This story has stretched me in the best way. And I wouldn't have reached THE END without the support and encouragement of so many. And here's the space I get to brag on them.

A huge thank you to the Barbour Team who believed in me and didn't bat an eye when I had to change the entire premise of this book. Thank you to my agent, Julie, for always championing my stories. My critique partner and dearest friend, Rebekah Millet—thank you for not getting tired of me and my neediness. Love you, friend.

Janine Rosche and Janyre Tromp, I'm so grateful for our friendship. Thank you for being so encouraging and understanding of my crazy life. To my Proverbs 17:17 ladies—Crissy, Joy, and Amy—thank you for being there and for all your wonderful encouragement. I will always love those nine hundred notifications from our group message.

Also I'm super grateful for my early readers, Ashley and Abbi. Your feedback always means so much. Natalie Walters, I promised to place you in every acknowledgment, and somehow it slipped through my last book. So I'm doubling up here—thank you and thank you! Grateful for you.

My husband has been my number one fan for two decades now. Not only in writing but in life. Scott McDaniel, I love you forever. To my kids, thank you for putting up with Deadline-Mode Mama. For being understanding on those weekends I had to stay home and write.

To my Jesus, Your story is my favorite and the one that gives me life.